M

Mike Grist is the British/American author of the Chris Wren thrillers. Born and brought up in the UK, he has lived and worked in the USA, Japan and Korea as a teacher, photographer, writer and adventurer. He currently lives in London.

HAVE YOU READ EVERY CHRIS WREN THRILLER?

Saint Justice
They stole his truck. Big mistake.

No Mercy
Hackers came for his kids. There can be no mercy.

Make Them Pay
The latest reality TV show: execute the rich.

False Flag
They framed him for murder. He'll kill to clear his name.

Firestorm
Wren's father is back. The storm is coming.

Enemy of the People
Lies are drowning America. Can the country survive?

Backlash
He just wanted to go home. They got in the way...

Never Forgive
His home in ashes. Vengeance never forgives.

War of Choice
They came for his team. This time it's war.

Learn more at www.shotgunbooks.com

HAVE YOU READ THE LAST MAYOR THRILLERS?

The Last Mayor series - Books 1-9

When the zombie apocalypse devastates the world overnight, Amo is the last man left alive.

Or is he?

Learn more at www.shotgunbooks.com

FALSE FLAG

A CHRISTOPHER WREN THRILLER

MIKE GRIST

SHOTGUN
BOOKS

SHOTGUN BOOKS

www.shotgunbooks.com

Paperback ISBN - 9781739951146

For Su

1

BLACK SITE

Christopher Wren liked his cell well enough.

It was small. Bed, sink, toilet. A CIA black site off the coast somewhere, probably, not bound by US law. No window, but he didn't need one. Enough room to exercise, when he wasn't too weary from the interrogations. Putting him through his paces; the old field guide, not the new one, all the 'enhanced interrogation' they could manage and twice on Sunday.

Waterboarding. Extreme stress positions. Deprivation of food, water, sleep, bodily autonomy. Beatings. Humiliation. Sometimes, questions.

It was awful. All-consuming. The best thing about it was it gave him no time to think.

Today it was the cold. He sat on the bed, naked and wet on the bare metal frame, and shivered. Sometimes the door opened, someone came in and tossed a bucket of icy water on him. A reminder. They were doing him a favor, really. Holding back the fear. He counted three months since his ex-lieutenant CIA Agent Sally Rogers had put a black bag on his head outside his wife's duplex in Frederica, Delaware.

Since he'd seen some shadowy figure raising a hatchet over his wife's silhouette in the duplex window.

He'd shouted in the van until they sedated him. Only as he'd plummeted down into the morphine dark, had Rogers leaned in and whispered through the bag, close enough that none of her team would hear.

"Your family are fine, Christopher. I swear it. I don't know what you saw, but it wasn't what you think."

Those words had haunted him ever since.

His family were fine.

It wasn't what he thought.

It was better not to have to endlessly think about what those words really meant. Taking them apart into their tiniest fractions and rebuilding them, every second of every minute since, deconstructing the tiniest hints in Rogers' inflection, parsing the instants as the hatchet came down. Trying to comprehend what it meant, what he could possibly do, on and on and on…

Torture next to that was a mercy.

The door slammed open. Wren looked up, expecting another bucket. It came, drenching him. Good. Core temperature had to be below ninety degrees now. A dangerous line to walk; much lower and his extremities would start to rot alive. Frostbite was a real possibility.

The door slammed closed. There'd be more questions soon. The questions were always the same, trying to break open his Foundation. The names of his members. The keys to his darknet. Everybody broke in time, of course. Wren was curious how long it would take for him. They'd be better off just leaving him alone in the dark with his own fears; he'd be begging to be let out within a week.

The door opened. He looked up. This time no bucket came.

Instead someone was standing in the entrance, looking

down at him. A blur at the moment, his eyes too frigid to work properly. It took long seconds of blinking.

"Christopher," the figure said.

Wren smiled through the shudders. It was genuine. He was glad to see him.

"H-Humphreys."

Humphreys just stood there. Director of the CIA. A big kahuna. Cabinet seat next to the President. Nice of him to make the time. He wore a new black suit, had a tightly trimmed black moustache and short dark hair in a crew cut, hands relaxed at his side; no gun at his hip, no shoulder holster. The Director didn't need a sidearm. That was just another sign of his power.

Once Wren might have gone for him in a bid to break out, but not now. Couldn't even if he wanted to. His legs would give out after the first step. Muscles palsied by the cold. Give him half an hour and some ketamine, he'd be game to give it a shot.

"I asked them to stop the torture," Humphreys said.

Wren almost laughed, but his lungs didn't want to cooperate. Filling with fluid; early-onset pneumonia, probably. You had to love Humphreys. 'Asked', like the Director didn't control everything.

"Th-thanks."

"They didn't listen."

It was hilarious. Wren let his head drop. It hurt too much to hold it up, to meet Humphreys' eyes. No shame in that. Correction; plenty of shame in that, but shame was par for the course these days. The only way to endure was to embrace it; to self-brainwash fast, before your old ideas of reality made your spirit crack, like freezing water poured into a too-hot glass.

"We need to talk."

Wren grunted. Probably this wasn't even Humphreys. The

3

number of times he'd hallucinated in here? If anything, that was the real threat. They'd tried him on various truth serums, some kind of lab-grade LSD. In his lucid dreams he'd spoken to Tandrews, to the Apex, to Adolf Hitler on one hand and Abraham Lincoln on the other, and his interrogators had written it all down, searching for meaning in the Rorschach test of his mind.

He didn't think he'd given up a single Foundation member, but there was no real way to know. Maybe they had them all already, locked up in parallel cells to either side. He laughed at the notion. Couldn't help it. Alli in a cell? Hellion in a cell? Forget it.

"S-So talk," he stuttered.

"It's about your Foundation."

Of course it was. He looked up. Humphreys' expression hadn't changed. Ah, Humphreys. Once he'd looked at Wren with respect, maybe a hint of fear. A legendary ex-DELTA cult breaker, the first Agent Without Protocol in sixty years, but no longer. Humphreys' face was totally blank.

It was good to see through to the truth, sometimes. Nobody stayed on a pedestal. The sooner you fell off, the better for all involved.

"They've c-come for me," Wren hazarded a guess, stumbling over his consonants. "R-rescue attempt."

Humphreys just stared at him. Disapproving, cold, beyond intense. "Worse."

He laughed. "You're on board. You're running th-things now."

"Last guess."

"The Apex b-became President. First executive order: b-burn yourself alive."

"Closer." Humphreys took a step in. "Your cult's gone mad, Christopher. It has to be stopped."

That woke Wren up. A dump of adrenaline helped with

4

focus. It would last for a few minutes only, but for that time the shuddering receded. His vision sharpened; he looked into Humphreys' eyes and thought he was telling the truth.

"What have they done?"

"They're trying to start a war."

A second adrenaline dump brought Wren up like a shot of methylphenidate. The last of the shivering paled away and he straightened. Humphreys wasn't here to gloat. Humphreys was here for something else.

"What w-war?"

"Easier to show than tell," Humphreys said, and four soldiers stamped in. Not Wren's torturers, not even CIA. A new team, a new uniform. Marines, by the cut. Humphreys' old gig, before he became Director of Operations Coordination. Wren scanned them; side-holsters, tactical weaponry. "Get up," the Director said, and strode out.

The Marines picked Wren up and dragged him along behind. They weren't gentle.

2

SHOW NOT TELL

The Marines carried Wren out of his cell, feet trailing uselessly along the concrete floor. The walls were raw cement here, his home for the past three months. Left along the corridor led to the interrogation room, right to the way out.

They went left.

The interrogation room had a table and two chairs, with metal eyelets on the table and the floor. Wren blinked against the harsh white light. In the last few months they'd bombarded him with endless questions, trying to worm their way into his head.

No dice. Wren knew all the tricks. He'd written half of them himself.

Humphreys took his seat. There was a laptop waiting on the table. The Marines seated Wren, cuffed him at the wrists to the desk eyelet, at the ankles to the floor eyelet, then stepped back. Restrained like cannon fodder.

Humphreys sat down, his face a slab of blank white alabaster. A perfect poker expression, giving nothing away. That was new.

"I can tell you're pleased to see me," Wren said.

Humphreys ignored him, opened the laptop, spun it around so Wren could see and hit play.

It was news footage playing in split screen. All the major news networks in their own quarter, CNN, CBS, FOX, NBC, all showing the same thing. Street protests. Signs. People marching, chanting, with banners scrolling along the bottom announcing their demands. The shots looked like different cities, different days even, judging by the weather, the timestamps, the headlines.

It took Wren a second to process what he was seeing. The messages on their signboards.

DUMP THE DEEP STATE

FREE THE FOUNDATION

RELEASE CHRISTOPHER WREN

He looked up at Humphreys. Speechless for a moment. "Release Christopher Wren?"

Humphreys gaze drilled right back into him. "You've gained fans."

Wren snorted. "Bullshit. You deepfaked these."

"To what end would I deepfake this, Christopher? Don't play games. This 'movement' is spreading across the country like a cancer. These people think you're a hero, thanks to your speech bringing down the Reparations." A hint of revulsion cracked briefly through Humphreys' stony exterior. "Video of your 'amnesty' announcement has been seen over a billion times. You've conned the whole country, Wren. Now they think we're the enemy, because we're holding you. It doesn't matter that you're an avowed murderer. They just love you more."

Wren didn't need to think about that. "So let me go."

"Well, precisely," Humphreys said, and clicked three times on the laptop, starting up another video feed. "Watch this one."

Wren leaned in. The feed showed a dark room with three

shadowy figures seated in the middle. It was a cheap and grainy visual shot at an odd slant; a low-spec camera performing poorly in the low light cast from a single swaying bulb. Dusty air, a hint of cement walls in the backdrop, no natural light. No date stamp, GPS, nothing. Some kind of prison.

"What am I looking at?" Wren asked, squinting.

"It's not a deepfake either," Humphreys pre-empted. His eyes shone now, watching Wren closely like he was waiting for a tell. "These people have been taken. The video is authentic."

The light brightened, and Wren felt the change like an electric shock down his spine as the prisoners were illuminated. He knew all three of these people. On the right was Steven Gruber, an NSA agent and member of the Foundation's Board, in the middle was Jay Durant, a trucker in the Foundation, and on the left was Sally Rogers, Wren's lieutenant at the CIA.

All were naked, shiny with sweat, with their hands bound behind their backs. Two members of the Foundation and the woman who'd put him away.

"We just received this an hour ago," Humphreys said. "I commandeered a Chinook to come see you. All the protests, that low-level BS in the streets, I thought it would blow over until I saw this."

Wren stared at the three seated figures, mesmerized by the swaying light. Ball gags in their mouths. Rogers sat upright, seemingly unbroken, blond hair pasted to her cheeks, powerful shoulders tensed. Heavy-set Jay slumped against his bindings like a beaten man. Gruber gulped at the air, mid-twenties and junkie-thin, eyes darting side-to-side like a lizard, until a figure entered the side of the shot; a towering, broad silhouette in some kind of military uniform. Jay didn't move. Rogers' eyes widened. Gruber began to hyperventilate.

The huge figure moved across the front of the camera, like he didn't know it was there. Footage taken illicitly, Wren guessed. The guy had ramrod posture, a confident gait, an assured manner. Left he went, then right, hypnotically. Instilling terror. Only Jay didn't react, he was too bowed already. With each step Gruber paled further.

"What is this?" Wren demanded, looking up at Humphreys. "What's going on?"

Humphreys met his angry glare with the same cold expression. "You tell me, Christopher. We already know these are members of your cult." He tapped the screen twice. "Jay Durant, 3-year coin; Steven Gruber, 2-year coin. We've had them and others under surveillance for months. As for Rogers," he tapped the screen a third time, "the public don't know she brought you in. To them, she's become a poster girl for your cult."

Wren stared. It was a lot to take in, and that pissed him off. "Poster girl? But you know she's not, so why have you renditioned her?"

Humphreys' steely gaze sharpened. "This wasn't us, Christopher."

Wren had no words for that. Not a CIA rendition? He looked back at the screen. All the tell-tale signs were there. "So, who-"

Humphreys just tapped the screen.

Now the big silhouette was holding a cigarette lighter. A small yellow flame burned in the dark, and Wren's vision instantly tunneled around it, abruptly picking out details like a drowning man grasping for firm ground. Gruber's eyes flaring, pupils dilating wide into the whites. Rogers gasping. Their skin shining, too slick to be sweat.

"This wasn't us," Humphreys repeated sharply. "It was you."

The figure threw the lighter. It hit Jay's chest, bounced

into his lap and he went up in flames like a flashbang grenade. Napalm, painted on his skin. Sudden phosphorous-white light temporarily blinded the low-grade camera. There was muffled screaming. Jay thrashed, fiery limbs flailing.

The video ended.

3

FALSE FLAG

A cold bomb dropped in Wren's belly. He felt instantly sick. The shaking came right back, bulling through the adrenaline so hard his cuffs rattled on the table.

Jay had a family; a wife, two kids. He'd made big strides in the coin system, turned his life around, become a man Wren was proud of, a man to make his family proud, and now...

It was hard to breathe. Three months in the black site had been heaven next to this.

"I know you're behind it," Humphreys said, cold eyes drilling into him. "The man with the lighter is yours. The ones burning are yours. It's all your setup, your people willing to die for the 'cause'. Now you're going to tell me how to stop it."

Wren blinked. Stop it? Behind it? That didn't make sense at all. His voice came out rusty and thick. "What are you talking about?"

Humphreys was unrelenting. "You're an expert in mind control. The best I know. You made your cult love you so much they did this."

Wren just stared. After-images of Jay going up in flames flashed across the Director's pale face. He swallowed hard. "You think I ordered my own Foundation to burn themselves alive? Why?"

Humphreys' expression didn't budge. "You're the only one who benefits. Ever since we locked you away, your 'Foundation's' been driving this victimhood narrative." He tapped the laptop precisely. "Release Christopher Wren. Down with the Deep State. They make you the hero, make us the villain. Now this execution is custom-built to make us look like monsters, and your people like innocent victims."

Wren flailed. He spun back through the video in his head: the concrete walls, the uniform, the military bearing. It looked like footage from past atrocities; Abu Ghraib or Guantanamo Bay. Like what the US government had been doing to Wren for three months, except here was Humphreys saying he hadn't done it.

"You think I've framed you," Wren said. "Set up a false flag attack."

"Exactly right," Humphreys said, his tone utterly flat. "We haven't touched your cult. We weren't going to until this, but the people on the streets don't know that, and to them this video is proof we're killing off the Foundation. They're taking it as a declaration of war."

Wren just stared. War. "What possible benefit do I gain from that?"

Humphreys just stared. Wren had never seen him like this before. The rage absolutely contained. Presenting nothing but a sheer rock face. "You build a groundswell. Turn the people against us. Force us to let you go."

Wren blinked. It was convoluted, but made some kind of sense. Except he hadn't done it.

"Just think for a second, Humphreys," he tried, seeking out the cracks in the Director's rocky façade. "How could I arrange something like this? It's a conspiracy theory at best. Am I such an expert on mind control that I could set up a false flag attack from prison?"

Humphreys was ready. "You set it up in advance. Left instructions in the event we locked you up. Your get out of jail free card."

Wren's eyes widened. There was no give there at all. Humphreys really believed he was responsible. "Instructions to do what," he blurted, "cosplay as CIA, find some craphole black site-looking bunker and run through an actual execution of my own people? Film it on some crappy burner phone then release the video so that the general public will, what, start riots trying to set me free?" He took a breath. "That's an insane conspiracy theory, Humphreys. Open your eyes! You really think I ordered my own people to burn themselves alive?"

Humphreys met the accusation hard. "Why not? You've done it before."

Wren flinched. Of course, Humphreys was partly right. On the last day of his father's cult he'd burned one thousand people to death. He'd only been twelve years old at the time, but he'd done it, painting the napalm onto their bodies one-by-one, lighting every match. He'd confessed to it in the Reparations videos, so everyone in the country knew.

"I was just a kid then. I didn't-"

"But you did," Humphreys spat, and now there was fire in his eyes. Anger building for years, nursed like magma at the center of this cold stone mask. "You are completely capable of this. You are responsible for what you've done and who you are. So take ownership of it."

Wren didn't know what to say. Humphreys had never liked him. They'd both known it. They'd exchanged their share of harsh words, but this was something more. This was a bridge forever burned, a refusal to acknowledge Wren as even human.

Humphreys' watch vibrated. He looked at it then flicked the notification away. "The riots have already begun. Crowds just broke a cordon in LA, flipped a police car, and it's still broad daylight. In your name. You still want to say it's a conspiracy theory? News stations are picking up the video and we can't slow them down at all, thanks to blowback from your assaults on the First Amendment. The social media companies are black boxes to us now. People are going to die if you don't tell me how to stop this."

"Jay already died," Wren countered, his mind racing on adrenaline fumes. If it wasn't him and it wasn't the CIA, then that left only one likely perpetrator. A genius manipulator, capable of coming up with a convoluted plot like this. The man truly behind the Pyramid burnings, twenty-five years ago.

"This has to be my father, Humphreys," Wren rushed on. "Apex of the Pyramid. He drove the Saints, the Blue Fairy, even the Reparations, and now he's driving this. He's framing us both, making us fight each other. You need to be hunting him!"

Humphreys listened in silence, the fire fading so his face became a crag of alabaster again; unmoving, unfeeling, cold. "Your lies don't work on me anymore, Christopher. You're a proven liar. Manipulator. Cultist. You want to talk about past attacks? It's always been you! You are a delusional sociopath, and I've been your patsy for years." His knuckles whitened. "But not anymore. You're nothing to me now. Not an agent, not a sympathy case, barely an entry in the record book."

Wren felt himself slipping. The rock face had no finger-holds, toe-holds, nothing. It was getting hard to breathe. If his father had really done this, it meant everything was coming to an end. Wren wouldn't be able to save the Foundation, or his family, or his country. The Apex would swallow them all.

All he had left were Hail Marys.

"At least get me to LA," he sped on, sucking in a fast breath. "Put me in an ankle monitor, whatever it takes, but get me in front of all the news channels walking with my hands out, peaceful, free. Take away his leverage. Give the people what they want and the riots will end."

Humphreys didn't bat an eye. His watch vibrated in the silence but he didn't look. If anything his gaze grew colder still. "You're saying you want footage of you out calming the five thousand, your arms wide, spreading peace through the masses?"

Wren saw it too late. A perfect trap.

"America's second coming." Humphreys went on, his voice choked up with rage. "A messiah for the new millennium. We could never lock you up again. You'd be above the law for life."

"That's not what I want," Wren tried to backpedal, "I'm saying-"

"I know exactly what you're saying." Humphreys stood. "I was a fool to think I could reason with you. I won't be your fool anymore." He snapped the laptop closed and started away.

Wren sucked in another sharp gulp of air. No purchase on the rock, only freefall into the dark. "At least look for my father," he said swiftly. "You think he'll stop at killing the Foundation and starting some riots in the street? Look at what he did to the Pyramid, Humphreys! He's a psychopath addicted to death; he won't be happy until there's a body count like you can't imagine, rivers of blood to drown us all."

Humphreys turned, and the ice in his eyes said it all. "The people don't love you that much, Christopher." He paused a moment, weighing one final blow. "And frankly, I don't care if your whole cult kill themselves. We'd all be better off."

Humphreys turned. Wren sagged. First Jay, then Rogers, then Gruber, then more. It wouldn't end, and he saw it all stretching ahead like a vision of hell. His father ascendant as America burned. The chaos of the Pyramid revisited upon the world.

There was just one Hail Mary left, the most dangerous yet. He took three more fast gulps of air, rocked back as far as he could in the chair, then slammed his face forward onto the metal table.

There was a crunch of bone and cartilage as his nose crumpled; blood burst down his throat and out over his shackled wrists. The shock trumped the pain, but he was already coming back up before either could bed in. For a second he saw the surprise in Humphreys' eyes, then he took another fast gulp of air and went in for the double.

His face slammed into metal and darkness snatched him down.

4

PIT

When Wren was only nine years old, the Apex had buried himself alive.

Out into the wild deserts of Arizona he'd gone, leading the Pyramid in a long, solemn procession. Wren, then known only as 'Pequeño 3', a half-caste child with wide eyes and a mop of unruly black hair, had run along at his father's side.

It wasn't their first procession into the wilderness, headed for new wonders. Excitement mingled with terror in Wren's young mind; another spike in the rollercoaster of his everyday life. What treasures was the great man about to unearth. What tortures.

The Apex stopped every few minutes, pausing to suck in lungfuls of air, survey the sight lines, toe the hard crust of sand. Each time his cult hushed and waited with bated breath. Soaking it all in. Guessing silently what today's lesson would be.

At last the Apex settled on a space a mile from the town. He marked a circle in the sand with his heel, eight feet in diameter, and ordered his cult to dig. It took a day, as his people dug by hand. They foraged for stones to bank up the walls as the pit sank down into the desert, mixing up mortar with their precious supplies of water. They placed and mortared the stones in one after another. Ten feet deep, eight feet wide, a dry well in the earth.

By nightfall the hole was complete. Nobody knew what its purpose was, until the Apex was lowered in alone. At ten feet deep, the walls were too high to climb out. The muddy mortar had set smooth and hard. In a midnight ceremony, he ordered them to pull three supply sleds over his head and seal him in with sand.

The Pyramid obeyed.

Young Christopher Wren stood at the side of the hole and tried to be brave as his father disappeared from sight. The man whose whims he'd lived by for every moment of his life now steadily disappeared from sight. Standing there at the bottom of the pit, arms spread and eyes shining, he looked like a miracle. Like the Earth turned at his hand.

Under flickering torchlight, the Pyramid wailed as they swept two feet of sand over the sleds. Mourning their leader already, for surely he was going to die. The walls were too sheer to climb. There were no gaps for air to trickle down.

For three days the Pyramid waited in the desert. Their scant supplies of food and water ran out, but no one complained. They were silent and watchful. Few slept, none spoke. With the Apex gone there was nothing to say. Wren hardly left the side of the pit, now a faint mound. He didn't eat a thing, barely drank a drop, rarely slept. If the Apex was suffering, so would he suffer. None were so devoted as little Pequeño 3.

Through those three days and three nights he came to think of the pit as an extension of the Apex's body. At night the sand swelled as he exhaled. Through the day it sank as he drew in deep, nourishing breaths. The sky swirled in time with his pulse, the clouds shifted as his slow eyes blinked, the wind blew as he licked dry lips.

He would survive. Wren knew it. Though only nine years old, he'd learned much from his father's experiments already, searching for the limits of the body and the mind. If you believed otherwise, why should pain be feared? If you had faith enough, what need was there for food, water, air? With sufficient strength of spirit, what need did you have of your eyes, your ears, your arms and your legs?

So Christopher Wren dreamed of the Apex in the darkness below, lying still as a corpse. His heart stopped because he willed it. His lungs fell silent because it was his desire. Proving to his people what wonders could be done.

Three days and three nights passed. The silences above ground grew longer and starker. A thousand people could not shift their eyes from the faint mound, beneath which lay their master, too afraid to blink lest they miss something.

At midnight, they finally dug up the pit. Eyes were wide with fear. What would they find? They raked their fingers bloody on the sand, scooping it hungrily, desperately. With grunts they dredged the supply sleds out, showering dust to the pit floor below.

Women wailed. Men cried out.

By torchlight, flickering as if afire, the Apex stood exactly as he'd stood before, arms spread and eyes shining with some inner light.

The Pyramid dropped to their knees and sang his praises. People entered hysterical fits, moved by the strength of his faith. Their Apex was alive. Their Apex was reborn.

It was only to little Pequeño 3 in the early hours of the morning, after the Pyramid had gone back to the façades of their fake town, that the Apex revealed the truth. In the perfect smooth wall of the pit, the Apex opened a gap. The mud mortar crumbled with ease, stones spilled out, and beyond lay a tunnel built with sturdy wooden boards, barely two feet below the surface of the sand. The Apex led and Pequeño 3 followed, crawling along together. The tunnel continued a hundred feet to an opening in the desert.

Standing on the surface in the moonlight, the Apex explained with a kind of furious glee. He'd crawled out as soon as they'd put the sleds above him. All eyes had been on the pit, so no one had seen him walk away. For three days he'd lived in the fake town alone. Enjoying the silence. Under cover of darkness as the third night drew in, with all eyes on the pit, he'd crawled back underground and re-mortared the wall behind him.

Pequeño 3 had only stared. The Apex's grin was infectious. Sharing the lie with his favored son. He'd sent his cult to dig the tunnel months earlier. Blindfolded, they'd carved what they believed was a channel for water. If anything, it was all a test of his Pyramid's devotion. Not one of them had left his side.

Wren remembered few details of the Apex; not his face, rarely the exact words he'd said, but he remembered the thing the Apex said to him then perfectly, as the smile fell swiftly from his face.

"But you know what's real, don't you, Pequeño 3?"

The smile came back just as swiftly as it had left.

But you know what's real.

For months after that, little Pequeño 3's dreams had been haunted by images of the Apex alone at the base of his pit, as cold and unmoving as a hibernating cicada. He always woke sweating and afraid, as if he'd somehow failed. He couldn't forget the tunnel and the Apex's grin, but next to the three days he'd spent standing watch over the pit, feeling the earth breathe in and out with the Apex's dying gasps, that memory felt false. It felt cheap, nasty and unreal.

So he hollowed it out. Like the Apex tearing down the

crumbling mortar, he erased the truth day by day from the inside out. He worked hard to believe the lie, until finally he made the false memory real.

Lying in the dark of his own shallow pit in the sand, after long months of practice, he effectively halted his pulse, stopped the flow of breath from his body, and entered a kind of hibernation. For three minutes he appeared dead to the outside world. It was called aortal flutter.

5

AORTAL FLUTTER

Wren's body flopped, head bouncing off the metal, shoulders rolling sideways, his center of gravity tilting him off the chair to fall taut on his outstretched arms, still cuffed to the the table.

On some level he could still sense the world; dim sounds, sensations, images through his glassy eyes. He'd worked to maintain some level of consciousness while entering the state of 'aortal flutter'. Hyperventilating the lungs, but only so far; inducing hyperarousal, the fight or flight response, through acute trauma, but only to a certain extent.

The right combination of stress and hyperventilation sent the body into a compensatory panic: pulse rising to catastrophic heights of three or four hundred beats per minute; breathing cut right back to an undetectable wisp; all motor and neural capacity lost.

To the outside world he'd appear dead. The chambers of the heart beat so fast and shallow that the aortal valve didn't fully close, gushing blood in an even stream that made a pulse indistinguishable. The fraction of air passing through his windpipe would only be detectable with a mirror held close to his mouth.

Dead to the world.

The risks were very real. If the state went on too long the heart could be irreparably damaged. Brain death could occur without ever waking up. Hallucinations, confusion, memory loss were common. A mad magician's trick, too dangerous for laboratory study. In all the world, there was likely no person as adept as Wren.

Seconds passed, minutes, and he was deep underwater throughout. They moved his body; first to sitting upright in the chair, checking his pulse, listening for his breath, but feeling nothing. Right there, they had a choice.

Let him die or revive him.

The next thing Wren knew, he was laid out flat. Wrists and ankles uncuffed. Someone was pumping his chest. Dangerous for a heart that was wide open. Breathing air into his overloaded lungs. More dangerous still. Wren felt a warm breeze on the bare soles of his feet; the door to the cell was open. Someone bringing a crash kit. He saw the Apex's face in the darkness; a blur, as ever. His father.

Time for the grand reveal, arms spread at the bottom of the pit.

He loaded the motions up in his brain before he moved. His reactions would be shot for an hour, longer maybe. The vascular hangover would last for days. Punch. Grab. Aim. Shoot. It had to happen smoothly, as there'd be no way to course-correct as he went.

His chest compressed again. Someone breathed in his mouth. He used the moment to bite down. There was a shriek, and his eyes flashed open; it looked like the world was filmed with candlewax. One of the Marines, barely the pink smudge of a face, was recoiling. Wren chased him with a jerky sit-up, his whole toned core driving the sweet spot of his forehead hard into the guy's jaw. Crunk, and the guy sagged.

For a second Wren reeled. Dizzy, fuzzy. Two more

Marines in the room, barely blue smudges on gray, one caught burrowing through a bright yellow plastic box. The crash kit. Humphreys a white face at the door. Shouting.

Wren's pre-loaded program rolled on. He grabbed the unconscious Marine and pulled him in like a shield, snatching at his tactical side-arm. It took three pulls, then the gun was in Wren's palm. Ten seconds, all in. Black metal before his eyes, a Glock M007, index finger pushing in the trigger bar, then the gun was barking in his hand.

One shot, two, three, cacophonous sound roaring in the contained space. Recoil sent his wrist every which way. Random.

Wren rose, on his knees. The Marine-smudges had their guns up now. Wren held his gun to the head of the one that was his shield, and breathed.

His pulse slammed in his head. Dropping from its frantic pace, valves closing and opening, blood tearing around his body. The chance of permanent damage every time. He blinked; the waxy film came off his eyes, sound rushed in, and he held the Marine in front of him. Almost fell, but the man's body kept him steady.

"Shoot him!" Humphreys was shouting, words in an endless stream, but the Marines didn't shoot. Three of them now, but none of them could shoot, not with their colleague between them and Wren. Training dictated otherwise. Give them ten more seconds and they'd figure it out; leave the room, lock the door and take control.

Wren couldn't give them the ten seconds.

He shot Humphreys.

Little time to aim. No way to stabilize his shaking arm as blood stormed through it. Spray and pray.

He hit the wall, the corridor, a Marine in the thigh then Humphreys in the arm. A crunch as the guy's femur blew apart; he shrieked and dropped. Humphreys spun in his tracks, clutching his bicep. The second Marine assessed quickly, saw Wren's gun trained on Humphreys, and went to his fallen colleague. Greatest threat to life, and all that. Admirable. The others held fast, weapons pointed at Wren.

Wren let the unconscious Marine go and rose slowly, his legs just taking his weight, his gun shaking on Humphreys. Director of the CIA, right-hand man to the President, big kahuna at any table. Absolutely livid.

Humphreys looked to the Marines either side, figuring it out. "I won't be your hostage," he hissed through gritted teeth, with blood leaking through his clamped fingers.

There was no need to argue. Wren strode the gap between them in a second, snatched Humphrey's injured arm and twisted it behind his back, wrist up between his shoulder blades. Instant pain. Instant compliance. Humphreys cried out and hopped up onto his toes.

"Resist if you want," Wren slurred, barely comprehensible, but the first thought Humphreys had to be thinking. "I'll dislocate your shoulder and use the other arm. Resist some more, you'll never swing a golf club again. Now march."

Humphreys grimaced, cursed, and marched.

Out into the corridor, Wren's mind worked feverishly. Two more Marines out here with their guns drawn, but they wouldn't fire either. Not with the CIA Director at stake, Wren's gun pressed to his head. Humphreys shouted something but Wren ignored it, running calculations.

Fresh adrenaline would last maybe three minutes. His legs might last five, his heart ten before he crashed. He hoped the black site wasn't big, and the Chinook wasn't far. That was all he could think. Beyond that, God knew what. Riots. Revolution. His father. His bare feet slapped noisily on the concrete floor, matched by the desperate clatter of Humphreys' heels.

6

CHINOOK

Humphreys wailed. Wren didn't listen; his legs were already giving out. Together they staggered along three tunnels of lichen-smeared greenish cement, two flights of murky concrete stairs, faces looming from open doorways and an alarm caterwauling. At last there was a heavy metal door, a crash as he shoved through, then a sudden burst of light.

Wren was blinded and squeezed Humphreys' arm tighter, tottering into the full bright of day. There was fine gravel underfoot, jet fuel exhaust in the air and the sun on his skin.

Three months underground with no sights, no smells, nothing real except what they'd given him, left him feeling like a shuddering cicada reborn naked into the world.

The thunder of the Chinook came to him like a manic pulse; the downdraft stinging his bare calves with blown sand. He forced his eyes wide open and saw the dual-rotor helicopter squatted like some massive beast in the midst of a strange, pitted landscape. Orange clay stretching into a distant heat haze, punctuated by strange berms in the earth like prehistoric burial mounds. His flagging mind ticked over.

Blue sky, a few clouds striated like torn muscle fibers, and now this.

Missile silos? Fallout bunkers? Wren dragged Humphreys with him. The man was barely conscious now, faint with blood loss. That made two of them. Far off stick figures ran out from one of the berms; red clay sloping walls, a metal blast door. Who knew what lay within?

Voices on tinny loudspeakers ordered him to stop, barely audible over the thunder of the Chinook's blades. Both sweat-soaked, pale and flagging. Wren charged at the massive creature: twin rotors, an olive-green shell big enough to swallow a squad thirty Marines strong. The side bay door hung open like a toothless mouth.

In seconds they came under the furious downdraft.

"Get in," mumbled Wren, and hoisted Humphreys bodily into the Chinook's steel belly, rolling in after. Cold metal on bare flesh. He caught a flash of the CIA Director's face; pale as alabaster, but disbelieving. A new relationship, now. Their phone calls would never be the same again.

Wren stood and weaved; there was webbing on the walls, low benches, equipment crates bolted down. A cornucopia of medicines, MREs, weaponry, gear, clothing kept in ergonomic cabins.

Humphreys went where he was pushed; up to the cockpit where the pilot was staring back.

"Get out," Wren said, and levelled the Glock.

A Marine pilot. He unstrapped the helmet calmly like he was untying his shoelaces, opened the door, shot Wren a disapproving glance then hopped out. Good training. Marines weren't hostage negotiators, and knew it.

Wren shoved Humphreys into the co-pilot's seat and strapped him in. People were closing in now, the loudspeaker voices growing louder. Wren fell into the pilot's seat, took the cyclic, pushed the throttle and the bird launched like a wobbling rocket. The roar of the rotors became a tornado.

Away.

He fought for control as the berms and silos fell behind. The voices and people and torture. The breeze felt good. He surged to one hundred feet then hit the automatic pilot, set the course to the flat orange line of the horizon and staggered into the back.

Moments passed him by like postcards in a zoetrope as he sucked down a strip of combat sharpeners, some methamphetamine mix that bought him a few more minutes; enough to strap Humphreys' wound tight, to tug on some black tactical kit and boots, to stuff a rucksack with MREs, water, meds, assorted gear. In the front Humphreys lolled unconscious.

There wasn't long. With Humphreys aboard they wouldn't shoot him down, but they would track the Chinook. Soon a jet would overpass, assume remote control of the helo and divert it. His window would be minutes only. He throttled the speed, down to twenty miles an hour, then leaned into Humphreys.

The man was barely conscious. Wren pushed his face right up to the whites of his eyes. "Go after my father," he hissed, then staggered away.

In the back he yanked a rappel line clear of its rotary dispenser spool. Hooked the end on to his belt harness. Below lay endless scrub, desert, red loam and clay. No more berms. Barely any cover. Heat haze, false oases, sharp spines of rock. The sun was high. Zero cover. His eyes blurred on the orange spread.

He jumped.

The rappel line caught. He paid it out fast, spiraling and falling. Nobody knew where; no way to know. His heart beat artificially fast, the meth hit taking it to the limit. Wired and flying. The Chinook soared, the dusty landscape seared up, then he hit.

At the last moment he cut the rappel line, and the impact came; his body tumbled like a skipped pebble, bouncing and rolling in the dust until he finally slammed to a stop curled against a spiny gray bush. He barely felt the pain. No time left for pain now, anyway. He dropped his cheek to the hot earth with the darkness surging, as the Chinook thundered away into the distance.

7

DESERT

Wren woke to the worst headache he'd ever experienced, hammering from his temples to the back of his head like hydrostatic shock, each beat of his pulse a bullet.

He curled his body tighter. Every muscle cried out in pain. These were his various tortures coming home to roost; the freezing, the adrenaline hangover, the comedown from prolonged aortal flutter.

Stupid. He groaned and opened his eyes on stars. How long had he been out? A slim crescent moon cast little light over the barren landscape. The pole star was high; early hours, at least past four in the morning, given it was summer. Dark, but now there were flashes of light spiking in the distance.

Searchlights.

He dry-swallowed, blinked raspy eyes, listened. Through the roar in his head there were distant rotor blades; as if the Chinook had never left the skies, as if Humphreys was up there still, circling...

Helicopters. Drones.

That meant thermal imaging.

He grunted and curled his body tighter. From a distance his heat profile, obscured by the spiny brush and huddled tight, could pass for anything. A sleeping coyote. A warren of meerkats. But the moment he moved, extended an arm or a leg, they'd have him.

He took stock.

Alone in the middle of nowhere, likely south of the border, absolutely decrepit and drained, with God-knew how many CIA squads out looking for him, unable to move. No darknet, no Foundation, no GPS to localize his coordinates, and no place to hide. As for Humphreys, he had infrared eyes in the sky and a clear line from the Chinook's navigation computer to follow. Now they'd be working their way back along that line, looking for the spot he jumped.

Judging from the sound, it was a thorough search. Fifty agents? Multiple support vehicles. Humphreys himself in attendance, arm bandaged up tight.

And assets? With minimal movements, he rummaged through the backpack, found a bottle of water and drained it. There was also a flashlight, some MREs, a compass, a mylar blanket, a tool kit, a lighter, and a holster for the Glock with several spare magazines. He'd have trouble aiming, though, given his condition.

Not great. The choices before him were abysmal. This was going to be touch and go.

Choice one was to run, but that was a non-starter. With thermal imaging they'd have him the instant he moved, and even if they somehow missed his infrared signature, they'd find his trail in the sand. He ran a hand over the gritty surface dust, still lukewarm from the day's sun. No way to hide footsteps in this. They'd drag him down like dogs on a wounded deer.

Choice two was to go to them. He envisaged the search pattern they'd be running, likely one broad search cordon, support vehicles in back. If he could somehow bypass the infrared, maybe he could sneak through the search cordon, try to pass as CIA on the other side, commandeer a vehicle and flee. But the chances of pulling that off and getting away clean were infinitesimal.

It left choice three. His fried mind raced. Some combination of the two. They had him on the Chinook's straight line; if he could get off that line and out into the open, without a clear trail or infrared signal to follow, they'd never find him. Drone coverage was useless when the area multiplied to many square miles. He just needed an escape vector that obscured both his physical trail and his heat signature.

The thunder of helicopter blades rolled closer. Minutes only, and his mind sped ahead. Back in his days undercover with Taliban groups in the Loe Nekan mountain range, Afghanistan, the jihadis had used multiple tricks to evade Predator drones tracking them via infrared: started fires, sheltered underground, hidden beneath thick goatskin blankets; anything to mask the heat of their bodies. In high summer even large rocks would work, holding enough of the sun's warmth to obscure a human's infrared signature and render American overwatch blind.

A rudimentary plan began to take shape in his head.

Carefully he got his knees under him, hunched over the backpack. From within he took one of the two spare magazines, field-stripped the bullets onto the back of the mylar blanket, then used twin pliers from the tool kit to prize the first bullet apart. In the darkness he operated largely by feel and sound, feeling it as the bullet casing 'pulled', listening as the black grains spattered down on the sleek mylar. He moved to the next as the searchlights splashed closer. Within minutes he'd pulled seven and had a small mound of black grains gathered in a crease of the fabric.

He took a deep breath. Everything that followed would have to be fast and precise. A blessed rush of adrenaline pushed the headache back and gave him room to breathe. Now he caught voices carrying through the still night air; clipped and professional, sharing constant status updates. Maybe five hundred yards away.

He pulled the backpack on, tipped the black powder grains into a natural crook of the spiny brush tree's roots, nudged the heap to spread out a simple 'fuse' one grain thick, then unfurled the mylar blanket. A thin and staticky silver material designed to trap heat, it spread out with a crinkly whispering that sounded like an engine roaring to his sensitized ears. He pulled it over his head, back and arms like a cloak of invisibility; instant cover from infrared overwatch, as long as he kept his core, his hands and his head largely hidden from above.

Slowly he shuffled backward two feet, waiting for a cry to go up, but none came. The blanket was working. He shielded his face with his elbow, held the lighter to the end of the black powder trail then pulled the metal dial across the flint.

It sparked. The black powder caught, ignited with a puff of smoke and ran up the makeshift fuse in a split second, giving a little explosive puff when it hit the pile, sending flames searing up the spiny brush tree's dry side.

Instant conflagration.

The tree caught and spewed out heat and light. Wren lurched to his feet, ducked low and sprinted parallel to the search cordon, getting off line. Ten steps, twenty, until he almost ran into a large rock jutting up through the sand. He dropped at once, hands to the rock's surface and feeling the captured heat emanating outward. An infrared island, offering additional cover.

Had they seen his transition? It was hard to say. He looked back.

They definitely saw the burning bush. It was an inferno now, burning like Jay, sudden heat flaring like a crocus through the cold air. Any stray heat leaked from the mylar should have been a ghost trapped in that explosion.

The helicopters were already thundering closer, their floodlights illuminating the night. Maybe ten seconds had passed. Shouts grew louder, feet were already stamping across the few hundred yards between here and there; call it two football fields, twenty seconds each at a dead sprint, longer over unknown terrain. That gave him less than a minute.

He pushed off the rock and ran right at the lights, mylar snugged tight. In ten seconds he was well beyond the bush's halo of firelight and charging headlong at the search cordon, twenty seconds and shouts tore toward him, twenty-five and he slid into the heat shield around another large rock like a runner into home base, pulling away the mylar blanket just in time for a streak of flashlight to track wildly down his side.

His dark outfit in the darkness offered nothing to fix on, with no reflective splash off the silvery blanket, and the figure ran on. Wren felt the stampede passing him by; outstripping their slower support vehicles in the race to catch Christopher Wren, driven by their own endocrine systems pumping out adrenaline. He heard the bark of a rifle report, chased by others. Even better; in the chaos of the chase, confusion was his friend.

He'd made his own gap; lodged now in a dark gulley between the bristling lights of the front cordon and the floods of the trundling support vehicles, maybe a hundred yards wide. He set off at a terrifying blind sprint into the dark, running perpendicular across their angle of approach, head low, risking a broken ankle off uneven ground and rocks with every step, putting his faith in his sense of the land and reactions until-

He hit an obstruction full on in the belly and staggered off line, spinning back to see what he'd hit.

A guy in the dark, rifle barrel extended, night vision goggles strapped to his head. For a moment only Wren stared and the guy stared back. Night vision gave tremendous clarity, but the peripheral vision was useless; he hadn't seen Wren coming. Now he did, already swinging his rifle barrel back around. There was no time for Wren to draw his gun, instead he spun the dial on the lighter just as the rifle fired and a bullet zinged by his shoulder.

The figure screamed as the lighter's flame flooded his retinas, scrabbled to get a hand up in front of the lenses, and into that gap Wren plunged. A shoulder in the guy's gut, hoisting him bodily off his feet and down into the scrub. Wren muscled his way on top, put a knee on the rifle stock, punched the guy three times hard in the chin, then yanked off his goggles.

Panting while the guy groaned, Wren took a second to reorient himself. Humphreys had really prepared; adding a second search cordon to patrol in the darkness. It was hardly standard operating procedure.

No time to waste. Now the helicopters were spiraling wider around the burning bush, looking to pick up his trail. He retrieved his mylar, wrapped it around his shoulders, snugged the tight goggles over his head and instantly saw everything. The dark gully lit up bright.

He ran into the light.

8

GULLY

There were two more figures in the gully but Wren bypassed them easily, in stealth-mode now, covered by the shouts and gunfire rattling off to the left. Seconds were counting down; as the agent he'd punched recovered, signaled on his radio, and they all figured it out. Wren just had to stay ahead of that bleeding edge.

He burst through the cordon with no fanfare. The inner core of vehicles and lights were all in back to the right, the choppers and flashlights strobed in back to the left.

Wren broke right.

Heat would be escaping around the edges of his mylar blanket by now. Nothing he could do about that but pray; that the analysts at their screens weren't inclined to buy a flicker of heat-spill as a person in flight. Tunnel vision ought to have their eyes trained on the immediate few hundred yards around the burning bush.

Every yard he gained now bought him time, out of the lens before they clicked the focus wider. He ran on for a minute or two, avoiding obstructions easily with the goggles, then stopped by a big rock parallel to the core convoy, slipped the night visions off and unwrapped the mylar, letting some of the heat escape while he had cover. Steam poured off him.

The core was five vehicles strong: three troop carriers, a big-wheel Humvee and a long support truck on caterpillar tracks. Where the hell did they get that? Flown in during the night, he guessed. Figures stood on the roof training floodlights ahead. They had no idea he was already flanking them.

He turned to the burning bush; its light carried through all the dark brush and cacti, and the two helicopters hovered over it like flies on carrion. Pretty soon they'd figure out his play.

He flung the mylar around his shoulders again, pulled the goggles back on, took a breath and ran into darkness. Two more minutes and he rounded the rear of the support vehicles. No foot patrols back here. He swung in tight to their trail; every wheel track and footstep frozen like a river leading back across the desert, caught in the silvery goggles' display.

They'd be coming for him soon. He turned to face the receding convoy and ran full tilt backwards along their trail, mylar blanket whipping around his face. Invisible, and if not invisible then barely a glitch of stray heat in the algorithms. Facing forward, his boot marks would be near-impossible to distinguish from the fifty pairs of boots and tire tracks that had come this way already; a trick he'd learned from his adoptive father Tandrews, in the forests of Maine some twenty years ago. Enter a river, you were covered. As long as your exit point was disguised, your trail was gone.

He ran backward hard, until his hamstrings burned and his knees felt they might jolt out of lock, until the helicopters were circling back with their floodlights spinning like disco balls. They knew they'd lost him, but they didn't know just how bad.

As they zoomed back toward him, he sidestepped fast to the 'river's' edge and leaped onto a long spine of rock. Five steps on he jumped to another rock, then another, then dropped back to the sand some twenty further feet away, obliterating his trail. He was a ghost.

One helicopter roared near as he ran full tilt into the wilderness, floodlights sweeping like Vegas skybeams. Humphreys' voice came over loudspeaker.

"I'll lock them all up, Christopher! Every last member of your damn cult. They'll never see the light of day again."

Wren ran on, hunkered low. Humphreys had already said all that. There was no new threat here. If it wasn't Humphreys taking out the Foundation, it would be his father. The crosshairs were on them all now, and imprisonment was better than burning alive any day of the week. The helo sped past his exit point on the trail and carried on.

Wren ran. The darkness unfolded for him, a sole meteor in the wilderness. Stars blazed overhead, painfully bright through the night vision goggles. The sound and light of the search teams diminished the further he went, boots stamping down, doing his best to ignore the myriad pains in his thighs, gut, head. Adrenaline fading, replaced by lactic acid.

Still he ran. At some point he shrugged off the mylar blanket, crunched it into the suit's belly flap and kept on at an even long-distance pace, putting miles between him and the convoy. Thirty minutes. An hour. Slow thoughts turned through his battered mind.

He saw flashes of Jay burning again. Of Humphreys making threats. Most of all, he thought about his father. Apex of the Pyramid. Out there somewhere, bringing ruin down upon America. Forcing people to turn against each other. The same old box of tricks, now amplified big enough for a whole country to swallow.

The moon and stars tracked across the sky. Call it eight miles. If they couldn't find his tracks, there was no way they'd find him now. The wind would help disperse whatever trail he'd left. Animals passing by.

He dropped to his side beside a boulder and gasped for air. He managed to pluck another water bottle from the bag, drank half of it in one go, then lay there panting until exhaustion claimed him.

9

CIVILIZATION

Wren groaned awake with the sun on his face. The heat was blistering and his lips felt scabbed over from exposure. His mouth was dry, his eyeballs were gritty in their sockets and his whole body felt pummeled.

But better.

He rolled up, blinking hard. A family of small brown roadrunners froze some fifty yards off, alarmed by the sudden movement, then darted swiftly away. Orange scrub sand stretched as far as Wren could see, broken by clumps of juicy-looking prickly pear cacti. There was no sound but the odd rustlings of animals and the whispering of a nearby ocotillo's hydra-like flower heads in the hot wind. The sky was swimming-pool blue and devoid of jet contrails, with the sun high overhead.

Early summer south of the border, in the desert drawing close to the twentieth parallel, about as wild as the surface of the moon.

He rose to his feet. His heart hammered, his breath rasped noisily, and he reached up to his face, remembering the slam into the desk. There were no loose teeth, but his nose was broken. He took a breath, took a grip, and gave it a twist.

Cartilage clicked and gristled. The blue sky grayed out for a second, blood trickled down his upper lip, then he could breathe.

A day and a night since Jay had burned.

He sifted through the rucksack, came up with a bottle of flavored water and two MREs. He drank half the bottle and slugged the first MRE down in moments. The hit of the sugar was immediate; his senses sharpened, his head cleared.

Time to go.

He dropped the MRE tray and looked around, taking in the flora, the heat, the sand, the smells. It felt like the Sonoran Desert. Not hot enough for the Mojave, with too much wildlife, which meant a straight shot up to Arizona, if he could trek a thousand miles through scrub. Aim to stumble upon a road or a settlement before then, get a vehicle, hit the border before nightfall, and the next body burned.

The clock was ticking.

He took a deep, hot breath. It was good to be out in the desert. It was where he'd been born, darting through the sands of Arizona spearing tarantulas, bark scorpions and ridgenose rattlers before he'd even learned to read, hunting and eating cactus wrens, packrats and jackrabbits like they were candy dropped from the sky. To some the desert was a place to go die, but to Wren it was just one big banquet table stretching out to the horizon.

No time like the present. He took a deep, hot breath, pulled the rucksack on and set off at a loping jog for civilization.

Three hours on and maybe twenty miles covered, Wren hit upon a trail. The sun had swung halfway toward its zenith overhead, his pack was one more bottle and an MRE lighter, and his muscles felt like they were singing, as the hangover of aortal flutter cleared out.

The trail ran roughly east-west, marked out in tire tracks. One pick-up, he figured, a desert hermit. The arrow treads headed west, so Wren started west

An hour or so along there was a shift in the air; a kind of intense brightness, as if an array of search beams had been turned up to the sky. He sped up, guessing what it was before he saw the first glint of light off silver atop a long, low wall of dark pipe scaffolds.

A solar array.

They'd been springing up in the Sonoran and Mojave deserts for twenty years now, fueled by government subsidies and the push toward renewable energy. Wren knew about them from his undercover work with the Qotl cartel; gangsters trying to shake down construction work for protection money.

The big companies usually paid. It was easier than rebuilding whatever the cartel pulled down, and less damaging for their reputation than images of butchered employees spread across the web. On one occasion, though, they'd gone to the US government, and they'd dispatched Christopher Wren.

He'd been tasked to deal with early sabotage of the Don Jose array. That had ended with a fresh deal being cut, two Qotl cartel members dead in the brush and a certain measure of peace in the desert.

He ran on toward the emerging wall of scaffolding, until he folded neatly into a narrow access alley between the array's giant black panels like a pinball in a slot. With his head and shoulders just bobbing above the angled plates, it felt like he was running through a choppy dark sea. The giant five-by-three panels stretched away in a massive oblong to the west, perfectly aligned to the track of the sun.

Up ahead lay the control hub; a two-story structure with large wraparound windows like an air traffic control tower. Wren reached the edge of the solar scaffolds and strode out without pause, gun drawn. A gravel parking lot, a transformer array buzzing behind a fence to his right, a blacktop road running off to the left, and two pick-ups clustered into the tower's scant shade. Through the second-floor window Wren saw one guy's eyes widen on him.

A man in dusty black tactical gear emerges from the array, gun drawn, what was the guy supposed to think? One hand already on the phone to the Federales. Wren levelled the Glock and the guy froze. A mop of black hair and an open mouth, staring out.

Cartel business, he'd be thinking. No two ways about it. Survivor of a hit, maybe. Nothing the police were going to do to help him. Nothing the government were going to do, either.

Wren shoved his way into the lobby. No security in the desert. A locked door blocked the stairs, card swipe in a plastic frame, and Wren kicked it through. Up the stairs, he came face-to-face with two guys in the control room; the one with wide-eyes, still staring, and another holding an antique Mossberg 500 shotgun, 1965 if it was a day, wooden stock with filigree, 12 gauge, 410 bore, enough whammy to blow a manhole-sized tunnel through Wren's chest, if the range was right.

Wren stopped in the doorway and smiled, let the Glock drop at his side, looked at Wide-eyes and spoke in fluent Spanish.

"¿Soy Qotl cartel. Hiciste la llamada?" I'm Qotl cartel. Did you make the call?

The shotgun guy answered, shaven-head but with a bald pattern growing through dark on his scalp like a monk's hair line. "¿Qué llamada?" What call?

Wren didn't look at him. He only looked at Wide-eyes.

Coffee stain on his rumpled white shirt, mid-thirties, maybe a doctorate in electrochemistry, cursing every day of this cattle prod gig out in the middle of nowhere.

"Federales," Wren prompted.

"No lo hice," the guy managed. No I didn't.

Wren grunted. Shotgun wanted to say something, but Wren acted like he wasn't even there. He put the Glock down on a filing cabinet and surveyed the control room, eyes skipping over the weapon pointed his way like it was of no more interest than a ripe banana. That was how you showed power.

Several workstations, signs of hotdesking, a used coffee mug declaring 'Una mala madre-', 'One bad mother-'. Nothing he could use. He looked sharply back at Wide-eyes, who flinched as if struck.

"¿Tienes ropa de repuesto?" Do you have spare clothes.

Shotgun took a step closer, maybe thinking to make his play. Wren took one step in too, away from the gun on the cabinet, still ignoring him. No threat. No fear. All his focus on Wide-eyes.

"¿Qué?" the guy asked.

"Necesito ropa de repuesto. ¿Tienes?" I need spare clothes. Do you have some?

Wide-eyes stared then nodded hard. "Sí."

"A ver." Show me.

Wide-eyes looked over at Shotgun. Wren didn't. The guy with the shotgun only had the authority Wren afforded him, and he afforded none. The man to listen to was Wren.

"Ahora," Wren said, and put a little sting into it. Now. Enough to get Wide-eyes moving. Shotgun tracked him, but that didn't matter. The time to shoot had been the moment he walked in.

Wren followed Wide-eyes as he bustled over to a locker. Ask just right, and he'd get clothes, a phone, a car, and these two would never tell a soul. Write it up as theft; company insurance out here, in bandit country, would cover it. You didn't cross the cartel, not if you wanted to live, and what else could Wren be, if he wasn't the cartel?

Twenty minutes later Wren climbed into one of the dusty pick-ups in the lot with both his Glock and the Mossberg, wearing tight borrowed jeans and a check cotton shirt, swigging Coke from a liter bottle.

The desert always provided.

10

DARKNET

S itting in the driver's seat with the engine running and the AC on, Wren booted Wide-eyes' iPhone and flashed a glance up through the windshield as it downloaded an anonymizing VPN. Both guys were peeking out of the window above, waiting for him to roll out.

They'd have to wait a little longer.

The app chimed and booted; Wren typed in the link to his Foundation darknet immediately and saw-

Nothing. He hit reload but it didn't help. He tried a random news site, it loaded, then he hit the back button but still no Foundation site.

His mouth went dry. There was no site there. It didn't even return a 404 Missing Link page, just blank white. He'd half-anticipated this, but it still stung to have it happen. There were redundancies, though, baked in by his uber-hackers Hellion and B4cksl4cker; back-up sites on their secret 'weathernet' which afforded them constant oversight of the whole Internet. Now he had to hope one of them was still live.

He typed in the first backup, and got nothing. The second and third both went the same way. He tried a few back channel links, direct routes into the deeper layers of his darknet, but they all returned the same.

It was worse than he'd thought.

His thumbs flew over the keys as he dredged up more links from memory, and every one hit a blank. The erasure was total. It left him utterly blind to the activities of his Foundation. Had the 'Deep State' already grabbed all his members? Had the Pyramid?

His heart pounded. He took a long pull on the Coke, calculating possibilities. He loaded up three different news sites and left an identical message on comment boards that were several years old: a secret trigger code and his new phone number.

Hellion, B4cksl4cker and anyone else in the Foundation core was free, they'd have an instant Internet alert set for the code and would call him as soon as it chimed.

He sat still, waiting for the phone to ring. Sweat beaded down his cheeks; the hot gust from the vents didn't help. Still no call. He checked the dashboard clock, 11:17 in Mexico made it 18:17 Central European Time. B4cksl4cker would just be getting started for the day. He wiped his forehead. Minutes stretched on.

Still nothing.

Bad.

He scrolled to the front page of a news site. It seemed the riots in LA had tamped down with the dawn, which was something at least. The same story was echoed across New York, Cincinnati, St. Louis, Berkeley, and other cities. Live casualty counts splashed in red banners: five dead in LA, thirteen hospitalized, including both protesters and cops; three dead in New York, seven in Cincinnati and more across the country.

At least there'd been no fresh burnings. Steven Gruber and Sally Rogers should be OK for now.

Still nothing from B4cksl4cker or Hellion.

Wren paged through headlines. The riots led every story, some critical and some in broad support. 'Deep State Brutality' was a popular logline. His name was mentioned everywhere: 'Where is Christopher Wren?'; 'Release Christopher Wren!'; 'Who is Christopher Wren?'

One name kept popping up, 'David Keller'. Apparently he'd been dropping hints about running for the November presidential election as an Independent. A successful CEO and millionaire, now he was out at every protest stoking the crowd to fight for Wren's release.

There was one thing he could do about that right now. He opened the phone's camera app and swiped to record video, turned the lens on himself, then began to speak.

"My name is Christopher Wren. I'm the leader of the Foundation, ex-agent of the CIA, and I am no one's prisoner. I am not being held in a black site, I am not being tortured, and I do not need your help to be released."

He took a breath. Thinking through what kind of message he wanted to send.

"Yesterday my Foundation member, Jay Durant, was murdered, but it was not at the hands of some imagined 'Deep State'. Jay was murdered by my father, Apex of the Pyramid, the suicide cult I survived twenty-five years ago." He fixed the lens with a glare. "The rioting yesterday is his end goal. I believe he wants more of it, in every city across the country, because he likes to see people die. Do not do his work for him. Do not be a vector for this disease. I am a free man. You are a free people. Trust that I will hunt my father down, and step back from the streets. Go back to your lives."

He stopped talking, ended the recording then uploaded the two-minute clip to several social media sites. For long moments he watched the video post, barely breathing, as it was watched, upvoted, and commented upon.

'Who is this guy? Is he for real?'

'He looks like Christopher Wren, but something about the audio is off.'

'The audio is way off, and look at the setting!! It's totally fake, green screen like a B-movie. This whole thing is more propaganda."

'Vote it down, sheeple! It's clickbait. Do your research!'

Within minutes, downvotes throttled the video. Accordingly the apps responded by making it invisible.

Wren just stared. He could make another video, but it wouldn't help now. The people didn't want to be calm. They didn't want to go back to their homes and wait to be saved from some shadowy manipulator. They were angry and they wanted blood, and nothing Wren could say was going to stop that now.

Still nothing from his hackers. At least the AC was pumping cold air at last. Wren started the engine and revved the pick-up out of the sandy lot, dialing another number from memory.

11

ROOTS

The phone rang and Wren tore down the buckled desert road flanked by solar mirrors, envisaging the landline ringing in the study of a timber-frame house far away, hand-built by Wren and the old man himself. Backwoods of Maine, a place to go when you needed a little 'me' time.

Tandrews had said as much early on, back when the young Christopher Wren had no sense of the cultural zeitgeist. What was 'me' time to a child fresh out of the Pyramid, still scarred by the burning of a thousand people alive?

The phone rang, an old rotary model, Wren remembered, trilling through the study and into the den, where he knew his once adoptive-father James Tandrews was most likely sitting, sipping a whiskey in the late afternoon, maybe listening to jazz, looking out through the glass into the dark of the forest.

The phone clicked twice; no doubt they'd bugged Tandrews' phone and were listening to every word, but Wren didn't care. He needed to think, and that meant bouncing ideas off a sounding board, and what better board than his 'other' father?

"Hello?"

It was the voice of an older man; still strong, just beginning the slow glide toward his seventies. Wren would recognize it anywhere.

"James," he said. Using Tandrews' last name didn't seem to hit the spot now.

It only took a second. "Christopher?"

Wren's throat seized up. Grit rattled in the wheel wells as he sped on. Grit seemed to get in his eyes even though the windows were closed.

"They told me you were dead," Tandrews said.

"I'm not dead."

Another pause. "Then they lied."

"Humphreys?"

"Him, or one of them," Tandrews said, like it didn't matter. "Christopher, is it really you?"

Wren rubbed his eyes. After three months of torture and twenty-four hours of being chased, the old man's voice came like a balm on his soul. Kindness always broke you hardest after cruelty.

"It's me. I know they're listening in. Don't get yourself arrested."

"Don't worry about me, Christopher," Tandrews said. "They don't know what I'm capable of. What you're capable of."

Wren couldn't say anything to that. He cornered hard out of the solar array and shot into open scrub desert like a rocket reaching escape velocity, heading north and swallowing hard. There were whole acres of regret assigned to Tandrews in his mind. The last time they'd spoken, the old man had urged him to make peace with his children. Well, he'd tried.

"You escaped," Tandrews said, putting the pieces together from the silence. "They were holding you."

"That's about it," Wren managed. "Mexico somewhere, a black site. I'm on the run right now."

Tandrews didn't reply immediately. Wren imagined him lifting his old bones up, stepping up to the glass to stare piercingly into the dark backwoods. They could've been father and son, if Wren hadn't been so broken. It hurt every time he thought of it.

"You saw the burning video?" Wren asked.

"I saw it. They're saying-"

"They're my people. The one who died, he had a family. The woman was my lieutenant at the CIA. The other's NSA, covert for me; he's a good man."

"I imagine you must be grieving for him."

Wren felt his eyes prick sharply. "It's my father," he said, bulling through. "The Apex. That rat bastard's doing this, framing me as a hero, framing the CIA and the rest as lawless to get the people riled up. I know Humphreys isn't behind it, though. He's not smart enough."

A pause. "Yes. I have met him."

Wren snorted. "I had him. I let him go."

"You did the right thing, Christopher. It wasn't Humphreys. He's only a pawn."

Wren blinked. "So you agree? That this is my father?"

"I'm certain," Tandrews said swiftly. "This is undoubtedly your father's work. You know I have studied men like him all my professional life. I have studied him in particular for thirty years now, long before I ever met you in the desert. I know his mind as much as any person can. I knew this was him from the moment the protests began."

Wren wiped his eyes. It was getting hard to drive for all the grit. Talking to Tandrews felt like tapping into a deep, cool well of strength.

"He is a master gamesman," Tandrews went on. "There are second and third-order effects of this latest onslaught he'll have planned out decades in advance. On some level, I've been expecting this ever since I found you in his fake town, without him."

Wren could only listen rapt as the pick-up charged roughly over the sand.

"He left so many signs, Christopher. The arrogance of his youth. Did you know he's a younger man than I? Perhaps twenty-nine back at the fake town; younger than you are now. I saw him once, or thought that I did. I think of that night often. Huckstering on a street corner in some off-Vegas town, performing card tricks for gullible tourists. We exchanged a glance. This was back when the Pyramid were actively recruiting, charming people on the streets and drawing them in. I thought to myself in that moment, this man's a killer. But I didn't act. I thought there'd be time to surveil him. He must have seen something in me too, because within an hour he was gone. We rushed out to their camp; all scrubbed and empty. My one chance."

Wren didn't know what to say.

"That's my guilt. I never told you this, but I've carried it. You have the spark I don't have, the ability to make snap judgments and act on them without hesitation. There's a ruthlessness there, an absolute obedience to the truth. How it ever endured in the smoke and mirrors he made of those people's minds, I'll never know. But I have been grateful for it."

Wren frowned. Grateful? He pulled north onto sandy blacktop and revved the pick-up to eighty.

"Watching you all these years has been a source of the greatest pride to me," Tandrews went on. "Even as a child you were as true as a compass, Christopher. When I doubted, you set me straight. Your obedience to absolutes hasn't made you many friends, I know that, but it is your greatest strength. The ability to see things as they really are and respond accordingly, immediately. I believe it is the reason you will defeat your father." He paused briefly, taking a wheezy breath. "He has no sense of what's real, Christopher. Only of what he wishes to make real. It explains all his bizarre experimentation; his tanks, his pits, the efforts to substitute his willpower for the thinking minds of others." Another pause. "Perhaps he is a psychopath, as the pop psychologists all said; I don't know if he was born or made that way, or burned any sense of empathy out with his own hand, but he cannot accept a shared worldview not authored by him. I think it pains him every day, to not be seen as the sole creator of people's experience. He could never tolerate the kind of leader relationships you constantly build, where all are free to challenge you at will."

Wren blinked. "You're talking about the Foundation?"

"I am," Tandrews allowed, "but not only them. Every person you meet, Christopher. Americans are afraid, and you and I know how frightened people lash out. It doesn't make them evil. It only means they need help. We have to help them see what's real, so their better angels can come to the fore."

Wren sucked in a breath. "But I've lost my Foundation. There's no darknet. I can't reach any of my teams."

"So make new teams," Tandrews answered, like it was nothing at all. "The people are crying out for a leader. Fight for them. Meet your father's poison with the truth. Inoculate, immunize, protect. It's what you do."

Wren ran a hand down his face. What he did. What did he do? Send out mass text messages. Smash vehicles into buildings. Kill people. He'd become so beaten down with slaughtering the Pinocchios that he'd lost sight of what it was all for. Now Tandrews was talking about something much bigger.

"I don't know how to do that."

Tandrews laughed. "Of course you do. You learned at the knee of the best. Your father is a genius, Christopher, but here's a secret I'll only share with you. You are smarter than him."

Wren squeezed the wheel tight.

"You are stronger. You are better. It's probably the reason he spared you, after you burned the Pyramid down together. He saw it and curiosity stayed his hand. He wanted to see what you became. Now he's made you central to all his plans, by branding you a hero. Use that fascination against him."

"I already tried. I made a video. It got crushed by downvotes."

"If only one video could hold back the flood..." Tandrews said in a tone of mock sadness. "You're not asking for permission here, Christopher. You take what you want from this man. He'll never listen to reason. You beat him until he's dead, then you salt the earth above his grave. The truth doesn't need to negotiate for terms."

Wren sucked in a breath.

It helped. Already his mind felt clearer. The truth. Reality. Tandrews hadn't suggested any strategy, hadn't laid out next steps or some grand plan to bring things to a head, but already Wren felt those things happening in the back of his mind. Gears turning, reality bending. Permission being granted.

"Thank you, James."

"Always, Christopher. You know I'm here for you. If I can help in any way, let me know."

Wren smiled. "They're probably going to arrest you now."

Tandrews laughed. "I have a few tricks of my own. But yes, I expect so. Humphreys will be in here, stamping and pouting."

Wren laughed too. "He does a mean pout."

"Put on a good show, Christopher. The world will be watching."

The world will be watching. He was counting on it.

He killed the call. All that lay ahead was desert, but Wren saw the true scale of this thing spreading into the distance. America. His father's plans. Three hundred twenty million people, and beyond that? Seven billion on the planet.

The Greatest Show on Earth.

12

BORDER

I t was an hour's ride on barely visible dirt tracks through El Destierro, 'The Abandoned' desert, before Wren rolled into a dust-scoured shanty town three miles south of Puerto de Libertad, north-west Mexico. A kid stood by the road at a cardboard shack hawking watermelon slices on ice. A wrecker's lot lay across the gravel road; acres of rusting Fords, GMs, Chryslers. An old woman knelt by a roadside shrine sprucing up flowers.

Wren stopped the pick-up, opened the window and took a deep breath. His heart fluttered threateningly. It had never been this loose before. Shouldn't have drunk all that Coke. He closed his eyes and settled in to wait, until-

Hands dragged him out of the truck, yanking him awake. He let them frog march him a blurry three yards into a waiting sedan, which rapidly pulled away.

"My man, Christopher Wren," said Hector Gutierrez.

Wren blinked. Skinny, wiry Hector was sitting in the passenger seat looking back. Qotl cartel, making a show of force. There was one big guy either side of Wren on the back seat, one big guy at the wheel.

"You're famous now, cuz," Hector said, grinning wide to

show his diamond inlays. "Everybody wants a piece of the great Christopher Wren. Honey, where you been all my life?"

Wren snorted. Hector was a Qotl coyote; born and raised in Baja California. Riffing a style of Beach Boys meets Biggie, he'd found a natural home pitching the wonders of the United States to all points south. Part snake-oil salesman, part desert guide, he sold a package of goods to souls broken by gang warfare in cities all the way down to the Guatemala border.

Once upon a time he'd been Wren's way into the Qotl cartel. Now he was the only guy left Wren could call in a pinch.

"You're too much of an uptown girl for me, Hector," Wren said, which cracked the skinny guy up.

"You hear this cabrón?" Hector slapped the driver's thick arm. The man didn't budge. "CNN got his ugly mug on the side of a barn, farmer's bragging he's some messiah, and this is how he talk?"

Wren had seen that in the news feeds; his face graffitied onto a barn wall in New Hampshire, with the now-standard message, RELEASE CHRISTOPHER WREN. It galled all the more now that he had *actually been released.*

"I'm no messiah."

"That's right, homes, you're just some sweet baby doll in the back of my truck, never been kissed."

Wren frowned. That wasn't quite how he saw it. "I'm hardly a blushing bride."

Hector cracked up, slapped the driver some more. "This guy, man. How you like to be renditioned, Mexico-style?"

Wren just gave him a look. "Three points I could've kneecapped you, Hector. These guys either side of me are dead in two point five seconds if I want." Wren made a show of looking. "Throat. Throat. God gave me two elbows for a reason. Headbutt in your face, take the driver's eyes, now I'm really feeling like a messiah."

Hector didn't stop laughing. "Oh, me. Christopher Wren. Release Christopher Wren!" He trumpeted this a few times. It seemed to bring him no end of joy. The two guys either side of Wren edged a little away.

It went like that for three hours on the ride north-west to the border town of Mexicali, passing through desert and little scrub towns, skirting the Gulf and watching the arid desert shift as the sun rolled overhead. Hector teased Wren, or tried to, invariably mocking anything he said using a fake bass voice, spinning tall stories about the work Wren had done taking out rival coyotes with extreme prejudice. Really putting to the test Tandrews' theory that Wren allowed people to challenge his authority.

Wren ignored him as best he could, setting up gigs via his stolen iPhone on various mercenary darknet sites, requesting intel hacks on FBI, CIA, NSA, DHS databases. He needed to get up to speed on the hunt for Gruber and Rogers ASAP.

Within an hour, after thousands of dollars spent in untraceable blockchain coins to blackhat hackers in cells spread around the world, all his hacks came back empty. Wren stared at the screen while Gutierrez rabbited on about how haunting Wren's eyes were, maybe he was part Chupacabra.

Results would be better if Hellion and B4cksl4cker were running the search, but maybe not by much. It seemed there was hardly anything in the 'Deep State' record about how Gruber, Durant and Rogers had been taken, they'd just disappeared.

He brought up what meagre pickings his mercenaries had scoured off traffic cams and prized out of intelligence silos: CCTV footage showed Gruber leaving his office in East Hollywood three days earlier just after noon, getting on the

#175 bus along Santa Monica Boulevard, then simply vanishing.

There was no explanation. Between stops, with no chance for Gruber to get off, he was just gone. Wren played the videos back and forth. One second he was sitting there at the window, the next second he wasn't. Sally Rogers and Jay Durant were even worse; complete black boxes. They'd gone home three nights back, Rogers to her apartment in New York, Jay to his home in Nevada, and never emerged. Sally hadn't turned up for work the next day. Jay never came down to breakfast with his family.

There was nothing to go on at all. So what did that leave?

Wren's thumbs flew over the phone screen. There was no way he could go investigate directly. Humphreys would be watching the bus route, all the drivers, Gruber's work, his apartment, but Wren had contacts still. People in the 'Deep State' who might still take his call.

He found the number for Robin MacAuley on a private repository site. She was a hotshot pattern analyst he'd requisitioned for his Agent Without Portfolio team under Rogers. They'd worked together for three months to bring down the Blue Fairy, and he'd seen something of the devil in her. Deeply loyal to Rogers, she might be amenable to bending a few rules if it meant getting her old boss back.

He prepped an anonymizing VPN that would bounce any tracking three times around the world, then made the call.

13

MACAULEY

The cell rang three times and picked up.

"MacAuley."

Business-like. Purposeful. Probably right in the middle of the Christopher Wren manhunt.

"Don't hang up," he said.

A beat passed.

"You're shitting me," she said. It was the first time he'd heard her curse. Back in their Pinocchio-hunting days she'd been a formal paragon of by-the-book behavior.

"You know who this is?"

"This is a joke, is what it is. I'm hanging up."

"Sally Rogers," Wren said quickly. "Your boss. My lieutenant. We both want her back."

Another beat passed. Figuring out how she wanted to handle this. "So give her back, you psychopath."

Psychopath? Still, a little heat was good. Better than hanging up. "Whatever you think I did, they'd want you to stay on the line. Initiate tracking, record this call, all that."

A second passed, but no longer. She'd always been quick. Doubtless she'd already rigged the record function, was now setting up tracking. "It's really you? I'm actually speaking with Christopher Wren?"

He smiled. For the benefit of the tape. "As I live and breathe. Now, there's something I was hoping to talk about."

"Of course," MacAuley said. "You want to play catch up, talk about old times, I've got all day."

"The topic's Rogers. Are you on the hunt for her?"

The by-the-book response came immediately. "I can neither confirm or deny any active -"

"I'm thinking yes," he interrupted quickly, "because everybody is. Did you know Director Humphreys came down to Mexico to see me? Haul me out of my black site cell for a chinwag, seems he thought I could help him out?"

Silence for a second. Thinking what to say that wouldn't get her fired. "That's above my pay grade," she settled on.

That was fine. He hadn't really expected her to talk; she'd be ending her career on a dime if she did. It was enough that she listened.

"So let me talk you through what I'm seeing. Your job is to keep me on the line, right? So don't react in any way."

"I won't."

"Perfect, don't." He pressed the phone tight to his ear, listening for her breathing, any gasps, any fluctuations. Play it right and he could get a read. "What I'm seeing is nothing. I've hired some brilliant hackers to dig into the Federal record, and they say you're blind. No trails whatsoever leading away from Rogers' apartment or Durant's house, and just the bus for Gruber. Am I on track so far?"

Her breathing quickened slightly. Just barely audible. Wren pumped the volume to max and ground the phone against his ear.

"So Gruber, he gets on a bus," he went on. "East Hollywood, the 175, and he disappears. Real magic trick, what's going on with that? My question is, is that you, wiping the footage? Swapping in deepfakes to turn anyone else off the scent?"

Silence. Not breathing. Then a breath. She'd held back for a second

"Not you," Wren said, tasting the words. Thinking through the possibilities. "So that's my father's doing, too. He's got himself a deepfake crew, running simultaneous alterations, good enough to fool the best you've got." Listening, but she gave nothing. "Good enough to hack traffic cams, municipal CCTV, also social media posts, videos, satellite footage, then cover the hack in ways you can't track back."

Her breath was quickening. "You're guessing," she said, and he almost thought she did it on purpose. Giving him a tell to read. It just confirmed everything he'd suspected.

"You really haven't got a clue, have you? How it was done. Who took them. You're genuinely blind."

Faster breathing still. A dead giveaway. It explained why Humphreys had come out to see him; clutching at straws, with rioters piling up in the streets and no way to dig themselves out. Now add Christopher Wren to the mix, on the loose and stirring up trouble?

"Tell Humphreys I'm going to fix this for him," he said firmly. "And when that's done, I'll come around for another little chat."

He hung up. Breathing a little heavily himself, now.

Hector turned around and started giving a slow golf clap. "Very impressive, hermano. The great detective at work!"

"Thank you," Wren said, which somewhat took the wind out of Hector's sails, then bent over his phone, mind racing.

Humphreys must have tried every trick in the investigative book to get a lead. There was no way he'd have come to see Wren until he'd exhausted every other possibility. So Wren needed a trick that wasn't in any book. Maybe something so far off-book that only a madman would attempt it.

A slow smile spread across his face. That was pretty much the government line on him these days, anyway. MacAuley had just called him a psychopath, so why not play the part? Tandrews had set him on this course, after all.

Greatest Show on Earth.

His thumbs danced over the phone. Firing up fresh gigs. Making new hires. Setting a new plan in motion.

"Hey, Christopher."

Wren looked up from the screen, finishing up his final orders. They were pulling in next to a ramshackle one-story shop on a dusty street. He oriented himself quickly; they'd arrived. The west side of Mexicali, some four hundred yards away from the new US border wall, beyond which lay the little American burg of Calexico.

"So what I get for all this?" Hector asked. "Coins?" He stared earnestly at Wren for a long moment, then cracked up laughing the loudest yet.

"Yeah," said Wren, and held out a hand. "Gun."

"Oh man, the stories I'll tell," Hector cheered, tears coming from his eyes now. "The infamous Christopher Wren, in my car! Yeah, give him his gun."

One of the big guys gingerly handed Wren the Glock. Wren checked the breech, magazine well, magazine then tucked it in his waistband and got out. He didn't mention the Mossberg shotgun and neither did Hector, but that was fine. He wouldn't need a shotgun where he was going.

"We'll see you real soon, cuz!" Hector called, leaning out the window as the sedan drove off. "Love you."

Wren watched him go. What a clown.

A wizened old guy was standing in the doorway of the shop, looked like a dye works. Wren looked around. A sun-bleached blacktop street set in the tight suburban gridwork of

Mexicali; telephone lines running overhead, freshly planted cypress lining a dentist's clinic, chunky palm trees and low buildings stretching on and on. You could almost be in the States.

"Por aquí," the old guy said. This way. Wearing cracked glasses and a long stiff apron that seemed more purple dye stain than original fabric. Wren followed him into the shop, barely two rooms big with ceramic dye vats on one side, bolts of cloth on the other, through to an outhouse door in back.

The old guy heaved and lifted a filthy toilet off the ground; unplumbed. A round metal platform lay underneath, polished like the top plate of a scale. A single piston industrial elevator. Maybe three feet in diameter. Just one of thousands of such rabbit holes under the border.

He stepped onto the platform and the old guy pushed the button to send him down. Twenty feet he descended, featureless dirt walls banked with steel brace rings passing up to either side. At the bottom he ducked and crawled off the plate. The tunnel ahead was tight; no more than compacted sand held in place with more braces. Sufficient unto the day. He lay down on a waiting trolley and the circuit kicked in, the rope attached to the trolley pulled tight and dragged him into motion. Six hundred yards to get under the wall, out of one country and into another.

Let Hector laugh as much as he wanted. With his head down and the anger just beginning to surge in Wren's heart, he felt like a bullet on an unstoppable trajectory. His father was going to pay for all the people he'd killed.

14

GREATEST SHOW ON EARTH

W ren emerged off the borehole elevator into a filthy bathroom stall in a two-pump gas station on the fringe of Calexico. An old leathery-skinned Mexican woman watched him from the station's counter, chewing tobacco. There were a few sun-worn buildings nearby, adobe and white plaster gleaming in the late afternoon sun, and blacktop roads running in a mostly bare grid. Nobody in sight. He blinked against the brightness.

The old lady pointed. Under the station's sagging canopy sat a ridiculous powder-blue two-seat micro car, barely more than eight feet long. The keys were in the front wheel well. Wren scarcely fit behind the wheel even with the seat racked all the way back. Hector's idea of a joke. There was an earpiece, a bodycam, a wallet with five hundred dollars cash and a hot pink Google Pixel smartphone in the glove compartment, wrapped in a simple note that spelled it all out.

THIS IS IT

Pretty much what he'd asked for. Wren looked up at the old lady. She just stared right back, a thousand yard gaze of her own. So this really was it. No more cartel help. No

Foundation. He was truly on his own, with only mercenaries to come at his call.

He stripped the battery from the iPhone, broke the handset, dumped both pieces by the side of the road then booted the Pixel. Curved screen. No buttons. Likely it was filled with all kinds of spyware, but Wren had a bypass for that, downloading a pirated Operating System over-install.

He checked in on the darknet gigs he'd ordered then set off. Out of Calexico onto I-8 heading west, he revved the little car up to its top speed of ninety miles an hour. It felt like overloading a souped-up golf cart; the chassis shook, the engine throbbed and the windows rattled in their frames.

Two hours to LA, arrival time around 4 p.m. He tuned the radio and listened to news of the protests growing in numbers. David Keller again; holding a rally in New York, whipping the people up against the 'Deep State'. Every time he mentioned Wren's name or his Foundation there was a cheer that came like a gut punch. Pundits suggested this rabble-rouser might actually have a chance in the presidential election. Five months out, there was no time to get on the ballot on any State, but as a write-in candidate?

Wren raced in the passing lane up the coast. With every blink he saw Jay burning again, until the suburbs of Los Angeles bloomed around him like bacteria. Desert sand and bare ocean gave way to impersonal strip malls, massive parking lots, windowless fulfilment centers and cement-lined flood control channels. An orange/gray exhaust haze hung over the metropolis like a poison fog, smearing out the horizon.

He tore up through Mission Viejo then Lake Forest on the five. In Irvine protesters were hanging out in brightly colored clots at intersections, yelling his own name back at him like hippies sixty years out of date. Black-clad Anti-Ca protesters wearing skull and bones handkerchief masks clustered side-by-side with groups of sun-weathered homeless. Wren pulled over and asked one such group for a mask and ball cap, ten bucks.

He got one of each, cinched the mask around his face like an Old West pistoleer, tugged the cap down low over his eyes and drove on. Good enough to obscure his face from traffic cam overwatch.

The air felt febrile entering Santa Ana, like the poison was deep in the bloodstream here. He saw it in burned-out storefronts tarped over with plastic, in handmade posters trumpeting his name plastered across the busted windshields of cars, in arguments firing up at crosswalks over nothing and sirens wailing out only a few blocks over. The stink of ash was in the hot afternoon air, and people were gathering on corners everywhere, holding signboards and wearing masks.

Wren felt a greasy, ugly tension building just beneath the surface. The last year of attacks weighed down the air with a thickening sense of dread, as people waited for the night, and the next burning video, and the violence to come.

Steven Gruber's place was a third-floor apartment on Baird Avenue, Reseda, twenty miles northwest of downtown. It was getting on for 6 as Wren passed into Van Nuys, rolling up Amigo Avenue one street west of Baird. He pulled into a parking lot beneath an elevated apartment block. Security cameras caught his license and signs warned RESIDENTS ONLY, but the most they'd do was issue him a fine. He rolled to the back of the dark lot, parked up and sat for a second feeling the anticipation swell up from his gut.

The Greatest Show on Earth. It all came down to this.

Through the windshield he surveyed the back corner of Gruber's building. Orange terracotta and brick, it had no real security other than the CIA agents likely staking it out. He figured they'd be parked on Baird across the way, maybe an agent in the room, a camera in the corridor. He brought up the building plans on his phone; Gruber's apartment, 306, was right in the middle.

He slipped the cartel earpiece in then tapped out a message on the ops task app and sent it to his mercenary team.

IN POSITION?

Multiple responses chimed in on the earpiece. Wren's heart hammered in his chest. Curtain's up. He got out of the vehicle, pulled his cap down firm and sent the order to activate mercenary one.

Somewhere in the shadowy lot there was a sound, and Wren focused on it; a woman emerged from the dark by the side of a tricked-out motorbike, carrying a sleek black suitcase.

"It is you," she said in a faint Israeli accent.

Wren said nothing. She was tall and willowy in black leathers, wearing a motorbike helmet. Rigged with all kinds of voice controls, he figured. Top of the deck when it came to tech, she went by Alighieri on the darknet gig boards. Two thousand dollars an hour for various hacker services. Ex-Mossad, he guessed, looking to cash in.

"You are Christopher Wren," she went on. "Infamous wrangler of the hacker collective H4cksl4cker, and a man much in demand. My rate just went up."

So she recognized him. He pulled the mask and the cap off and let them drop. He wouldn't need them now anyway.

"We had a deal."

"Forget that deal," she said. "The new rate is ten thousand an hour. Decide."

It was extortion. Wren didn't care. You couldn't buy loyalty. He had funds enough for this. "Put it on my tab. Now, how's the lighting in here?"

She started over to him at once, hips rolling sinuously, the suitcase swaying by her thigh. Wren saw strong cheekbones through the visor, wide almond eyes, over six feet tall.

"For ten thousand an hour, I brought my own lighting array." She lifted the case, popped the clasps and held it up flat, then opened the lid and gave the command. "Rise."

A light buzzing came from the case, two-toned, and within seconds twin micro-drones rose into the air. Four rotors each on four molded radial arms, central housings no larger than a kitten, hovering in the air in front of Alighieri's face. She closed the case and let it drop back by her side, while the drones remained hanging in the air. "Lights," she said.

The smaller drone flashed to light; a triple array of high-powered beams, one for full flood, two for fill.

"Camera?" Wren asked drily.

"Action," said the woman.

The drones moved in concert, covering the short distance to Wren in a second and swirling around him as Alighieri slid a tablet from the case and took control.

"Ready to go live," she said. "On your word."

Wren grunted. He'd prepped a single live video stream with a request written in a banner over the top, soon to be broadcast out through his Megaphone app across all the video streaming apps. Time to capture some eyeballs.

"Go live," he said.

The camera drone blinked red, and Wren let it survey him for a few seconds, the lights playing across his face. The more light, the more motion, the less chance they could explain this away as a deepfake.

"My name is Christopher Wren," he growled in his gravelly bass, "and I'm looking for my people."

That was enough. No need for a long speech this time. Actions spoke louder than words. He turned, and the drones swerved through the air as if on a gimbal, tracking him as he vaulted over the low wall out of the parking lot and started toward Gruber's building at a run. At the same time, Alighieri would be activating his second mercenary, a man on a pizza delivery moped waiting at the bottom of Baird Avenue.

Wren reached the building and jumped to grab the first balcony, pulling himself up. The drones rose with him smoothly, capturing the action. The sun beat down. The pizza guy should be at the building's entrance by then, even as the third mercenary should be pulling up Baird in a stolen vehicle. Wren had requested the theft of a sports car, but it was a lottery what model he'd get.

He hauled himself up to the third-floor balcony, Gruber's apartment, careful not to silhouette himself through the sliding glass door. Pressed against the wall, he listened carefully. Pizza guy had to be heading up the stairs now. Seconds ticked by.

"He's in the corridor," came Alighieri's clipped accent in his ear. "Five seconds."

Wren braced. Twenty feet away through rebar and plasterboard, the pizza delivery guy would be reaching for the doorbell. A second later, he heard the chime faintly through the wall. He risked a glance through the sliding glass and saw the man waiting for him inside. He was bulky with protective Kevlar beneath a suit jacket, the clear profile of a pistol in a shoulder holster. Easily as big as Wren, maybe bigger. Heading over to the door now.

"Music," Wren said.

"Of course," answered Alighieri.

From out front his third mercenary turned the stolen vehicle's high-powered speakers on, churning out raucous death metal at full volume. Enough noise to drown out a gunfight.

"FBI stakeout have activated," Alighieri said. "Two black

suits getting out of gray sedan, they look angry. I'm calling in the police. Time to go."

Wren hit the sliding door with the Glock's grip. The glass crashed through, barely audible over the music, though the agent heard it and spun. Wren already had the Glock trained on his face. The guy's eyes went wide; trying to figure out just what was going on. Pizza. Music. Now Christopher Wren?

Wren slipped one hand through the broken glass, popped the lock and worked the sliding door. At the same moment the guy moved fast like a QB, getting off-line behind the kitchen partition. No doubt radioing through to his team, but they wouldn't hear him now, not with the death metal booming out.

Ten thousand dollars an hour and then some, just to buy Wren three darknet mercenaries and five minutes uninterrupted in Steven Gruber's apartment. The drones followed him in. Let the show commence.

15

BIG GUY

W ren scanned the apartment in a second: dust marks on the desk where Gruber's computer had been, pin marks on the walls where notices had been untacked, the bed stripped back, the wardrobes hanging open. The Deep State had tossed the place thoroughly and snatched up any evidence of Gruber's disappearance, but that was fine. Wren hadn't come here for evidence.

The drones buzzed at his side; the noise louder in the contained environment.

"Where is Steven Gruber?" he shouted at the wall where the agent had taken cover. The agent answered by putting a gun around the corner and firing.

Wren was already in motion, getting offline so the bullets crashed through the sliding door. Mid-stride he snatched the lighting drone out of the air like he was plucking an apple and hurled it in an angled curveball. It flew through the air, rotors revving manically as the internal gyroscope struggled to equalize, cornering perfectly around the wall until it hit-

The agent let out a yelp; struck by the blades, maybe

blinded by the sudden light, then Wren was on him too, slamming a knee up into his groin while isolating his right arm, forcing the gun away. Three bullets discharged into the wall in a half-circle; parabellum rounds from a Taurus G2S subcompact. The guy was huge, strong, but in the throes of shock he wasn't thinking tactically, too focused on the gun.

Wren got his left hand on the guy's wrist, right hand on the barrel and pushed the safety in before the guy could bring it back to bear. The hammer clicked uselessly on the safety, and Wren gave him no more time, driving ahead like a linebacker. His shoulder slammed into the guy's gut and drove their combined mass of some four hundred fifty pounds into and through the thin plasterboard wall to Gruber's bathroom. Wren caught a glimpse of tasteful raw rock paneling, a rainforest shower, then the big guy was back on the beat and dropping a brutal elbow into Wren's shoulder blade.

Wren roared, pulled back in a spray of choking white plaster dust and sent a big right cross that glanced off the guy's temple.

Hand-to-hand fighting trumped a firefight for drama any day, and drama was what Wren wanted now, yanking eyeballs to his video livestream. The big guy didn't know about that though, and from his lodged position in the wall clicked the safety and tried to bring the pistol back into play again. Wren stepped inside his outstretched arm, grabbed his elbow and wrist while ducking his own shoulder into the guy's armpit, then with a gargantuan roar and squat hoisted him bodily into a massive judo throw.

The guy scooped out of the wall like a roll of vanilla ice cream, sailed overhead with his feet scuffing a line down the plasterboard, then pounded down to the sleek gray carpet. Wren held his forearm in isolation, spotted the drones watching him tight, then performed an almighty grunt as he yanked the gun away.

Good so far.

"Delivery boy's out of the building," came Alighieri's disinterested voice in his ear. "Your stakeout agents are focused on the music; the driver's refusing to cooperate. I see police three minutes out."

Three minutes. Wren mimed an incapacitating elbow lock long enough for the big agent to recover sufficiently to throw a punch into Wren's chin. Wren slipped it but oversold his reaction; tumbling five big steps across the apartment, judging it just right so that he came down hard on his back across a classy glass coffee table, anticipating a big dramatic smash.

The glass didn't shatter. It just hurt like hell.

The agent didn't come for him either, or go for the stripped gun. Instead he went for the door.

Wren cursed and surged up. A more dedicated controller like Hellion would be stepping in right then, using her lighting drone to block and confound the guy, but Alighieri's allegiance was clearly to her gear. The guy had the door open by the time Wren put a jump knee into his back, flat across the spine; impressive to see but no more damaging then a firm shove. The guy bounced into the open door then stumbled comically back into Wren, who pulled him down into a tumbling ball.

"View count rising," Alighieri said dispassionately.

Not quite the greatest show on Earth, Wren thought absently as he tumbled. More amateur wrestling, but people loved wrestling. Wren himself was a huge fan.

"Who took Steven Gruber?" he roared above the death metal blare, as he tussled with the big guy on the ground. The agent tried to throw elbows and gouge Wren's face, but Wren rolled the blows and controlled the guy's grasping fingers. The drones circled above them, filming two men sweating and tussling.

Not too much of this, Wren figured; shapeless clinching on the ground didn't make for good television. Time for a power move. Wren prompted a surge and steered the fight up to their feet. The guy was strong, with some grounding in jujitsu he was just beginning to utilize, but Wren had been born redirecting force, and it was an easy thing to control the flow of the battle. He ducked his head to the left, which drew the guy into another ill-advised elbow, committing his weight onto the front foot. It gave Wren the opportunity he needed.

He punched both his thighs into an upward drive even as he scooped his right arm between the guy's legs, his left arm trailing across the guy's right shoulder, and lifted. The guy gave a squeak, flailed madly as Wren hoisted him bodily, rotated him, then body-slammed him squarely on his back onto the hardwood floor with a resounding thud.

"And they say wrestling's fake," Alighieri said sarcastically.

Wren stood panting, soaking in the moment, the hero or the heel, surveying his fallen opponent. The guy curled up instinctively, more shocked by the slam than anything. It was a lot of punishment, though no lasting damage. It was what people wanted to see.

"Tell me everything you know about Steven Gruber," Wren boomed in a fake deep voice. "Who took him, where he was last seen?"

The guy stared up numbly. Maybe he was beginning to grasp that Wren was performing. He'd know that Wren could have killed him three times over by now, but hadn't. He saw the drones circling and had to put the pieces together.

"What are you-" he began, but Wren descended and threw

three massive blows at his head which, to the audience watching, would look tumultuous, but which Wren actually pulled, faking the noise of the impact with his foot stamped on the floor.

The guy stared. Barely believing he was still conscious after that.

"I-" he managed.

"Tell me who took him!" Wren bellowed. The drone zoomed in close, rotors spinning barely inches from the faces of the two heaving, sweating men. Wren so intense. The guy frowning in confusion, not sure what on Earth he'd fallen into.

"I, I mean..."

It didn't matter. Wren didn't care what he said; that wasn't why he'd come. What would a guy left to guard an apartment know that Humphreys himself hadn't? Nothing. But somebody out there knew, somebody had seen who'd taken Steven Gruber, and Wren just had to reach that one person and win them to his side.

Greatest Show on Earth.

"You better tell me what I want to know," he roared, gave the guy a look as if to say 'sell this', then hit him with a massive backhand. It didn't connect. The guy rolled with it well, though. Maybe some amateur dramatics in his past. The drone reeled to keep track of the action. Wren dragged the agent up, trapped him into a headlock, then pulled off a crunching DDT headslam into the floor, cushioning the guy from the worst of the blow. Getting ridiculous now, maybe. They both shouted and tumbled. Breathless. Faking was harder than he'd expected.

"Tell me!" Wren hollered. The guy just stared.

"Police are in position," Alighieri said in his ear, bored-sounding. "View count spiking. Ready for phase two."

Wren let go of the big agent. He just sagged and stared.

"Saved by the bell," Wren rumbled, then scrambled for a closing one liner as he stood over him. "Tell your mother I said hello." It was the first thing that came to mind, and only baffled the guy further. It wasn't Wren's best work. Still, he knew he'd cut a powerful figure as he strode toward the door.

16

GTA

D own through the building followed by the drones, Alighieri's voice came in Wren's ear.

"You have several thousand watching your stream now."

Several thousand wouldn't cut it. Passing the first floor landing he growled back at her. "Any comments on the request?"

He'd written it and she'd overlaid it atop every instance of his video:

DID YOU WITNESS THE KIDNAPPING OF STEVEN GRUBER, SALLY ROGERS OR JAY DURANT? DID YOU SEE THEM BEFORE THEY WERE TAKEN? WHERE? WHEN? BY WHOM?

"Nothing meaningful yet," she answered. "Just compliments on your bodyslam and requests for a piledriver."

Trolls. Wren grunted and pushed out through the building's front door. Late afternoon light washed over him; Baird Avenue looked much as before, though there was now one patrol car pulled up beside a Porsche; source of the banging death metal. Wren's eyes widened; a two-seater Porsche 718 Boxster, mid-engined, sleek, silver, gorgeous.

He'd spent another ten grand on the theft, and the guy had really delivered.

Now he was sitting in the driver's seat while two cops were squaring up to two FBI agents, flashing badges and making demands, while the music continued to pump out.

"Get him out of there," Wren said as he took the steps down to street level in large bounds.

"He's moving," Alighieri came back.

The guy in the Porsche abruptly hopped over to the passenger side, opened the door and ran off. The cops and the agents watched after him in confusion, and Wren strode right into that. The drones buzzed at his shoulder and drew the attention of the nearest cop, whose eyes widened. His jaw dropped and he tapped the roof of the patrol car to get his colleague's attention, temporarily struck dumb. Within two seconds they were all looking.

Christopher Wren, the man all the protesters were talking about, in LA in broad daylight. The FBI agents raised their weapons first, barked some nonsense about stopping, but Wren was already right between them, at the Porsche's door. Move fast and you could bull right through confusion.

He slipped in, slammed the door and revved the engine. They pointed their weapons awkwardly through the window at his face, but Wren figured they wouldn't shoot. No crime, as of yet. He didn't hang around to find out, though, slamming the stick into reverse and punching the gas.

The Porsche burst away like a bottle rocket. The cops fired but it was too late. The FBI were already getting in their vehicles. The death metal pounded like a grand mal seizure in Wren's ears as he accelerated away backward.

Stage two.

"Do you have me?" Wren shouted.

"I have the dashcam," came Alighieri in his ear, clear and sharp over the screaming music. "Just syncing now."

Wren hit the end of Baird where it butted onto Rayen Street and pulled a hard handbrake turn, burning rubber across the two-lane so the car rocked to a halt facing east. Wren wound the windows down and looked left; there were seconds only until the pursuit was on him.

"Where is it?" he barked, scanning the skies over Gruber's apartment.

"Any second," Alighieri said, and Wren cursed under his breath. Hellion would have had it mounted and ready to roll. His foot twitched over the gas pedal, then-

There it was; a much larger version of the micro-drones, shooting up over Gruber's building and coming straight for him; a DJI Inspire 2, the fastest commercial camera drone money could buy.

"Got it," he said and slammed the gas; the Porsche blurted onto Rayen and accelerated with phenomenal speed, hitting sixty within seconds and forcing Wren into another big handbrake turn south onto Reseda Boulevard. A quick glance in the rear view mirror showed the Inspire tracking him easily, hovering just above the FBI sedan.

"You have twenty-seven minutes flight time on the battery," came Alighieri's voice.

"Are you on these intersections?" Wren barked back, swerving madly around slower-moving vehicles. Already he'd torn through a red light at the four-way with Gresham Street and was closing rapidly on Parthenia Street, also showing red.

"One second," said Alighieri.

Wren didn't have a second; he flew onto the intersection blind at sixty, scanning to left and right. A semi thundered in and missed him by inches.

"Alighieri!" he shouted. "If I die you don't get your bonus."

She said nothing, leaving Wren to accelerate and lane-jump toward the Chase Street intersection on his own.

"Done," she came back, and the red light ahead flipped to green seconds before Wren shot through. "Police frequencies are scrambling all cars your way. There's a call for road blocks on major lanes ten blocks out."

"And the request, do we have witnesses?"

She was silent for a second, and Wren inched the Porsche up to seventy. People flew by either side; mouths wide, fingers barely raising in time to point his way. Another intersection blew by green, seven more until he hit anything like a road block.

"Alighieri."

"It's a lot of data," she answered, sounding flustered. "Comments are coming in too fast. I can shunt them to a subteam. It'll cost you another ten an hour."

Wren laughed. A great time to tell him that, in the middle of the chase. "Do it. Get me that data."

"Working."

Wren buzzed another intersection, too fast to pick out any details now. At least it was green, at least there was no one on the crosswalk. Blue lights flashed everywhere now as the LAPD swarmed; side streets, in back, firing up ahead.

Another intersection blew by, then a squad car shot out of a side street ahead and swung out wide to part-block Reseda. Wren swung the wheel, worked the handbrake and fishtailed a lane to the left, shearing off the squad car's front fender in a spray of sparks. The drone buzzed along in back, capturing everything.

Wren corrected and accelerated, taking the Porsche closer to eighty as Reseda emptied out ahead. Now he could see the road block going up; four intersections south, call it a mile, looked like three squad cars pulling end to end across the street. He could probably blow right through the middle, but that wasn't the plan.

"Anything yet?"

"Yes," Alighieri answered after a delay. "Feed up to fifty thousand viewers, most streaming apps are carrying you on the front page. You're getting comments, lots of garbage, we're working on relevance."

Wren grunted. Fifty thousand was just the beginning; he hadn't expected anything else. Full saturation would require an OJ Simpson-level event, squad cars trailing him for over an hour, but bigger than OJ's slow roll.

Another intersection blew by. He swung hard around a guy on a lowrider.

"Is network news covering this?"

No answer. Two intersections left.

"Alighieri."

"You just went up on CNN. Fox have you on the banner. Sounds like they're redirecting a pool traffic helicopter your way."

That was better.

"Send the drone ahead and shoot me tight from in front for this," he directed over the thump of the music. "Transition in five, four-"

The cops were standing in front of their barricade now, weapons up. The drone hammered overhead as Wren reached Sherman Way and yanked a huge handbrake turn across the whole intersection, scorching burned rubber trails in an arc that bounced him off the south-west curb even as bullets starred then shattered the windshield.

Wren bobbed back up and raced west, the drone hovering just ahead and pointing back at his face, taking in the contrail of pursuit vehicles. Wren saw them in his rearview: the FBI sedan, the original squad car plus some others he'd picked up along the way.

"Reaching a hundred thousand on the stream," Alighieri said. "Network's picking you up, interrupting regularly scheduled programming. That's a lot. My price just went up twenty thousand."

It was ridiculous. "Fine," Wren said. "Hang the drone back after this. Anything on the comments yet?"

"Nothing statistically viable," said Alighieri, "except several reports he's been seen in East Hollywood. Looks like he was last spotted there on the afternoon of the fifteenth."

"I know that already! Get me something new. Where did he go?"

"Working."

Two hundred yards ahead the road opened up to left and right. At one-fifty the thumping blades of a helicopter sounded over the death metal, at one hundred the officers fired and at fifty Wren wrenched the Porsche left, swept across oncoming traffic, tore through a chicken wire fence and down a brief grass embankment then hit air.

The Porsche flew for a second, two, as it fell fifteen feet into the Aliso Canyon Wash; a concrete-lined flood control channel with a trickle of water running down the center. The Porsche tipped front-heavy, Wren braced then took the impact.

The fender struck sparks then shattered, the license plate spat out its screws and flipped away like a spent shell casing, the chassis barked and bounced as it took the full momentum of the car, followed by the bodywork grinding on concrete like balsa on an industrial lathe. The front tires hit next and jammed into the top of their wheel wells, mangling the hydropneumatic suspension with a vicious double screech, and the Porsche skidded for a half second on its nose before the rear end slammed to earth like a jackhammer, bursting the back rear tires and shattering the axle.

Wren's head lashed forward and was punched back by the airbag even as he pulled left, forcing the jammed front wheels to pop out of their wells just enough to turn a dead-slam against the wash's solid wall into a brutal graze. The right headlamp and indicator blew out on concrete, the side mirror spun off like a tossed coin and the glossy silver bodywork scratched down to the bone in a flurry of sparks.

Wren kicked the gas and forced the battered vehicle on, shooting out from beneath the hovering Inspire 2. He was woozy from the impact but watched in the rearview as the pursuit vehicles variously stopped on Sherman, overshot or risked the leap to the floor of the wash.

The FBI sedan made the jump and hit the concrete wall flush, dead-ending their momentum with an engine block forced up through the hood. A patrol car made the leap and would have landed it clean, if the sedan hadn't already tangled up the narrow landing strip. Instead it tumbled and rear-ended the sedan with a tremendous metal bark.

No others jumped after that. Immediate pursuit ended.

Wren turned his eyes to the front and pushed the Porsche ahead on all-wheel drive, dragging sparks from the busted back axle as it accelerated along the concrete channel like a Tomahawk missile up a launching tube.

17

ALIGHIERI

In thirty seconds the Porsche hydroplaned across a broad skin of water then burst onto the grand sweep of the Los Angeles River: a concrete canyon splitting LA in two, easily as wide as a four-lane highway with a deep water trench down the center. Either side lay sloping banks of yellowed grass leading up to green backyards.

Wren pulled east and pushed the gas all the way down. The Inspire 2 strained to catch up with him in back, accompanied now by a small blue weather helicopter, beating low. More eyeballs meant more heat. He imagined this pursuit running fast up the chain of command, fresh roadblocks being authorized, the Deep State wading in and riot police being called, while on the news excited anchors puzzled over what in hell was happening.

OJ Simpson's slow haul in the white Bronco had hit 95 million viewers at its peak. Wren needed to go bigger; big enough to pull in just one person who'd seen Gruber snatched on the fifteenth from East Hollywood. The biggest call for witness testimony in history.

"Alighieri, how many now?"

Nothing came back on the earpiece. He edged the Porsche

down from its clattering breakneck pace, sixty from eighty. Bare bones white cement bridges flew by overhead, people staring down.

"Halt the vehicle immediately!"

A police helicopter hailed him on loudspeaker from above. Wren ignored it. He flipped the radio and found Freebird by Lynryd Skynyrd, just starting to rock out as it headed for the guitar solo. The sound washed over him and out like flames trailing a comet. The police helicopter dropped in front of him, flying backward so close he could see the pilot's eyes. In his rearview a stream of blue light vehicles poured down the embankment.

"Alighieri," he said, but still she didn't reply. He spun, but the Inspire was gone now too. That was a bad sign; without analysts riding herd on his comment feed, this whole show could be for nothing.

"Another ten an hour," he shouted. "Twenty, Alighieri! Do this or I'm coming after you."

Nothing came back but wind through the blasted windshield, Skynyrd's wailing guitar, the chop of the helicopter and the chorus cry of sirens. He brought up his phone and scanned the comment feed. Best guess, a few hundred thousand were watching online, with a lot more on cable and network news. The comments thread was a firehose, too fast for him to read.

Still, nothing he could do about it except hope Alighieri would come back soon. For now he needed to focus ahead, already drawing in on the Sepulveda Basin Park, three miles of green on all sides that would force him down a narrow channel ending in the Sepulveda Dam. The Porsche wasn't going to make it, but he could do something about that.

He tapped the app to activate his fourth contractor directly, now waiting in the parking lot of Pedlow Field Skate Park to the left. There was no time to watch for a confirmation; he shot under the narrow bridge for White Oak Avenue, hauled left and sent the Porsche up the river's inclined bank.

The front tires creaked on impact then strained as they took the full weight of the car, with the back wheels dragging lamely in back. By the top of the bank his momentum stalled out and the transmission finally snapped with a back-breaking crack, leaving him rocking at a dead stop. He kicked open the door and strode out just as the Porsche began to roll back down. Now there were five helicopters circling overhead, and a tide of emergency vehicles sweeping in some thirty seconds behind.

He ran. Into the skate park's long, crowded parking lot he sprinted; farmer's market to the left, Army National Guard base to the right, and the skate park dead ahead; grey peaks and troughs in cement like a convoluted swimming pool, filled with young people pulling off ollies and rail grinds. Wren ran along the edge tracked by a sky full of helicopters, and was greeted by stunned expressions and rowdy catcalls as the skaters stopped, recognized him and held up their phones.

"We're with you, brother!" one of them shouted.

"Release Christopher Wren!" another cried redundantly.

"Stick it to the Deep State!"

Ahead he picked out a fresh inflow of unmarked vehicles into the lot; intelligence agencies, Wren figured, on standby waiting for a moment like this. Between them and the charge chasing him in back, there was just about no way through. Except-

His stage three transport was parked right where he'd ordered; a twelve-foot tall, twelve-foot wide hot blue roll cage atop bulbous 66-inch tires, five tons if it weighed a dime, pushing a supercharged fuel injected big block American V8 engine, with two tall flag poles off the roof trailing picnic blanket-sized Old Glory flags.

A monster truck. Far from street legal. An expensive, off-book 'birthday rental' from a rally at the Staples Center; getting it in position had taken a double-wide trailer truck. Another fifteen grand right there. Now Wren's contractor, a custodian with access to the Monster Truck lot, saw him and the helicopters coming and clearly had second thoughts, hitting the gas just as Wren sprinted up, forcing him to leap like a hobo hopping a freight train.

Wren banged off the passenger side and barely grabbed one of the roll cage's bars, then righted himself, forced open the door and stared at the guy inside.

"Get out," Wren said. "Sell it and you'll keep your cash." The guy grimaced, clearly regretting his life choices, then made a show of throwing up his hands, kicked open the door and tumbled out as the huge truck kept rolling.

Wren swung into the driver's seat and hit the gas. Two of the unmarked vehicles were coming right for him then, agents holding pistols out the windows, and Wren steered right at them. They fired and bullets pinged off the truck's undercarriage and massive axles. Too late they realized what was going to happen.

The truck's huge wheels ate up the first car's hood like it was made of grits, crumpling the A and B columns under its tank-like weight and forcing the agents inside to hunch down in their seats like anchovies in a crushed can, then he was over and rolling onto the next.

"Crush the Deep State, man!" came the cry from the skate park.

The second vehicle fed under the huge truck's wheels like a giant corn dog, doors cracking outward like deep-fried batter, agents firing pointlessly into his hand cut half-ton rubber treads as their windshield shattered and their roof caved in. Wren's truck bounced down on deep coilover shocks then sped across the lot at thirty miles an hour rising

89

to forty, and met the tide of squad cars just as they breasted the top of the river's bank. He had just enough time to strap in his flight-style safety harness before he hit them square on.

The left wheel sprang off a squad car's hood, the right wheel caught a roof coming up and bounced, then the rear wheels clipped and sent the truck into a forward spin even as it launched into the air. For a second Wren flew, ten feet above the cavalry charging in below, ten plus vehicles strong, then the dive steepened, twenty feet now to the inclined bank with him rolling headfirst into a somersault. The front wheels barely touched down on the third rank of roofs before the truck overbalanced and sped into a cannonball roll.

Wren lolled like a ragdoll as the truck tumbled taillights over bumper down the slope, crushing cars beneath it like matchboxes until it hit the channel floor and found its fat, sticky tires once more.

Wren hit the gas and sped away, leaving a trail of wreckage in his wake.

18

HELLO, CHRISTOPHER

Wren tore into the Sepulveda Rec Area with the oversized flags streaming from the truck's twin poles, maxing out the engine at sixty miles per hour, ball fields to the left and Encino Village to the right, two miles and two minutes until the dam and still no clue where he was going. Helicopters buzzed everywhere like summer flies now, but he didn't anticipate any more barricades until Burbank Avenue and the other side of the dam.

"Alighieri," he shouted, even as he clicked frantically through screens on his phone, "do you read me?"

He brought up his master video feed; with the Inspire 2 drone gone, it had been set to auto-grab pertinent footage from news sites, and it was doing that with gusto. Four split screens showed the 'chase' from both above and behind as he raced down the tree-lined concrete channel.

"Alighieri!"

He slammed the wheel and cursed. He'd considered multiple points of failure but not her. The Foundation had spoiled him, having Hellion and B4cksl4cker always there in his ear, pulling magic strings in the background.

A minute thirty, the dam, and then what? Without someone corralling the thousands of comments his escapades were generating, sorting the trolls from the wackos from the truly deluded, his 'Greatest Show on Earth' strategy was leading him nowhere; at worst seven feet under, at best irreparably damaging the 'Christopher Wren' brand.

A minute twenty, seconds ticking down relentlessly. Beyond the dam they'd have him. You couldn't outrun the cops forever.

"Alighieri, give me something now!"

Still nothing. Wind whistled in his ears, the chop of the helicopters hunting him down. He veered round a bend in the pinball launcher and saw the dam up ahead.

"Alighieri!"

"Hello, Christopher."

Wren blinked. The crisp voice in his ear was not Alighieri. He held a finger to his earpiece and craned to hear. Had he detected a Russian accent?

"Christopher, yes, I see you can hear me. Wave for the cameras."

His jaw dropped slack. Could it be? "Hellion?"

"Yes, it is I, your best friend."

Wren tried to frame words but they wouldn't come.

"While it is a special pleasure to see you struck dumb," Hellion went on swiftly and sternly, accompanied by the familiar sound of keys clacking in the background, "it seems you have gotten yourself into quite a pickle. That naughty bitch Alighieri has made off with your money, and now what are you to do? A lucky thing your hacker friends are here to save the day."

Wren tried to force his mind to catch up. "But, how are you-"

"Christopher," came B4cksl4cker's rich Armenian baritone, "perhaps there are more important matters at hand, yes? For now, let us say we have just become aware of your newly-freed status. You are seeking a trail for Steven Gruber, is that correct?"

Wren just stared ahead. Hacker gods descending from above, stealing access to his earpiece and riding shotgun in his head? He wasn't sure they were even real; wasn't strange voices in your head just how madmen thought the lizard people spoke to them?

"Gruber or the others," he managed to say. "I haven't got anything."

"So you are canvassing the country in a clown car," B4cksl4cker said. "Very innovative. I am working on your comments now, Christopher. We will find something."

The relief that brought was unexpected, to have his hackers back on the case. They said kindness was always the thing to break you after any ordeal. He wasn't through this ordeal yet, though.

"Good," he managed, then shot beneath the Burbank Boulevard bridge and onto a broad and shallow concrete floodplain. The art deco Sepulveda Dam stood barely two hundred yards ahead. The concrete flood plain rose sharply to meet it in a steep ramp, interspersed with six sleek cement columns holding up the narrow bridge.

Barely twenty seconds until he hit.

"I have banished thief bitch's toy drone," Hellion said. "Say hello to your new fleet, Christopher."

Abruptly the air ahead swam with drones, all shapes and sizes buzzing up from beyond the dam like a firework display. Fifteen seconds, and Wren just stared. Greatest Show on Earth. She'd seen what he was trying to do and slotted right in. Alighieri would never have come up with that. Where had she even gotten them all?

"You should see your face," B4cksl4cker said with great

amusement, then there were just five seconds and Wren braced.

The monster truck hit the dam's forty-five degree ramp at sixty and bounced hard on its tight front suspension, only stopped from hurtling into a backflip by the propulsive force of the big rear wheels driving it on. Wren was crushed into the seat under sudden intense g-force, the roll-cage cab sprang tall as the truck breasted the dam's shallow peak in milliseconds, then he was launched into the air with his flagpoles streaming.

He flew.

Wheels roaring. Wind rushing. The truck soared like an artillery shell, the sharp upward ascent of a projectile before air resistance and gravity had their way, climbing still, all his forward momentum jolted into this massive upward trajectory.

Drones captured it all. The whole of LA spread before him; flat, gray, limitless. Another barricade was going up ahead, a couple of SWAT vans and a commandeered news truck underneath a slip road for the 405 Freeway, building a tall wall of metal topped by concrete that the truck couldn't bust through. He saw rifles aimed his way, radios raised, blue lights flashing, but they all looked like toy soldiers in some extravagant child's playset.

Three seconds of flight, four, and he felt the precision stamp of bullets smacking their tiny heads against his plate steel underbelly, trying to drill their way through. It was glorious.

Then his stomach sank as the monster truck began to fall. Two long seconds, maybe thirty feet, but the truck was perfectly balanced for jumps and didn't nose down like the Porsche; rather it landed rear wheels first with a cushioned thump, the front wheels swiftly followed and bit easily, sending up sprays of gravel like a bull pawing the arena's sand.

"Beautiful landing," B4cksl4cker said.

"Save the commentary," Wren shouted as the truck tore into incoming fire. "Cover me."

"Covering," Hellion answered, and her mismatched array of drones flung themselves forward like a volley of arrows, moving in perfect unison. Within seconds they formed into a triple-layered shield flying just ahead of him, effectively intercepting almost all of the incoming fire.

Ten seconds until he hit the barricade. Stray bullets worked their way through the buzzing cloud and pinged off his roll cage

"Clear the way, please," he shouted. "Nicely."

Half the drones shot ahead like a spear strike and instantly swarmed the barricade line. Wren had seen Hellion run this play before, battering drone housings and blades against the bodies of the Pinocchios in Idaho, killing a handful and injuring dozens. Wren could only hope she'd interpret 'nicely' to mean non-lethal.

The truck charged into the chaos of the drone storm as her keystrokes clattered like a manic drum solo, putting her four hundred actions-per-minute skills to good use and single-handedly pacifying the SWAT line. Wren braked hard and the big wheels screeched away his momentum, leaving him to thump broadside into twin vans. Wren was already releasing the safety harness and climbing up through the roll-cage.

"Hurry, Christopher," came Hellion's voice. "The storm's dying."

He stood atop the cage and jumped, caught his fingertips around the lip of the slip road's low wall then hauled himself up.

Abruptly he was standing in a whole different world. LA traffic lay before him, vehicles bumper to bumper in the evening rush hour. The roar of the drones and the shouts and the crash of gunfire seemed very far away. He turned and jogged along the row of vehicles.

"Tell me you have a destination."

"In theory," B4cksl4cker answered. "Perhaps. Head east."

Wren grunted, then found what he was looking for, another theft he'd requested and paid richly for, a superbike. He wasn't disappointed to see a sleek black Suzuki Hayabusa on its kickstand at the side, all molded chrome frame and fiberglass fairings, a truly beautiful piece of machinery capable of outlandish speeds.

A skinny guy stood there, looking terrified. Wren strode up, took the keys off him and hopped on. The helmet fit neatly, the engine fired up with a beautiful rush, and he roared away down the line of traffic.

19

MUCH TO SAY

Wren flew east on the 405 alongside six gridlocked lanes at a hundred and climbing, tracked by a single paramilitary drone.

"Talk to me," he said.

"There is much to say," B4cksl4cker answered. "First, you are ten minutes from your target at current speeds."

"I'm accelerating."

"Then perhaps eight minutes. Time enough. Christopher, we have been searching for you ever since Agent Rogers renditioned you from Great Kills. That event has since had unforeseen ramifications."

Wren blitzed over Mulholland Drive and into the Topanga foothills at one hundred and twenty, buffeted by the wind and trailing a chorus of car horns. "What ramifications?"

"A crackdown on the Foundation. They came for us on every vector, Christopher, online and off; hunting the darknet, your known associates, your most visible members."

"Like Gruber?"

B4cksl4cker's voice took on a chiding tone. "They have been watching Steven Gruber since he drove to the NameCheck campus in a yellow Prius during the Reparations.

Likewise Jay, Teddy and Cheryl and many others. Your government turned passive surveillance into a coordinated effort to break us. As such, we have had to take unusual precautions."

Wren wasn't sure he liked the sound of that.

"Firstly, darknet site is not down, but cloaked," B4cksl4cker went on before he could ask. "You of course know about our second skin on the Internet, taken from Lance Gebhart? It has given us ability to 'float' an Internet domain, just as he floated Pleasure Island. The Foundation site is currently floating in cloud, rendering us invisible, unless we want to be seen."

"But I tried-"

B4cksl4cker pressed on. "We saw your efforts to reach us from Puerto de Libertad in Mexico nine hours ago. There have been hundred such attempts each minute, every minute for past two months. Trying to hack us, Christopher. We could not allow any of them through."

Wren sucked in a breath. It was a lot to take in, but really, he'd known it already. Humphreys had hinted at the level of anti-Foundation feeling in the intelligence community. "So you didn't see my first video either?"

"It caught our attention," B4cksl4cker said. "But there have been similar deepfake attempts before. Only this grand 'show' is proof. As soon as we were sure, we kicked out Alighieri and took command."

"Her operation was slack, Christopher," Hellion chimed in angrily, and Wren couldn't help but smile grimly. "Neither of you should have attempted 'God mode' without capable operator."

He grunted. That was fair criticism. This was 'God mode' and then some.

"Seven minutes left," B4cksl4cker went on. "Now, you know that Gruber, Durant and Rogers went missing three days ago, on the fifteenth. Yes? We began searching for them immediately, but hit only brick walls. Hard locks went up around CIA, NSA other agencies, as if they knew we had backdoor. Air gaps, Christopher, requiring physical intercept to breach data moat. We were in process of phishing agents for access when this death video came into new app ecosystem."

"The video of Jay burning."

"Exactly. We doubled our search, but we are limited, Christopher. If I tell you extent Hellion and I have gone to for safety, I would have to kill you."

Wren snorted.

"There is nothing out there," Hellion said. "Nothing on kidnaps. Data record is wiped clean in real time. Rogers, Gruber, they have become ghosts. CCTV, dashcam footage, social media posts with them in background; they are X-ed out completely, as if they never were. Perfect deepfakes, leaving nothing for us to find."

Wren was topping one hundred forty. The sky was clear of helicopters now. Move fast enough and nobody could keep up. Scrub desert hills raced by on either side. "Alighieri said as much."

"On this she was right. It seems you have stumbled upon only possible method of tracking these people down: the human record."

Wren considered taking issue with her use of the word 'stumbled upon', but decided not to. "Now we're getting up to date. So you have a lead for me. Where am I going?"

"Wilshire Federal Building," B4cksl4cker said. "Hellion is preparing your way. Two-tail analysis of over hundred thousand comments on your video indicates this was last place Steven Gruber was seen. As you may know, Wilshire houses LA field office of FBI. Yesterday's riots began here. Perhaps you have seen news reports covering crowds gathering outside? Your country has split around you and Foundation, Christopher. Coming riots will be worse, expected as soon as second video comes. LA has 9 p.m. curfew, but crowd shows no signs of thinning. Three-block radius is locked down, many troops wait in surrounding buildings, ready to stamp down any violence."

"You're saying it's a death trap."

"It certainly could be," Hellion joined in. "I am taking measures to prepare, but they take time. This is our only lead. You won't have long before FBI find you, Christopher. There are three people in that crowd who claim to have seen Steven Gruber passing through. One gave deep level of detail. We have exact GPS coordinates of his phone, and I will direct you, but you must get out when I say."

Wren saw it now, up ahead. The Wilshire Federal Building, a thick white block stippled with dark windows rising seventeen stories high, like some grand mausoleum at the head of the long LA National Cemetery, off to Wren's left.

"Or not," he said, thinking through the possibilities.

"Or not?"

Events unspooled in his head, a chess game played many times per second across three dimensions. "If the heat's in the crowd, maybe I can bring them down."

B4cksl4cker laughed. "Have you ever seen crowd in this riot, Christopher? These are not people interested in listening."

"So I'll use a big voice. If it comes to that. For now, what's my extraction?"

"This is next on to-do list," Hellion said, and her casual tone almost made him laugh.

"Well, as long as it's on the list."

"Yes, it is high priority for me," she said sincerely.

Wren gave up on sarcasm and bore down. The long braille-like lines of the Cemetery's graves were running toward their end. Thirty seconds and he'd almost be in the Federal Building's lobby. The number of chess moves filled up his mind. "And my target?"

"I'm sending witness coordinates to your phone," Hellion said. "No photo yet. I will find additional ways to direct you, if necessary. If this fails, we can turn the crowd to violence as a cover."

"Don't do that," Wren barked sharply, then jammed the brake and pulled left onto a circling slip road. "In and out without bloodshed, unless I say otherwise. Is that understood?"

"Loud and clear," B4cksl4cker said, which didn't inspire Wren with confidence. Hellion was the one to watch out for. "We suggest you drop bike here and enter from above."

Wren slammed the brake all the way and the Hayabusa squealed around the slip road within fifty feet of the Wilshire, peeling rubber until it skidded to a halt. Wren leaped clear before it could topple, climbed onto the slip road's low wall and jumped.

20

WITNESS

Wren caught himself in the middle branches of a spruce on the edge of a tent village spreading underneath the 405, on the west side of the Wilshire. For a moment he held position and surveyed the scene ahead; a sea of tens of thousands of people spread out across the parking lot, interspersed with the blackened hulks of burned-out cars. The sheer scale of them dwarfed the Federal Building, like a long shadow cast at sunset.

Some were carrying signboards like he'd seen in Humphreys' video back in the black site, some were pumping their fists like the thousand legs of a millipede, some were singing and shouting in a wild chorus, with the chief slogan of them all: "Release Christopher Wren!"

Some but not all. In any riot it was the quiet ones you watched for. The ones carrying weapons, waiting for the moment to instigate violence and precipitate the rest, like crystals forming in distilled methamphetamine.

That moment was coming. The raw ferocity of the crowd felt like a blast furnace on his skin, a mixture of dread, anticipation and rage far denser than he'd felt on the open streets, like pure nitroglycerin sweating out of old TNT. All the anger and fear of LA had metastasized into this five-hundred-yard block, itching for that one spark to blow.

"You're too visible," came Hellion's sharp voice in his head. "People are starting to notice. I'm cutting all video."

Her drone hovered a hundred feet ahead now, overseeing everything. She was right, people were starting to point at him, looking back and forth from their phones as realization dawned. Of course, if anyone had been watching his video stream, it was the people right here.

"Don't cut it," he said, and dropped swiftly through the branches to the ground. "We may need it, just stream my bodycam feed only; they'll never know where I am. They already know I'm here, let's use that."

"Then point your face down," Hellion ordered sharply. "Look only at your phone. Trust me."

"Done," he said, and tilted his head forward, held his phone clamped close to his chest just below the bodycam so he could take direction, and pushed through bushes and into the crowd. Voices rose up around him in recognition, but the people were too dense and he moved too fast for the message to carry.

Bodies thumped on his broad shoulders and against his chest and back like hard waves off the hull of a ship. People were turning now, trying to pick him out in the crowd, but he kept his eyes down on the phone screen as Hellion sent him blinking arrows. Straight ahead. Veer left. Seconds passed and he pushed on, watching as she added a distance countdown.

80 feet.

His name was a deafening roar on the lips of the crowd now, as they unified around his presence. Elbows jostled him, the air was a forest of waving arms holding phones playing his video back. More people were wearing masks. He smelled gasoline, saw bottles; the people here were ready for havoc.

"Christopher Wren! Christopher Wren!"

"Plainclothes agents just emptied out of a fire door on the Wilshire's east side," came B4cksl4cker's voice. "They are heading in approximately your direction."

Thirty feet now, the phone said, bearing dead ahead. Wren pulled the black cap out of his pocket and pulled it down tight. No time to affix the mask. The phone said twenty feet, the arrows blinked straight ahead. He felt mob hysteria descending across the crowd as they cried out his name. He had to get out soon or he'd be swept away.

"Almost there," Hellion said, though her voice was scratchy with interference. "Christopher, I am losing resolution. There is jamming effort to take out my drone. I am pulling up."

He heard the buzz saw of the drone recede into the swelling cries of the crowd. There was a pulse throughout them now, bodies moving like a tsunami tide drawing back, preparing to surge.

Ten feet. "Release Christopher Wren!"

Then he was there. The phone blinked '0 FEET' and Wren looked up. Figures all around him.

"Hellion," he shouted over the roar.

Nothing came back. They'd jammed her. How long until agents saturated the crowd and got eyes on him? It couldn't be long. He spun and searched the faces nearest to him. He didn't have a name or a photo or even a gender, so instead relied upon his years of pattern analysis, seeking signal in the noise of the Apex's moods.

The primary expression on the faces around him was surprise, as recognition spread one, two, three people deep the longer he stayed in position, like ripples around a dropped stone. Eyes bugged wide, shock distorted mouths into 'Os', voices began to call his name and the first few clamoring hands slapped on his shoulders, but none of that was what he was looking for.

He was looking for anything like fear. Not fear of him, but fear of being called into the fierce spotlight beam of his gaze. Comments on the video had been anonymized, but this was anything but anonymous. He pocketed the phone and clamped one hand over the bodycam; now looking for anything like relief. He spun hard, jamming the people pressing in nearby, until-

There he was. A tall guy, thin, four bodies deep and staring at Wren like he was a wild animal on the loose.

"You," Wren said, and shoved through the crowd. The guy was dark and tall, maybe Wren's age, wearing an afro cap with long twined braids hanging to his waist. Wren reached him in three seconds and put a hand on his shoulder, making the guy flinch. "You saw Steven Gruber here, three days ago. Tell me everything you know."

The guy's mouth opened then closed, too stunned to speak. Wren understood it; twenty minutes ago he'd posted an anonymous comment on a video that was too good to be true, now Wren himself was here shouting in his face. Wren had dealt it with before and provided a jumpstart, taking the man's arm and leading him away from the throng of protesters who'd recognized him, aiming to break the spell.

"Steven Gruber, my Foundation member," he shouted over the cheering of the crowd. "Before he was stripped naked and forced to watch another man burn alive, he was here. You saw him. What did you see?"

It helped, and the thin guy gulped and nodded, getting a grip. "Yeah, brother Wren. Mr. Christopher, I mean. I saw him out thattaway."

He pointed. Wren spun; back the way he'd come and left, under the 405. "Tell me."

"It was strange, my brother," the guy said, hint of a lilting

Jamaican accent. "The reason I remembered him; I saw this man on his knees, taking off his jacket, you know? I thought, what's this? Then he just had another, some kind of hoodie, he pulled it on, balled the other into one of them tents." Another vague hand wave. Wren didn't care about the jacket.

"So he swapped it out?"

"That's right, brother Wren. Man was on his knees. Strangest thing I ever did-"

"And he was definitely under the freeway?"

"Right there, my friend. Man crawling on his knees."

"Crawling?" That sent up alarm flags. "Which way?"

"That way, brother man. Right over there."

Wren followed the guy's long arm, pointing underneath the 405 Freeway and beyond, across another parking lot and directly toward...

Suddenly it all started making sense.

From the beginning, the notion of Gruber leaving his office in the middle of the day to come to a protest site hadn't added up. Protests weren't Steven Gruber's scene at all, and this one in particular was a terrible move for an NSA agent, given his actual Foundation affilation.

Then crawling? Swapping clothes?

Wren had already been questioning the notion of a daylight kidnap from the thick of a protest crowd anyway. Too visible, too many witnesses. There were ways, of course; knock Gruber out with a fast-acting neurotoxin, extract him with a team wearing EMT gear and explain it away as a case of fainting from too much sun, something like that, but even that would have stood out.

More people would have seen. More eyes would have been drawn.

But on his knees, changing his jacket, heading to a second location? It left one srong possibility.

Steven Gruber had kidnapped himself.

Along with that realization came an overwhelming flood of secondary realizations and emotions; that Gruber never would have taken such efforts if he was just jonesing for an orgy. The Feds, if Gruber had even been aware they were watching, wouldn't have cared about his sexual exploits.

No.

That meant he'd come here deliberately to shake them off, and there was only one reason he might have done that. Guilt filled Wren suddenly to the brim. One of the dark ramifications of him letting Rogers black-bag him was this; the members of his Foundation had been left swinging in the breeze.

No coin check-ins. No Foundation oversight. The structure that Wren's presence in the Foundation offered, suddenly gone. Even worse, based on what Hellion had said, none of the Foundation had contacted him either. Steven Gruber had been quarantined, infected with the Feds' attention, and that had left him completely isolated. More vulnerable to coercion than ever.

Gruber would've been easier than ever to bait out. One text message from someone pretending to be Wren, and he would have come.

That was sickening. Gruber had willingly gone, and now everything flipped in his head. No longer was Wren looking for a panel van extraction and a team disguised as EMTs; all he was looking for was Steven Gruber himself, running an avoidance routine, and who would he draw on from that?

Christopher Wren himself. Double-laundering. Do it fast before anyone could respond. Actions matching his own MO, which meant Gruber had, what? Gone to the VA Hospital to muddle his trail? He'd want to get out fast, no electronic record, probably by hailing a city taxi.

Wren spun ahead as the crowd surged around him. Even if the CIA or the FBI had thought to hunt that taxi driver down, what would they have found? Hellion had said the data record had been scrubbed completely, and Wren believed that would certainly extend to the GPS tracking and travel logs kept by whichever taxi company Gruber had flagged down. His father was nothing if not meticulous.

Which meant the only trail left lay in the one human who knew where Gruber had gone that day.

The taxi driver.

He focused back in on the witness. "What color was the hoodie?"

"What, my brother?"

"The hoodie, what color?"

"Uh, blue?"

"And what-"

"And a red hat. Sorry, I forgot. A red wool hat?"

Wren nodded sharply. "What time?"

"I, uh-"

"Rough guess."

"I'd say 4:30? In the afternoon?"

That was enough. More than the FBI had when they'd gone searching for Gruber; an outfit, a time, a location, a likely means of egress. If Gruber had run the avoidance technique right, they'd never have even known he'd come this far.

Wren abruptly snagged the bodycam and plucked it off his chest, flipped the lens and aimed it at his face.

"Three days ago on the fifteenth," he started, shouting to be heard over the throbbing cries of the crowd, "my Foundation member Steven Gruber fled the protests here at the Wilshire Federal Building in LA. I believe he ran to the VA Hospital on the other side of the 405, passed through the building, then flagged a cab at approximately 4:30 p.m.. He would have been wearing a-" Wren paused, staring at the witness but not really seeing him. If Gruber had had the good sense to wear a different hoodie for the walk to the VA, wouldn't he have had the good sense to switch out again on the way out?

"Wearing a t-shirt," Wren settled on. He'd seen Gruber's wardrobe back at his apartment; even stripped, he didn't seem to own a single collared shirt. "Now I'm looking for one specific person in all of LA; the cab driver that picked him up. If you know a cabbie, ask them. If you are one, ask your friends. I need to know where that cab went, and I need to know right now."

Even as he said it fresh cries went up around him.

"He's right here!"

"Christopher Wren is here!"

He tuned back in to the crowd; voices screaming ecstatically, bodies tumbling over each other to be near him, a pulsation spreading through the masses and rising to-

He saw the movement at the last possible moment, reflected in the eyes of his witness, which flashed to the right. There could only be one reason for that, and it gave Wren all the warning he needed. He flung himself forward, and just felt the sharp whip of twin taser darts flash by the back of his head.

Someone to the side fell beneath a massive electric shock. Wren picked out one guy two bodies away, taser extended over the shoulders of people who even now were pulling away like receding tides, momentarily stunned by the violence. It opened up the path for three bulky figures to bull through, each carrying tasers, strapping guns.

The spark to light the dynamite.

21

DYNAMITE

F ight or flight, and Wren decided in a split second.
Fight.

If he ran they'd chase him, they'd shoot, and people would be hurt. The only hope was to take these three guys out fast and get away.

Half a second; Wren let gravity bend his knees and tilt him forward, then he exploded toward the lead guy like a torpedo. Powerful thighs thrust him head-first, arms at his side, the top of his skull the first thing to make contact, two hundred-fifty pounds of mass cannoning into the guy's jaw like a lead jack-in-the-box.

Parasagittal posterior parietal bone meet mandible; thickest bone in the head plays the weakest hinge in the body and takes all the cards. Wren's crown struck and transmitted force directly up through his trunk line: thick neck corded with muscle, dense spinal column wrapped in squat trapezoids and deltoids, like being hit in the face with a steel battering ram.

The guy dropped cold and Wren fell on top of him, catching his weight in a break-dancer's bridge, already redirecting his momentum to jerk his left leg around and under his body, entering a classic capoeira spin. His left foot hit the incoming calf of the second guy, rocked but didn't trip him until his right leg followed and insisted.

The guy's leg swept and he fell, bringing Wren to a dead stop flat on his back, looking up at the one guy still standing, already training his weapon flush on Wren's face.

Not fast enough.

"Hands behind your-" the guy started shouting, until some object sailed in across Wren's field of vision. A red, green and yellow bird, maybe, or some kind of fabric. The witness' afro cap. It flopped against the agent's dour face and made him blink, just long enough for Wren to pull his right leg back and shoot it out like a piston.

It hit the guy's calf square and pushed through, sending his whole left leg back, lurching his full weight forward onto his right, which momentarily buckled. The gun came off target in an involuntary reel for balance, and Wren snapped off a whipsaw sit up to catch the guy's right leg in a tight bear hug. Another half second, and Wren jammed his left elbow in the back of the guy's knee, braced his right bicep hard against the front of the guy's shin, clamped his hands together on the other side and twisted.

The guy's knee bent and his foot lifted up off the ground, leaving him suspended in the air. He let out a wail and fell dead ahead, trying to get his arms up to break the fall. Wren didn't wait; as the guy went down he pulled into a hard 'ashi garami' entangled leg lock, one of the four barred judo maneuvers, and wrenched.

The knee popped. Ligament damage. The guy screeched and hit the deck. By then the second guy was getting up from the leg sweep and bringing his weapon to bear. Wren rolled tight and pulled the third guy on top of him, coiled his legs into the guy's solar plexus, then thrust, flinging the guy like grapeshot from a catapult.

He flew a good four feet, hit the second guy who barely caught him, then Wren was on the way, sending an elbow to the second guy's temporal lobe that put him down.

Wren caught a sharp breath. Three guys down. Twenty seconds, all in.

"Holy shi-" said the witness.

Wren spun. All around were wide eyes and phones held up to film him. Others would be coming in any second, and still no word from Hellion.

"You," he snapped at the witness, "don't let anyone take their guns. Keep the crowd back. Wait for the authorities. We're not at war with each other."

Somebody gasped. "Not at war, are you serious? After this?"

Wren spun. A big guy with a stunned look on his stubbled face. On camera now, a bit player in the bigger drama, and Wren took the opportunity. This was more antidote, essential to get it in now, while he could.

"The 'Deep State' didn't take my Foundation," Wren said. "They're not the ones I'm after."

The guy's stunned look became disbelief. "What? So who the hell are you after?"

"Whoever took them," Wren answered, then spun to run west, shoving through bodies and scanning for his fastest route out. Bodies, the freeway, the VA hospital beyond, slip roads and access roads and-

He fixed on a flashing light beneath the freeway overpass, not a blue light but a red one, hovering flush in the air. The drone! Relief rushed out with his heightened pulse. Hellion had figured out an exit route.

He ran on through the fraying edge of the crowd, tapping the hard plastic of his earpiece. "Hellion?"

A bullhorn fired up in back, bigger than any protester bullhorn, ordering him to halt. At the edge of the crowd his

ear crackled; a signal coming back into range. He vaulted a metal fence and came down in a service road leading to the VA hospital, shadowed by the Freeway, where the drone hovered above a Mercedes-Benz A-class in deep mahogany red.

"Are you roadside assistance?" a girl asked.

Wren had a second to take her in; yellow t-shirt with some nerdy pop culture reference, skintight black jeans paired with beach sandals, lingering awkwardly beside the Mercedes.

"Am I what?" Wren barked, then Hellion's voice rasped back into his head like the dulcet tones of an angel.

"Your route out," she said swiftly. "I hacked Radio Frequency ID of this Mercedes, Christopher; now it is all yours. This dummy thinks you are roadside support."

"My system just shut down," the nerd girl was saying, "remote engine lockout, it said, and then this drone told me to get out and is that something you can fix?"

Wren yanked open the Mercedes' driver side door and dropped in. Massage seats, calf leather, walnut dash. "I'll have it back for you in no time, ma'am," he said, as Hellion swiftly re-initialized the system. The central display booted, the engine fired up, the anti-theft wheel-locks unclamped and Wren hit the gas and took off without looking back.

22

FALSE POSITIVES

Wren hurtled out from under the 405, past the VA Hospital where three days earlier Steven Gruber had fled looking for him, and folded onto Wilshire Boulevard to cruise at a steady pace, keeping his head down, talking to Hellion and B4cksl4cker the whole time.

"All cabs accounted for," Hellion reported as Wren crossed San Vicente Boulevard, well within the speed limit and obeying all traffic lights. "We have checked the online logs, fare records and GPS tracking on every private hire vehicle within a mile of the Hospital across a two-hour window on the fifteenth. B4cksl4cker is cross-referencing to traffic cam footage, but we do not see Steven Gruber."

"And you won't," Wren said, making a smooth left turn to keep track of any possible pursuit. The drone was gone, no longer tracking him. "You said they've erased the digital trail. I'm counting on the cab driver or any witnesses reaching out directly."

Hellion was replaced by B4cksl4cker on the line. "This is highly unlikely, Christopher. We also hesitate to say this, but have you considered taxi driver has also been, how shall I say, erased from picture?"

"Yes," Wren said flatly. He hadn't.

"In such case, this would leave no trace for us to find. Nothing in human record."

"Technically," Wren said, and made another left turn. Working a loop.

His hackers paused; probably conferring between themselves. "Is there any way to see this other than technically?"

"With a little faith," Wren said. "Is anything coming in?"

Hellion hit the keys. They were both hardcore atheists, and faith didn't come naturally. "Thousands of comments a minute, since you took out agents. You are on every news channel, 'breaking the Internet', so they say. We are receiving," keys clacked, "many taxi sightings, but this is all meaningless. There are many taxis in LA."

"Is there anything meaningful?"

More keys clattering. "Several reports of Gruber in VA Hospital; three say he was wearing blue t-shirt, one red, one green. Of those, two report him climbing into yellow cab. That would make sense, as VA Hospital has contract with city. Only yellow cabs with shield can line up."

"We're making progress," Wren said.

"Progress to nowhere," Hellion said. "These witnesses do not know where he was going. There isn't enough for us to map out journey."

"Still nothing from a cab driver?"

"Nothing."

Wren spun the wheel right, making another loop. Still no follow cars. "What about missing yellow cab drivers? If they actually erased the driver, not just the image but the actual person, somebody must have filed a missing person's report. It was three days ago."

"Checking DoJ, FBI, LAPD... One moment... It looks like, yes. One. Two days ago, his wife called in to police, I'm seeing- "

"Get his photo up alongside Gruber's," Wren interrupted, as a new idea took shape in his head. It was a long shot, but long shots were becoming his stock-in-trade. "You said you were getting taxi sightings; let's double down on that. Change the request on our video feed, I want sightings of Gruber and the driver in a-" he paused "-what did he drive, straight yellow cab, yellow with blue sides, sedan or people carrier?"

A second passed. "Sedan, yellow and blue."

"Get their photos and the vehicle up. I want sightings from anywhere in the city across this time window."

It took a moment.

"Christopher, you cannot be serious." B4cksl4cker said. "Two men in taxi, three days ago? Nobody will remember this. Even here in Kyiv these taxi cabs pass by one every thirty seconds. You will receive nothing but false positives; people who wish to help but remember incorrectly."

Wren was way ahead of him. He wasn't wrong, but he wasn't completely right either. Some people remembered more than others, and there was always a signal in the noise; you just needed a way to cancel out the false positives. "Hellion, I need you to 3D model a rolling reconstruction of known yellow taxi cabs around the VA during that period of time, using existing travel records, GPS, CCTV, social media footage, the usual. Can you do that?"

There was silence for a second. "Yes, Christopher," Hellion said. "But this will not reveal anything to us. The taxi is ghost. They have used advanced algorithmic deepfake technology to erase it from all video footage. I cannot find them this way."

"We're not doing it that way," he pressed on. "Please make the model, as precisely as possible, then B4cksl4cker, map any sightings of Gruber's cab onto that model and see where they don't fit."

"But-" Hellion began, then eased off. It took a second. Wren took another turn, heading back toward the VA. It was the only clear sighting they had of Gruber, so Wren didn't want to stray too far.

"I see," B4cksl4cker chimed in. "You are tracking the ghost with crowd sourcing, yes? The human record, again. This model is filter layer to remove false positives."

"Exactly. We establish a baseline, that's Hellion's model. We know those are real movements. Onto that we map witness testimony from the human record. Any vehicles that deviate from the baseline model are suspect. If we get enough, all pointing in the same direction? Bingo. We draw a line of best fit through the data and see where it takes us."

Another second, as they digested that. It didn't take long.

"Ghosts cannot be seen by technology either," B4cksl4cker said. "Only by humans. Unless you count orbs."

"I don't."

"Compositing a 3D model," Hellion said, with the familiar sound of keys flying in the background. "Layering in GPS routing data, CCTV, private hire firm logs. Populating with vehicles..."

"It is very clever," B4cksl4cker said appreciatively. "However, you will need smart AI to turn this flood of random comments into useable data. Even then, it may all be useless. Garbage data in, Christopher..."

"Garbage data out, I know, but we're going to try. You can write an AI to do that." Wren didn't know, was just willing it to be true.

"Yes," said B4cksl4cker confidently, "I am perhaps one of only handful in world who can do this on such short notice. And yes, I will do it for you, Christopher."

"Thank you."

The VA was coming up on his right. The sound of the crowd was swelling to unearthly levels, washing over the street. He picked out a few words, 'Release Christopher Wren' and 'Free the Foundation' blurring into a wall of sound. Traffic lights held him and he obeyed, watching the distant swaying banners of the crowd. No agents rushing up to arrest him, yet. How long would that hold?

The lights went green and he eased ahead.

"Anything yet?"

"I am programming AI, it has already begun self-training on comment feed. Dismissing sightings of all-yellow cabs, cabs called by app, cabs outside time range, cabs without positive ID on Gruber or driver. Now cross-correlating to known cabs from Hellion's model, running backward and forward on time scale, searching for line of best fit. These results are fascinating, Christopher, we should really-"

"Is there anything?"

"First results suggest cab turned left out of VA lot," B4cksl4cker said.

"Then I'm going the wrong way."

He didn't wait for more, just spun the wheel and pulled a U-turn across three lanes of traffic. Cars honked but that was nothing beneath the thrum of the protest crowd.

"Next?"

"I am programming as we speak, Christopher. Self-training is delicate. Hellion, can you?" Like he was handing Wren off to a babysitter.

"Comments on your video stream are accelerating," Hellion took over smoothly. "Your bodycam is transmitting still, but I have muted audio and am hiding your exact location. We do not wish to be followed, do we?"

"Not now, keep us muted, but keep the feed live."

"Good. Our viewership has risen to tens of millions.

News stations are amplifying signal tenfold, replaying your fight in crowd."

"Two minutes and I will have something," B4cksl4cker said.

"Good." Wren thought ahead. "Hellion, where's the drone?"

"Tracking from above, Christopher. There is no pursuit yet."

That was something, at least. Without technology to 'ghost' him from the CCTV record, though, it wouldn't last long. "How are we playing on the news?"

"In your favor," Hellion answered. "There is man called David Keller on many channels now, speaking from political rally in New York. He claims to know you."

Wren sucked a breath through his teeth. "Never met him. He's a nobody."

"He is very handsome," Hellion said flatly. "You could take fashion tips from him; nice suit, proper shoes-"

"Not the time," he rasped.

She continued unfazed. "He is pointing out you did not use lethal force, that you do not blame US government. This is good propaganda, I think. He is on our side, we should consider reaching out."

Wren snorted, passed slowly through an intersection. Driving in stop-start traffic after the mad race down the LA River felt surreal. "He's on his own side. Don't reach out. B4cksl4cker, how's that training coming?"

"Very rapidly," B4cksl4cker answered. "There is good research batch of sightings to build from. I am feeding regression analysis tools into AI; it has incorporated Hellion's model for screening out false positives, and is now generating 'clean' data that produces range of potential routes. It seems there is sixty percent chance Gruber's vehicle turned right within next twenty blocks."

Wren laughed. "Twenty blocks?"

"I do not have confirmation of precise turn, but there are multiple constellations of sightings in north-west."

"So I just turn right when I feel it?"

"As the spirit moves you, Christopher. Have little faith."

He gritted his teeth and pulled right.

23

MANDEVILLE CANYON PARK

I t took twenty-five minutes for the AI to lead Wren up into the low hills of Mandeville Canyon Park. There were left and right turns that he had to correct for, but the further he drove the firmer the route became, built from many thousands of individual sighting.

"There is just one sighting in the parking lot ahead," B4cksl4cker said. "A marketing executive napping in his vehicle. He only saw the cab leave, but thought it was strange."

Wren charged into the lot. 7 p.m. and tingeing toward dusk. His heart beat hard, adrenaline flushing into his system. The lot was almost empty, just a few cars parked at the edge and overlooking a gorgeous sunset vista of Santa Monica with the sun sinking pink toward the Pacific. Wren rolled through, swiftly sighting the overgrown entrance on the left. There was a heavy-duty chain stretched across, bolted with a chunky padlock.

This had to be it. He stopped the Mercedes, kicked open the door and strode out with the Glock already back home in his palm. New padlock, new chain. He stepped over it and ran up a winding trail of bamboo strangled by Japanese knotweed, until-

"The Jeddah Mill," Hellion said in his ear, just as he saw the ramshackle old structure looming large over the trailhead: cedar boards turned gray with age, a hole-pocked tin sheet roof, willowy saplings springing thickly all around. No vehicles out front. "They used to do logging here."

"Get on the routes out," he said, circling to the entrance. "Same algorithm, same AI, same time window. I want ghost-proof sightings on all vehicles on this road. Find me where they went."

"Compiling," said Hellion, then Wren reached the mill's oak door and booted it open.

Inside lay a dim and empty hall, tables to the left with one old saw-bench in place, the wheel missing, crates and broken furniture to the right, antique gear hanging on the walls. This had to be someone's pet project, a kind of personal living museum. Dust motes plumed thickly in the last stray beams of afternoon light.

Wren scanned the floor. Footsteps in the dust everywhere. It wasn't confirmation, but given the lack of graffiti and beer cans, meaning no one came up here just to hang out, he figured these might be his targets.

"Are you recording this?" he asked, aiming the bodycam directly.

"Captured. Go on."

Wren strode in. The hall continued some thirty feet until the timbers gave out in a spray of fallen branches. A toppled jacaranda had come through the roof, still clinging to its roots and spraying sweet purple blossoms in the gloom. There was a door to the right and Wren kicked it through.

Nothing. A store room once, perhaps, now stacked with just a handful of terracotta plant pots. No chairs under a swaying light, no greasy stink of napalm in the air, no ashes, no Rogers or Gruber. He kicked through another door and found himself teetering over a drop down to the canyon slope. Not a long fall, but neither a comfortable one.

He cursed under his breath. Not here. That had been a wild hope anyway; unlikely, but worth clinging to.

"The drone is on overwatch, Christopher," Hellion said in his ear. "This structure is small and broken, the two rooms you have seen are all there is. No heat signatures within except your own."

He caught the far-off buzz of the drone and turned to look up. Barely visible, it was so high. "Can you pick out vehicle data from the wheel tracks in front?"

"I can try. Also with the footsteps in dust. I am running through pattern analysis."

Wren ducked back into the structure, tucked the Glock into his waistband and strode over the ancient wooden boards, bringing up his phone and turning on the flashlight to study the walls, floor and ceiling with fresh eyes. There was no immediate threat now, but that raised the next question; had Gruber even come here?

"B4cksl4cker," he rumbled.

"The AI is only becoming more certain," the hacker answered. "If this is a false trail, it has obscured the real route."

Wren grunted, thinking through a snatch-and-grab operation on Gruber. It wouldn't take much; Gruber wasn't a tactical threat to anyone but a geriatric. Call it a three-person team, one vehicle, some easy means of sedating the target. The hard part of a kidnap operation was the waiting. They would have been in place several hours in advance, and waiting brought out bad habits.

He pushed back into the main hall, already getting darker, and swept the phone's torchlight back and forth across the dusty boot prints, trying to figure out a pattern. Perhaps there was a cluster near the door.

He strode over, putting himself into the mindset of a Pyramid snatch squad. If they were anything like the Pyramid of the past, they wouldn't make mistakes. The Apex told you to stand perfectly still for days on end, you stood still. You wanted nothing more than to prove your defiance of reality.

There'd be none of the usual tells here; cigarette butts, chip packets, empty cans. No DNA, almost certainly no fingerprints on any surface. Twenty-five years ago the Apex had vanished without a trace; he wasn't about to start leaving trails now.

Ghosts.

"Anything?"

"Analysis of the boot marks is fascinating," Hellion said. "I found a wonderful program that relies on-"

"What did it find?"

"Two things. Three shoe sizes, but overlaid. One matching Gruber, based on his height, barely entered. Footsteps at the entrance, then no more."

"Snatched," said Wren.

"I concur. Another set of footsteps, they go everywhere, more recent than the others. The dust lies over them. The third, size 17, this is a giant man, Christopher. Six feet six and counting, taller than you."

Wren paused, studying the dusty footprints.

"One man?"

"Or a very large woman. They exist."

He grunted. One man, sure. Gruber wouldn't put up much of a fight to anyone. But why only one? He stepped back outside, stood on the rickety porch overlooking the approach road, partially blocked by saplings, and racked his mind for any other way to extract clues from the scene. Satellite overwatch was worth checking, but would likely be a null spot, likewise the human record, if he didn't know what vehicle they'd driven away in. Nobody was coming up here.

Except...

The interior had been immaculate. There'd been a fresh padlock and chain blocking access. Freshly bought within the last three days. And that second set of footsteps, checking everywhere...

"Hellion," he said, "who owns this mill?"

"Checking."

While she worked, Wren circled. The structure was dilapidated, but there was no trash anywhere. No beer cans, needles, graffiti. That suggested an attentive custodian, the kind of person who would absolutely notice if intruders had come in. Maybe, if he was lucky, the kind of person who kept off-grid closed circuit security camera oversight of the mill, the lot, the approach road.

Wren's heart skipped a beat. Would the Apex have overlooked something like this? No, but then was he dealing with Apex directly, or was this another one of his lieutenants, who might overlook one such tiny detail?

Wren had to hope it was the latter.

"The city owns it," Hellion said, "overseen by the Department of Parks and Recreation."

"And who's their custodian?"

"I'm looking at their website. Looks like three for Topanga, but, OK, she's on maternity leave, the other one's so old he can't be active, that leaves one guy."

"Name and number."

"Dodge Smitt. I'm calling him now. Check your phone."

Wren pulled up the pink Pixel. The last app he'd had open, his Greatest Show on Earth app, was still blinking as if live. He shunted it away and put the phone to his ear.

It was ringing. It answered.

"Hello?"

A young guy's voice. Mid-twenties.

Wren held the phone to his left ear and adopted a slightly nasal, pen-pusher's voice. "Mr. Smitt, my name's Gerald Humphreys, I'm calling from," he paused a second, thinking what would get him an answer fastest. Referencing national security would likely get him tied up in the guy's command line. "Bat Conservation International. We had a bat house located on one of your properties, the Jeddah Mill in Mandeville Canyon?"

It took a second. "You had a what? A bat house?"

"Yes sir," Wren said brightly. "It's like a box, in a tree. To help bats, which are endangered." Hellion laughed in his right ear and he ignored her. "Well, we installed it some years ago, with permission of course, and we've been monitoring it remotely ever since, but three days ago the signal died out. I'm on the property now, but the box is gone. I'm afraid it may have been stolen; bat hunting is a real scourge of our times. I was wondering if you had noticed anything unusual in that time, any trespassers on the property or things of that nature, and if you have any record of this."

"Well, I-" Dodge Smitt composed himself. "I suppose, if you already had a bat house there? I can tell you. Yes, there were some trespassers. They cut the chain, I had to buy a new one just two days back." He sounded laconic. "I didn't know what they they were doing, but now I see they must have been bat thieves."

Hellion laughed.

"Indeed. This is a serious matter for us here at Bat Conservation International. We're trying to build a case. Could you possibly send us the footage, as soon as possible?"

"I can get it," Hellion said.

"Well, I-" Dodge Smitt began. "That's actually city data. I don't know if I can just release it-"

"Of course, I understand. I'll file the proper paperwork,

but we're actually in the middle of a class action civil suit right now, suing the largest bat-leather production facility in the LA County. The final deposition is in several hours, in fact."

This confounded him. "Bat leather?"

"It's a terrible problem, a real scourge. Designer brands, you understand, influencers. I'd appreciate if you could send that footage to me directly, and I'll forward the paperwork first thing tomorrow. This could make a real difference, if we have some proof."

"Well, I-"

"Think of the bats," Wren said.

Hellion laughed louder.

"I suppose, I-"

"Thank you, Mr. Smitt. This will make a real difference. Please send it to this number in the next ten minutes, or I'll miss my moment at the bench."

"I, but, I'm not at work."

"Within the hour then. Again, you have the deepest thanks of Bat Conservation International."

"Well, OK."

Wren hung up.

"I can get that data," Hellion said.

"Faster than him?"

That silenced her. If it was on an open system, she certainly could, but then if it was on an open system these 'Ghosts' would have ghosted any record of it already. She'd have to phish for a contact, and he'd already done that.

"Christopher," came B4cksl4cker's voice, interrupting the squabble. "I'm afraid I have bad news. There is another video streaming right now."

That stopped him dead. All thoughts of bats fell away as another cold bomb went off in his stomach. Almost certainly another death; Rogers or Gruber.

"Who?" he asked.

"It has just begun, I'm sending the link to your phone."

The phone chimed. He looked at it, the same dark setup, raw cement walls, swinging ceiling lamp, Rogers and Gruber naked and glistening either side of the ash pile that was Jay Durant. The same huge man parading up and down in front of them.

One huge man. Wren didn't need to see any more, already stringing together the sequence of events to follow. The crowds at the Wilshire would watch it. Hopped up further by Wren beating up the 'Deep State' right in their midst, the eruption to come would be epic.

He'd provided the perfect warm-up act, just like in the old Pyramid days, dancing for the crowds in some down-at-heel Midwest town while the Apex worked his magic and the cute girls moved amongst the crowd, signing up recruits.

Always playing into the Apex's plans.

He ran.

"Get me drones above the Wilshire," he ordered as he stamped down the bamboo-lined trail, "and get the livestream tight on me now." He reached the Mercedes in twenty seconds flat, fired up the engine and tore away.

24

BURN

South onto the narrow Canyon Road as the sun sank purple over the Hollywood Hills, Wren amped the Benz up to fifty then sixty, passing vehicles around tight bends, barking instructions to B4cksl4cker and Hellion even as he brought up the feed on his phone.

"Ten minutes," he finished, then focused on the road and the video.

The man was right there. Head Ghost, striding up and down. Wren flew past a Dodge pick-up then chicaned hard right to get out of the way of an oncoming semi. Horns thundered behind him.

The video's visual quality was worse than before; grainy and too dark, but was there audio? Wren cranked the phone up to max and made out the rustling of voices.

"Feed it through the car speakers," he shouted.

Hellion said nothing, but a second later Wren could just hear the whispery mutters coming through the speaker system. He spun the volume dial to the max and the mutters became far-off shouts.

"-where exactly you last saw him, and what exactly he

directed you to do, or I won't be held responsible for what happens."

The man was focused on Rogers. She didn't move. Her head was slumped over her lap; very different from the defiant glare she'd shot this man before. Just a day ago now, a day and a half.

Wren strained to catch what she said, but perhaps she said nothing. The Ghost leaned in, grasped her by the hair and pulled her head back.

Wren almost swerved off the road when he saw her face. Rogers didn't look like Rogers. Pale, sweating, hair stuck to her skin, but that wasn't the worst part. The worst part was her eyes; the life was entirely gone from within them. They looked haunted, dead, utterly broken.

"That's not my Rogers," he said. He didn't want it to be.

He'd seen that look before, signaling absolute internal destruction. The moment cult brainwashing took full hold and the victim began to really believe; that everything they'd ever thought was true was not true, that there could never be sanity again, that reason and logic would only damn them and the last remaining answer was to confess to their sins, admit guilt and sell themselves out completely.

Two plus two equals five. The moment on the other side of despair when you don't only say what needs to be said to survive, you start to believe it too. It could take weeks of isolation, beatings, deprivation, humiliation to reach that point.

It had only been three days.

"What do you mean, Christopher?" Hellion asked.

"I, uh, I didn't think she'd break like this."

"Hmm," said Hellion. "I will look into this."

Wren barely heard her. The man shook Roger's head, and sweat droplets sprayed along with napalm. He pulled his left hand back like he was winding up an axe, then smacked it hard across her face. Wren jolted in his seat, but Rogers barely seemed to register it. Not drugged on anything other than despair.

"Tell me and you'll be a hero," the man said. "You'll save your country. This man lied to you. He twisted you around inside."

He was pouring words into an empty vessel now. Wren took both eyes off the road for a moment to swipe the screen and zoom in. Her eyes were black holes. Her lips moved. There was no way Wren could hear it. The movements were too slight to lip-read.

"Can you extract any of that?" he called to Hellion.

"Attempting," she answered.

Wren swerved around a slow-rolling Lamborghini with its downlights on, a garish red on the dark blacktop, and blinked sweat out of his eyes. Rogers was slumped again now, blond hair draped over her knees, shoulders slack. Wren wracked his mind for what she might have confessed. Rogers wouldn't know where any of his cult members were right now. She didn't have the location of his hackers, not even Wren knew where they were.

But perhaps...

Another cold bomb went off in his belly, hard enough that his foot briefly came off the gas and he cruised for a moment at seventy, barely reacting to the turns of the road.

His family.

Rogers had refused to tell him where they were. Back in Great Kills, New York, just before she'd taken him in, he'd asked and she'd refused to say. They didn't want to see him, that was all she'd said. Some kind of witness protection. Then she'd put the bag over his head.

Wren's heart ramped up to a hundred-twenty beats a

minute. Add that to the aortal flutter, he could give himself a heart attack. Implode from within, take the Mercedes off the road, end of story.

He gulped air. "Get Humphreys," he ordered. "Break through his Internet, his phone, whatever it takes. Flood DHS, the FBI, the CIA with this. The Apex has my family's address. They need to be moved right now."

Hellion said nothing, but he heard her fingers flying. He spun the wheel and punched the gas again, feeling his pulse in his fingertips as the huge man leaned back, pulling a glint of silver out of the pocket of his military fatigues.

"Let this be a lesson," he said, and Wren heard Gruber cry out.

The ghost dragged his thumb on the lighter's steel wheel, and it sparked on flint. The wick took the spark and flamed. Wren's mouth was dry, his vision tunneled, overwhelmed by the cocktail of rage and terror pouring through his nervous system.

The ghost flicked the lighter. Such a slight motion. It cartwheeled lazily in the air. Wren saw every frame of the juddering footage. It couldn't be real, he thought. It was too real. For twenty-five years he'd done everything he could to throw off the shackles of his father's touch, and now-

It hit Rogers. She went up in flame.

She screamed. She thrashed. The sound of it came loud and clear through the car's speakers for almost a minute.

Wren couldn't think. He flew down out of the dark hills and wrenched the car east onto Sunset Boulevard through a red light, sideswiping a limo and plunging toward the Wilshire Federal. Six minutes. The phone dropped from his hand as he pushed the Mercedes up to eighty, swerving without thinking across lanes, on and off the sidewalk, in and out of the oncoming traffic lanes, letting rage rise up to throttle the terror.

Fear was fuel. Anger was everything. You could burn fear to rage, and rage would get you through. The Wilshire was coming. Wren felt the city heaving around him like a tsunami tide, a year of helpless fury overtopping the levee and not one single person wanting to slow it down.

25

WILSHIRE

The protest crowd seethed as Wren pulled around the slip road, crossed under the 405 and raced headlong down South Sepulveda Boulevard until he couldn't go any further.

People here were spraying out of the central mass and swarming on targets like angry breakers: dark figures in the dusk smashing the windows of a parked Ferrari and pouring in gasoline, tossing fiery bottles and rocks toward the tactical cordon of riot police closing in from the Wilshire.

Wren rammed through a gap in the government line before it could seal over and plowed flush into the sea.

"The whole block is encircled," Hellion called in his ear as he stalled the Mercedes and booted open the door. The sound of the mob had become overwhelming, shouts and screams forming a rushing white noise that carried its own feverish pulse, his name mixed in with threats and patchy slogans and bullhorn voices demanding the crowd disperse at once.

"They're pouring out of nearby buildings," Hellion shouted. "Hundreds of armed police. Two helicopters inbound with a steady stream of troop carriers from the north, looks like the National Guard." Wren could barely hear her over the mob. The drone buzzed right above him, livestreaming his feed, but the sound was lost in the whirlwind.

Wren took a breath and reveled in it. To his left the Ferrari erupted in flame, prompting cheers. The riot police were driven back by Molotov cocktails bursting into flame by their feet. This was the same rage he was feeling, brought into reality, and it buoyed him on. Dusk had fallen fast across Los Angeles, and in the darkness justice would come.

He pushed into the crowd, heading for the heart of the tempest. Bodies shoved from all angles as the animal instincts came out, but Wren leveraged his height and mass to force a route through. From above floodlights lanced down; he glanced up to see twin helicopters hovering low. In their lights Wren saw Rogers burning again, saw the soul-death in her eyes, and pushed on harder.

Gunfire rang in the air, Wren hoped rubber bullets. A breeze blew off waving flags. Islands of fire sprang up in the midst of the mob as rioters set cars in the lot to blow, followed by the first deep explosions. Every person he saw wore a mask now, t-shirts repurposed to cover their mouths, screaming for blood. Flashbang grenades went off in the distance, by the fringe, unleashed like lightning. The bitter tang of tear gas breezed on a hot wind, stinging his eyes. Everywhere were faces split with rage, some stained with ash and blood, crying out their resistance and thrusting ahead to get into the fray.

Wren pushed on, checking the air above him; the drone was right there, buzzing low.

"Am I in the center?" he shouted.

"As near as possible," Hellion answered. "It's spreading rapidly in all directions."

"Tight on me," he barked. "Zoom out as the effect becomes clear."

"Understood."

Wren stood in the mob's thumping heart, feeling the rage swell through him. Two people murdered by a barbaric, unaccountable 'Deep State'. Of course they wanted justice. Of course they deserved it. Their bodies tumbled around him, jostled by unseen currents in the thickening dark, hurling projectiles, lighting rags stuffed in bottles of gasoline, aiding fellow members with blood streaming from head wounds, pouring milk in eyes fogged by tear gas.

He could feel the twin booster rockets of anonymity and rage propelling the mob on. Nobody knew who they were. Their cause was righteous. Like a reduction of naphthenic and palmitic acids into napalm.

All that had to be undone.

He scanned the faces nearest to him; men, women, young, old. They weren't thinking, only reacting, deep into the battle. He picked the biggest, a bearded man, 6' 6" and wearing a denim jacket, stabbing the air with a sharpened stake and thrusting toward the front line.

Wren grabbed him by the shoulder, spun him around and pulled him in close.

"Look at my face," he shouted, inches away from the guy now. "Do you recognize me?"

The guy's eyes were wild, lodged in the ecstasy of the crowd, with his thinking mind left far behind. He grabbed Wren's shirt and shook him back. "Hell yeah, man, I recognize you! Do you recognize me?"

He shook Wren again. Moved by the spirit. Wren rode it out and held on, locking eye contact and willing the guy to make the connections.

"No, really, look at my face! Do you know who I am?"

The guy stared, and Wren saw the anger turning on him.

There was no recognition there; no room for it. "Get the hell off me!"

The guy didn't wait for a response; already primed, he sent the first haymaker, a big right. Wren smoothly ducked it, the punch sailed harmlessly to his right, and he rose up into a neat side chokehold, forearm across the guy's throat and left arm up beside his head before he knew what was going on.

The guy went berserk. Lashing out. Spinning. Roaring, pulling others out of their own private fury and forcing them to take notice. Several pulled out their phones to film the struggle. A floodlight from one of the helicopters splashed down to illuminate the scene; better than Wren could have asked for.

A bullhorn bellowed from above, but Wren ignored it, restricting the guy's blood flow, until he began to veer and one knee went out. Wren let the grip drop, spun around while the guy was still dizzy, kneeled in front of him and took hold of his temples.

"Look into my face," Wren hissed. "You know who I am. I'm the reason you're all here. What's my name?"

The guy weaved. Someone in the crowd nearby shrieked, it could have been a name, but too high-pitched to make out. Here was always the moment that took a leap, forcing the brain back to rationality. Dragging people from the grip of extreme emotion and return them to being thinking people again, capable of assessing the impact of their actions.

The guy's lips framed words. It looked like anger. He was winding up for another punch, then something shifted in his eyes. The rage tamped out, replaced by confusion.

"Wait," he slurred, "you're..."

"Say it," Wren encouraged. A tight-packed crowd had circled to watch them now, with the helicopter lights highlighting the performance, and Wren's drone closing in filming it from above.

"Christopher Wren," the guy said.

A gasp went through the crowd. Wren raised his voice, now he was speaking to them all. "Again."

"Christopher Wren!' the guy shouted.

"And do you know why I'm here?"

Making them think. Forcing the anger back into its cage.

"I, uh," the guy's eyes rolled. "To crush the Deep State?"

"No," Wren shouted, then flung the question wider by looking up at his new audience, picking out their eyes one after another. "Do any of you know?"

They didn't. Someone a row or two back shouted something about saving the Foundation. Someone spilled choice curse words. No one in the front row spoke, because they were right there, because Wren could see their faces, and when you were an individual, not a mob member, you transformed. You were suddenly responsible for everything you said and did, and the spotlight glare of Wren's gaze was burning the fury off them.

"To save them," Wren said, growing louder as he went, channeling his own anger into this. "The Deep State. And to save you. I said it on the video and I'll say it now; you are not each other's enemies. They are not my enemy. They may think they are, but they're children, and I don't fight children. Are you children too?"

Wren looked back at the guy. There was something like the light of understanding in his eyes. Converting in the moment, gifted faith by the cult leader's touch. Maybe sign him up for the Foundation when all this was done.

"I said are you children too?"

"No," a woman shouted. Angry at him now. Young, maybe a college student, smart enough to see when she was being insulted.

"Then don't act like children! This is what he wants. He wants you fighting amongst yourselves, so you don't see what he's doing. How many people die here today, do you think? Does it end here, or does it just get bigger, spreading across the country until it's all we can think about, and who's watching our backs when that happens?"

They were struggling to keep up. Good. Rational thought was what he needed most of all now, filtering into their adrenaline-addled minds.

"I know you're outraged by that video. You should be, but think for a moment. Do you really believe your government is burning my Foundation alive?" He let that hang. "Do you really think they've got balls big enough to take me on?"

Somebody laughed. A beautiful reaction. If you were laughing, you certainly weren't rioting. Time to push that home.

"They're not geniuses," Wren went on, looking around at his audience. "They don't know what they're doing, so you have to take responsibility for yourself, and right now you are on the brink of the biggest mistake of your life. Do you want to kill someone today, and carry that for the rest of your life? Burn a car, loot stores, destroy innocent people's livelihoods? Will you tell that story to your kids, maybe, or your mother on her deathbed? I'm giving you the chance to turn that story around and get on the right side of this. Don't you want to take that chance?"

They stared. He had them. He was the guy this was all for, after all, the man whose name they'd been screen-printing onto their t-shirts and painting on the sides of barns.

"So stop," he said. "That's all I want. Take one knee like my friend right here." Wren released the guy's jacket and patted his shoulder. "Take a knee in silent protest and teach the rest how it's done. Don't sink to violence against children. Don't exhaust yourself fighting ghosts."

They stared. Wren stared back. It would just take one. His eyes snapped back and forth between the angry girl and the boy who'd laughed. Likely they'd be one of his leaders. It was neither in the end. It was an elderly woman wearing a red cape and white handmaid's bonnet.

"Sort these pigs out, Christopher," she spat, then knelt with more gusto than Wren figured her knees could stand. She then immediately began to harangue the others to kneel too.

They did. Every one of them.

Wren stood. Now he could see a little further over their heads. The riot was climbing higher; there were fires everywhere as more cars went up, floodlights spiraling, smoke and tear gas stinging in hot helicopter downdrafts, gunfire cracking out along with the thunder of rotor blades, bullhorns blaring with shouts and screams answering back, but right here there was an oasis of calm.

"Thank you," he said, then pushed through their line and back into the crowd to do it all over again.

26

ACTION

Faces blurred into a stream around him. He hooked more large men and worked the same trick. Some listened early, others listened late, but they all listened when he made them. Each group took minutes and exhausted him. Bringing down furious people took all the energy he could muster.

"The circles are spreading," Hellion said in his ear as he staggered through the crowd, meeting rage-burnished cheeks with his gentle hands, meeting rage-filled eyes with his own calm gaze. "Thirty percent."

"And the drones?" he called back, staggering now into a circle of people nursing injuries; people beaten by batons or struck by rubber bullets, people with eyes streaming from tear gas and blood streaking down their skin.

"I'm corralling as I can," Hellion answered. "There are four main off-shoot groups from here, one each way up Wilshire Boulevard, one along the 405, one spreading around the VA Hospital. Across the city we've got dozens of smaller uprisings; a shopfront's burning in Westchester, there's gangs hurling Molotov cocktails in Watts, cars upturned in Fashion District."

Even hearing the areas took it out of him. His lips felt numb, his throat hurt and his heart pounded dangerously fast. "Are they listening to you?"

"They listen when the drones start talking. They look at their phones and some are kneeling. The message is spreading across the country, Christopher. New York was lighting up, but that's slowing now. Indianapolis has riots, but the temperature's dropping. Keep doing what you're doing."

Keep doing what you're doing.

He worked the injured people. No chokehold was required to keep their attention, but it was hard to see their wounds and their shell-shocked faces. They were angrier than the others, maybe, more afraid, more outraged. The riot police, the Deep State, they didn't seem like children to them. Wren couldn't make the same arguments, so he made new ones, giving away more of himself with every passing second.

At last they kneeled, and he lurched to the next section of the crowd to begin again, keeping the chain reaction going by sheer force of will, barreling past 'overdrawn' and 'running on fumes' to the stage where he was running only on memory and willpower, barely thinking, each time scooping deep inside to serve up enough honesty to earn their belief.

"It's all over the news," Hellion crowed in his ear. He didn't even know where he was anymore, lost in a perpetual fog of violence and fire. It felt like he'd been doing this for a lifetime, like there was no end in sight. "They're showing your feed live. Nobody can believe it, they've never seen anything like it before. The tide is turning against the Federal response, Christopher, and picking up speed. This thing is swinging fast."

He kept on. He didn't feel it. The fires still burned, the air still throbbed with chaos. His own words lost any sense of meaning but still he kept saying them.

"Looks like seventy percent and spreading, Christopher," came the high voice in his ear. "It looks beautiful from above, like fractal crop circles in a field of corn. You have to see it."

He couldn't see it. All he could do was stumble to the next group, to the next, to the next, heart hammering, legs giving out, head pounding.

"Christopher," Hellion cautioned, "you're moving too close to the riot police. You need to back off."

He didn't hear her. Even if he did, he had no idea what she meant. This ocean of people was infinite, his own penance for all the violence he'd done. Endlessly talking people down from a rage he felt himself. Face after face, group after group, he was the cautionary tale to turn them aside and he couldn't stop working now. Stop for a second, even change direction, and he might collapse. He had nothing left, but Rogers' dead eyes drove him on, bursting into flame every time he blinked his eyes.

"Christopher!" Hellion warned.

Then he was there. At the edge, staring into the grim faces of riot police officers holding their shields in a tight line. They wore tactical black with visored helmets, rifles at their sides. Like a scent trail of ants, said Wren's broken mind. At their back vehicles rumbled closer, floodlights on their roofs.

He was back in the Sonoran Desert escaping Humphreys again. All the lights focused on him now. The helicopters swung around above, tracking him. No escaping from this. Forced at last to answer for his many crimes. Show the darkness to the light, and let the napalm burn.

The lights grew brighter than day. He became aware of a spreading silence. Beyond the churn of the helicopters, the gunfire had stopped. The cries of the crowd, the bullhorns, the screams, they were gone. The grandest stage of his life, with no energy left at all for the performance.

How many cameras pointing his way now?

The Greatest Show on Earth.

He remembered what his father had whispered to him in the desert, and it forced a fresh burst of anger.

'You know what's real, don't you?'

Here was where it happened. Bending the world. He turned to face the crowd

An ocean of faces stared back at him. All kneeling. Stretched back across the lot as far as he could see. People up on the 405 gazing down, where traffic had stopped. People on nearby rooftops, people leaning out of windows.

So this was what it felt like to be a real cult leader. Time to say something good.

He raised his arms, and opened his mouth to speak.

27

SOMETHING GOOD

"**I**'m your poster boy," he boomed, following his intuition into the dark. No amplification, using only the cult leader's firebrand voice he'd inherited. "I'm Christopher Wren. You painted my name on your barns. You screen-printed my face on your t-shirts. You're here for me and my Foundation, so listen to me when I'm telling you, this whole thing stinks. You're fighting the wrong people. We are not enemies here today. The 'Deep State' works for you."

He spun back to the cordon line of riot police. "These people here are not your enemy," he bellowed. "You serve at their pleasure. You should be protecting them, not fighting them, sowing wounds that will take generations to heal." He paused and ran his gaze along the police line. "I think we will all regret what happens here tonight, if we don't stop now. We will regret turning on each other, when the real hard times come, when the real enemy shows his face, because you think this is bad? He's just getting started. You don't want to know how dark this is going to get."

He gazed into the eyes of the police officers in front of him, through the glaring lights and past their tinted riot visors direct to their brains.

"My father ordered me to kill a thousand people in Arizona, and I did it, even though I knew it was wrong. A thousand people dead in the streets, how could that not be wrong?" Abruptly he beat his chest. "I should have stopped, but I didn't, and now I carry that shame forever. You don't want that. The Apex wanted me for his messenger, so here is my message."

He took a breath. It came hard. The flow of energy pouring off the crowd and through him was tearing him to pieces.

"Stand down."

Several flinched. None took a step back.

"Stand down," Wren repeated. "Unless you want to incite a massacre like nothing this country has ever seen. Ignore the voices in your headset ordering you on. There's nobody to defeat but ourselves. We have to be bigger than this, we have to stand together, or we will all fall when the true storm comes."

He could feel them beginning to bend. As riled up as they were, they didn't want to fight for nothing.

"Stand down," he said for the third time. "You are not my enemy, so stop acting as if you are. These people are not your enemy. My father is a genius at disinformation, a real Wizard of Oz for the modern day, but we get to choose if we listen to him. We don't have to let him push our buttons. There's a better way, and we'll all be stronger for it."

Now there were ripples through the crowd at his back, clamors agreeing with him, an attempt at a 'USA' chant. Wren pressed on.

"I don't think you want to assault these citizens. You will regret it for as long as he lets you live. Stand down, and I promise you there will be no riot. We chalk this one up to experience and we move on."

Wren saw the sweat pouring down the officers' cheeks. It

was a hard sell. Just moments ago this mob had been hurling fiery bottles, smashing their bodies against the shield line and coming back for more. It required trust.

"Intercepting their comms," Hellion said. "I think I hear Humphreys' voice, shouting at the group commanders. I warned you about him, Christopher."

Wren didn't say anything, he just held the moment, fulcrum upon which the riots swung.

"He's dead against this," Hellion went on, "says it's the visual he wanted least of all; you with your arms outspread, the messiah spreading peace throughout the masses, indoctrinating the country into your cult."

Wren snorted.

"Not much he can do about it, though, is there?" she added. "Idiot."

Wren took a step forward. That was enough time spent listening to Humphreys; time now to move the fulcrum point. The line had to break somewhere, and it was always easiest dead ahead.

"Please," Wren called. "Don't only listen to your commanders. They're blind with anger and pride. You have to have the clear heads now. Illegal orders are illegal, and it's your duty to know the difference. These people don't want to fight you." He waved his arm at the kneeling masses. "They want you on their side against this injustice. So be on their side!"

A shudder passed through the riot police line. Wren drove into it. "This could be the greatest moment of your life. Look at the people ahead of you and make the right choice."

The moment stretched out. Wren stared at them, willing it to happen. It would just take one, then others would follow.

"I don't think it's going to work," Hellion said in his ear.

"It will work," Wren answered quietly.

"I can hack the line with a fake Humphreys voice, order them to-"

"No," Wren rasped. "Don't even think about it."

"It would work, they'll-"

"It needs to be their decision! We can't fake this, Hellion."

She went silent. Wren just stared. He couldn't hold the mob at bay for much longer. If he didn't get a result, the rioting would start up again. He'd be washed away in the tide.

"Stand down!" he tried one more time.

It was enough. There was movement on the left of the riot police line. Helicopter floodlights shifted, the drone above Wren's head flew over. The shield wall had broken. A police officer was backing away, shield discarded, hands up. The others pressed close to fill the gap, but still the crowd cheered. Wren held his hands up for silence and they quieted.

As if in response to that another shield dropped on the right, and one dead ahead, then suddenly the wall just melted. On camera. The power of the 'Deep State' deflected without force. Everyone saw it, and Wren felt himself melting along with them. Heart racing. Barely able to hold himself up a moment longer.

"It's happening everywhere!" Hellion cheered. "Christopher, you were right, and I could kiss you."

It took everything he had to keep standing. Grim-faced, like the sculpture at the prow of a ship as the black wall dissolved.

"Humphreys is throwing a hissy-fit!" Hellion sounded overjoyed. "I think I will-"

"Don't do anything," Wren said low but firm. "No celebrations."

"But-"

"Hellion. Trust me on this."

She grumbled and more keys flew. "Now the President is

overriding her advisors. The order's been made official. The National Guard are pulling back."

Wren grunted. The first of the helicopters yanked its floodlight off him and hammered away.

The applause rose up. He thought to try and halt it, but he didn't have the strength, and maybe that was all right, it didn't feel like gloating. He turned slowly, and now the sound roared like a hurricane, spreading with the relief of what had just happened.

Not exactly victory. Not exactly defeat. Bigger than either. The sound washed over him like a cool rain, hitting harder than he could have expected. It plucked out tears that rolled down his cheeks unbidden. Always it was the kindness that hurt the most.

"My God," said Hellion in his ear, different now, the gloating of victory replaced by something like awe. "It is all of them. Christopher, what have you done?"

It took him a moment to understand what she meant, then he saw the first of the police officers walking into the crowd. Kneeling people opened a path before her, uncertain still, maybe afraid, until the woman turned and dropped to her knees amongst them.

The cheering reached another level. More riot police officers followed, their shields and batons dropped behind. They were greeted with hearty claps on the shoulder and such an upswell of joy.

Wren kneeled to join them.

The storm became an avalanche. A celebration of oneness. He was no better than them, no worse than them, just another one in their midst.

After that everything blurred. His legs moved, and he found arms helping him along. Strong hands lifted and guided him forward.

"Hellion," he managed to say, faint with the exertion. "I'm going to pass out."

"The Mercedes is clear," she answered. "I'm blocking all video coverage of you right now. There'll be no footage leading back. Looks like your cheerleaders have you until then."

He tried to snort but couldn't muster the breath. Nameless, faceless cheerleaders. No Gruber coming to pick him up in his yellow Prius this time. No Rogers winging in on a jet. Tandrews had told him to build a new team; how was this?

The crowd passed him hand to hand like he was floating on a cloud, like they knew exactly where he was going. The Mercedes was waiting. Sinking into the driving seat felt like falling into a dream. The engine revved like a purring cat. Only Hellion's voice giving the turns in his ear kept him afloat, as LA became a streaming black blur at his back.

28

ALONE

Wren woke in the Mercedes to dark and silence, haunted by memories that felt too fresh: faces burning one after another in the fake town; his children staring at him in the wreck of their den in Great Kills; Sally Rogers' lost eyes as she erupted in flame.

He was slumped in the driver's seat, halfway cranked back. Through the windshield all he saw were stars, wheeling slowly across the sky. In the Pyramid he'd learned all the constellations, then re-learned them when his father had spent a summer renaming every last one.

His body ached. He reached up and tapped his earpiece, but there was no sound. He had vague memories of Hellion directing him out into the desert, driving him just a little further, a little further until at last the battery gave out and he kept on until the Mercedes coughed to a halt, somewhere off the highway amongst sand and cacti.

He shuffled in his pocket for the phone; dead. Everything in the car was dead. He felt like he'd been buried alive beneath a sky full of lies. He'd held off his father's plans for one more night, the unstoppable desire of the Apex to burn America down, but this wasn't the end.

Steven Gruber remained, next in line to die.

For three months he hadn't thought once about his father. The interrogations had kept him too busy, but this freight train of pain had been coming for him anyway, its lonely horn sounding all across the still country, and now the weight of it hit him at once. Rogers and Jay were dead. The Apex was back. His family were not waiting for him to come home, like he'd led himself to believe.

He was more alone than ever. He watched the stars slowly scroll across the sky. The grandest things happened so slowly. It had taken twenty-five years, but now the Apex was coming back.

He closed his eyes. He was too tired to do this now.

A barrage woke him. It took long, pounding moments to recognize what it was. Rain, falling across the dark desert. The sky was a murky black silt, like industrial run-off smothering the stars. He couldn't afford to sleep any more, even though his head felt ready to burst, his back throbbed, his temples, his hips.

He opened the door, held his hand out and caught a puddle of rain in his palm. It tasted like dust. His lips were cracked and dry.

Around 2 a.m., judging by the fuzz of light from the pole star. Dark desert lay on all sides. His mind turned slow. Not the Sonoran. Drive for hours out of LA and he'd hit Joshua Tree, the Mojave, even Death Valley. He didn't remember the directions he'd taken, only Hellion urging him on.

He'd get out and walk. He couldn't be far from the highway. Hitch-hike, get another phone, another vehicle and keep on trying. He tried to get up, but couldn't.

His legs didn't respond, like he was frozen in place. Not just his body, but his mind was drained. He felt wrung out and used up. Five minutes, he promised. In five minutes he'd go. For now he just lay there, one arm out the door with the cold rain falling across his chest. The air felt charged, like a storm was coming on.

He closed his eyes to the pain, and unconsciousness pulled at him like heavy wool shackles. He barely noticed the rain as it stopped streaming down his cheeks, though he heard the steady pattering sound of it on the roof of the Mercedes still, shushing over the sand and stroking the bulbous arms of Joshua trees.

When he heard the voice say his name, he didn't even need to open his eyes to know who it was.

"Christopher."

She was standing over him with an umbrella open. He hadn't heard her approach, as ever. She looked much the same as when he'd seen her last, after he'd brought the Blue Fairy orphans to her camp in the Arizona desert, sprung up in the ruins of the Pyramid's ribs.

Maggie.

Something good from something bad.

She wore the same tans, browns and burned ochre shades as always, a scarf, a blouse, a Shaker-like shawl; part archaeologist, part professor, part pastor for the past.

"A woman named 'Hellion' called me," she said. "She said it was urgent, that you needed help."

He could just about handle that. As long as he didn't try to say anything back, he could handle the kindness; Hellion calling Maggie, and Maggie responding. Even the look in her eyes, part pity, part affection that he hadn't earned, he could handle that too, as long as she didn't-

"I didn't think I'd find anything out here, but here you are. Come on now, Christopher. It's time to come home."

Home. That broke the dam.

"Here," she said, and took him by the arm. She was stronger than she looked, and pulled him to his feet. She held the umbrella high to shelter him from the rain. He stumbled along at her side, too hurt to say a word. There was an RV nearby, a blue VW bus with people in it. Children? Wren could barely see for the tears.

She fed him into the back, where there was a gurney laid out. He sagged onto it. Little hands touched his cheeks, children he'd rescued so long ago, now guiding him down into the dark.

29

ESSENTIAL BAROMETERS

Until the age of nine, the life of little Pequeño 3 had been split like day from night into halves: the times when the Apex was there in the town, issuing demands, coming up with experiments and providing dawn-till-dusk lectures; and the times the Apex was away, out seeking converts to the Pyramid way of life.

Pequeño 3 had lived for the days when the Apex was away. He'd played in the desert for days, sometimes weeks at a time, utterly carefree. When the Apex was away, it always felt like the fake town was breathing out in relief. There were still countless tasks to be done, and discipline was strict if you were caught disobeying, but there were no daylong lectures, no three-day gatherings around some pit in the desert, and he'd learned to use those times well.

There were countless adventures to be had in the endless sands of Arizona. With his elders chasing him, he'd race between stands of prickly pear cacti and hydra-like ocotillo stands, weaving a path they never could keep up with. He'd always been fast and quick-witted, hiding when he couldn't run, tossing sand or stones as distractions when he couldn't hide, and none of the cult tried too hard to chase him down. He was the Apex's favored son, after all.

At the end of each day, burnished bronze by sun and sated with wild adventures amongst the roadrunners and snakes, stuffed on hand-roasted bark scorpions and stone-peeled prickly pear fruits, he'd always come back to the town and accept his beating with a down-turned head and the deepest penitence, only to spend half the night plotting his escapades for the days to come.

And he was not always alone.

Few of the town's children adventured as widely or as frequently as he did, but then few of the Apex's children were treated so favorably. Next in line were the other Pequeños, five older than him, three younger, but his elders were teens who'd been granted 'true' names and took their town responsibilities too seriously to play.

'Keeping records of essential barometers', the Apex called the tasks he gave them, and always scrutinized these records with great interest upon his return: how many times clouds passed across the sun in any given day, notched into pieces of wood; how many fireflies lit up in the town at night, recorded as knots in a length of string; how often the townsfolk said simple words such as 'Good morning' to each other, transcribed as grains of sand heaped upon a tin pan.

These were all important works, little Pequeño 3 understood that as well as any. The Apex occasionally gave long recitations of the results, and used them to develop predictions of days to come. Those were some of the better lectures, and always felt like flights of fancy, like his adventures in the desert, battling the evil forces of the 'FBI', monsters who wore the faces of men but in truth had black hearts filled with grasshopper legs.

Pequeño 3 looked forward to the day he too would be entrusted with the transcriptions, but until that day came, he largely ignored his older brothers and sisters, just as they ignored him.

The younger Pequeños were barely more than babies. The eldest was four, and even Pequeño 3 knew you didn't take a four-year-old out exploring in the desert. They were for the cages behind the façade of the saloon, where experiments were conducted around the clock.

There were other children in the town though, not only Pequeños. These were granted a sliding scale of respect and freedom based upon complex calculations the Apex himself worked out over time, based on their needs, his needs, and the number of bullfrogs croaking on a given May night. The Apex always had a number for everything.

The best of the children all had been 'Grace-In-our-Times', or simply Grace, as Pequeño 3 liked to call her. She was his age or close to it, a 'naughty little mulatto' the Apex would often affectionately call her, and she loved nothing more than escaping out into the desert and making mud pies.

Their conversations were simple and straight-forward. Between her water-gathering duties and his role in gathering all the black stones from the sands around the town, they only had to give each other a meaningful eye, and mouth the word 'Pies', to set off a rush of excitement that soon saw them charging out into the sands, carrying empty water bottles.

"I figure you ain't a real Pequeño," she'd say sometimes, as they walked hand in hand through the towering yellow chollas, handwaving yuccas and spidery organ pipes toward the old red stone creek.

"I am a Pequeño," he'd protest.

"I figure you's more of a mulatto," she'd answer. "Pretty boy like you."

He'd laugh. Everyone knew 'pretty boy' and 'pretty girl' were pet names the Apex reserved for his own use.

Her hand was always hot in his own, like she was forever

157

running a fever. She had lovely dark brown hair that framed her pudgy, chaff-brown cheeks. Sometimes, before they got to the dried-up creek under the big red cliff, he'd just walk along looking at her face, thinking what it might be like to call her his 'pretty girl'.

He'd never been a 'pretty boy' for the Apex. The others weren't allowed to talk about it, so he didn't really knew what it was, but it always ached like a beating on his heart.

"Race you to the creek," he'd say, and give her a shove, and they'd race away. As revenge she'd dunk his head in the puddle of mud, once they'd spent a good hour mixing it up with various seeds, bits of colorful sand, scrapings off cacti and pieces of broken insect shell.

The mud was always warm on his head. He'd scrape it off and say, "Mmm. Delicious."

She usually fell for it. Her big round eyes would get all wide and she'd lean in. "It is not."

"Try it yourself," he'd say.

Long moments of delightful anticipation followed. After 'cooking' the pie for an hour, bustling back and forth collecting and preparing the ingredients, how it tasted became the most important thing of all. And every time it was different.

Pequeño 3 licked his lips. It never tasted like anything much, but that wasn't how you played the game. Like the Apex's experiments, this was all about 'being the master of your own senses'. He'd talk about that endlessly in his long lectures.

"Strawberries," I figure, Pequeño 3 would say, and Grace would make a sweet face like she didn't believe him, wrinkled up and full of doubt.

"Bet you've never had a strooberry!"

He laughed because she said 'strooberry'. It didn't matter how many times he corrected her.

"I so did. Strooberries and bug juice."

Her eyes widened again. "Good bug juice or fat bug juice?"

"Good bug juice with biscuit bits."

She shuddered and hugged herself.

"Try it yourself," he'd say again, and there'd be a big back and forth about her not wanting to, not daring to, being afraid to upset the Apex if he ever found out she'd eaten strawberries without his permission. Finally, she always would, and waiting for her reaction became the best thing for little Pequeño 3, watching her eyes like he was Pequeño 4 studying the sky for kangaroo-shaped clouds.

She knew it too, and would always drag the moment out. The waiting was wondrous in itself, moments filled with possibility, when they weren't prisoners in a desert cult, beaten on the Apex's whims, abused, humiliated and neglected. In those moments, reality belonged to them.

When Grace was done drawing it out, she'd loudly pronounce, "Delicious, just like strooberries," or be more scathing, saying things like, "it tastes just like poo!"

You couldn't win them all. Whatever the taste, it always ended in a mud fight, then a race and some climbing up the red stone, then the long trek back to the town, where he'd take his beating and she'd be tucked into bed without any supper.

She was the best thing about the Pyramid to little Pequeño 3, so when the Apex came back one day from one of his long trips away, and said there would be another pit, and this time the pit would be filled with children as a test of their purity and faith, he knew he had to go into the pit with her.

30

ONIONS

Wren was on his feet before he was fully awake. Dreams of some distant past rushed through him, but he shrugged off the old pain and turned, seeing wooden walls, a chair, homespun blankets on a farmhouse bed, rustic cupboards, a window. He shook himself, strode to pull the curtain open, and saw something that struck him dumb.

The fake town. Transported as if from his dreams.

Bright ochre sand flowed like a river down the broad central avenue, lined either side with wooden structures straight out of a cowboy movie; the hardware store, the bar, the brothel, the saloon with swing doors, all rebuilt, with the cavities where he'd burned buildings down now filled with fresh, raw wood façades.

For long seconds he stared, taking it all in. It felt like just moments ago that he'd been in LA settling the crowd. Now he was here, back where it had all started. He rubbed his eyes and spun the map in his head. North, south, east, west. He had to be in the hotel, now. Site of some of the Apex's worst experiments.

A shudder ran through him. Back then the hotel had just

been a wooden face propped up with scaffolding. The real action happened in trailers pulled flush to the walls in back. The challenges set to all the children of the Pyramid, the ways he'd spend their lives on long observations of meaningless trivia.

He'd forgotten, but it came flooding back, and he shook his head to clear them. The memories surged still, shaken loose twenty-five years later. If he stared at the main street long enough, he started to see the ghosts of the past moving along it: the other Pequeños, the other children, the girl he'd known only as 'Grace'.

Enough. The past belonged in the past.

He pulled on a pair of jeans and a t-shirt resting on a chair then pushed open the door. There was the sound of music lilting from nearby. He strode along a wooden-walled corridor, passing several classrooms where children sat at desks studying, or sat circled practicing musical instruments. There were teachers in each room. The children were hushed and focused; none of them noticed him peering in.

That hush pushed into him too, like he had no right to interrupt any of this. Mid-morning, he guessed. A clock on the ground floor confirmed it, just past 10 a.m., well into the school day. Why should anything change just because he was here?

On the ground floor he saw more classrooms and a large empty hall, and at the end of a corridor a bustling kitchen where three cooks were busy chopping vegetables and braising meat and pouring ingredients into large pots. They glanced his way then looked back to their work.

Seeing this brought on more flashes to the Pyramid days; the vats behind the hotel where people were once half-boiled alive, with the Apex watching and taking notes in fascination, filming so as not to lose a single second of data.

He rubbed his eyes. The ghosts were everywhere still.

"Excuse me," he said. "I'm looking for Maggie."

One of the cooks turned to him. Dark-skinned and broad cheeks, maybe a Native Mexican, twenty-five, with her hair pulled into twin pigtails. There was a flash of annoyance in her eyes, and Wren found he enjoyed that. After the mass audience at the Wilshire, it felt good to be treated like he was no one.

"Did you check in at reception?" she asked sharply.

He bobbed his head slightly. "No ma'am, I came in last night. I'm a friend of Maggie's."

The woman snorted. "She's your friend, why she's not here when you wake your big old head?"

Big old head? "If you could just tell me where she is, then-"

"What you think, I'm her secretary?"

"No ma'am," he answered gravely, "I can see you're a cook, no doubt a fine one, what I'm-"

"Now you call me a cook? ¡No mames, puto! I'm a chef, big head, not a cook."

Puto? One of the other cooks laughed. "Ma'am, I'm a Federal agent in pursuit of-"

"Federal agent my ass!" she shouted. "Everybody know you're some lost soul, boy, don't be faking yourself up." She wagged a wooden spoon at him. The effect was unintentionally hilarious and somehow cheered him up.

"Ma'am, please, if you'd put the spoon down-"

"She's only teasing you," one of the other cooks interrupted. Wren turned to her; short and round as a ball cactus, white as Arctic charr, but with a spreading smile. "We all know who you are. Coral over there's just angry because you choked her brother half-to-death six months back. She doesn't forgive easy."

Wren blinked. It took him a second to remember; the first

time he'd come here, he'd taken out one of Maggie's men with a clothesline to the throat. He turned back to the angry cook, Coral. "That was your brother? I am sorry I did that. It was my misunderstanding. I hope he's all right now?"

"None the better for knowing you, pendejo," she spat.

Fair.

"Actually, Maggie said you might pop in here," the cactus ball cook said swiftly, cutting off the awkward exchange.

"That's great, can you tell me where she is?"

"Out," she said. "And there's no use you chasing her, she said to tell you as much. She's gone to fetch you tiny batteries."

That confused him for a moment. "Tiny batteries?"

"That's right." She pointed at a dish on the work surface nearby, which contained his earpiece, his bodycam and the pink Pixel phone. Wren picked up the Pixel and pushed the power button, but it was just as dead as it'd been in the Benz the night before, likewise for the earpiece and cam.

"We don't have the batteries for any of them," she went on, "so Maggie's gone to buy replacements."

Wren nodded. Tiny little batteries. He slipped the gear into his pocket, thinking ahead. A trip out from the fake town wasn't like a stroll to the nearest convenience store; it had to be a hundred miles to the nearest town, on dirt roads through Hopi Reservation land. That presented a problem, because he needed to get up to date right now.

"What about your phones, could I use one? Or a computer with an internet line? I don't know what Maggie's told you, but there's things I need to urgently-"

"I'm sorry," said the ball cactus woman. "There's no internet here. It's part of the deal. We're off grid."

Wren stared at her, like she was speaking Ancient Greek. "No internet?"

"We focus on the now." The third cook, a heavyset man in back, raised his head from chopping potatoes just long enough to make eye contact. "It's good for the children."

Good for the children. No internet. Wren searched for an out. "You must have something for emergencies."

"There is an emergency phone," Ball Cactus allowed, briefly raising Wren's hopes. "But Maggie took it. We've got everything else we need here; doctors, supplies, equipment. But Maggie should be back in an hour or two. Until then, there's not much to be done but shell peas for lunch."

Shell peas? "I may not be a Federal agent anymore, but this is a national security emergency. If I can't get hold-"

"No national security emergency's gonna conjure up a phone," Coral snapped abruptly, wagging her wooden spoon at him again. A piece of mashed potato flicked off the end. "You wait for Maggie like you been told, and you make yourself useful, you chop while you wait."

She pointed the spoon at a wooden crate piled with brown-shelled onions.

"I need a vehicle," he said.

"We could do that," Ball Cactus said. "Except last I heard, Maggie plans to requisition the old weather 'copter out of Eloy. If you wait, that'll be faster getting out of here than any pickup we can loan you."

Wren's jaw tightened.

"Make yourself useful," said Coral, and tossed him a long kitchen knife. She looked disappointed when he plucked it expertly out of the air. "Them onions aren't going to chop themselves, and some of these kids can't chew for shit."

Wren looked at the knife; it was decent, cold pressed steel, no kind of guard, but it'd serve well enough. He slipped it into his pocket without thinking further. There was a fruit bowl beside his phone; he scooped up two oranges and an apple, nodded at Ball Cactus, then strode out.

"Did that big head fool just take my knife?" Coral's outraged voice floated after him, along with the laughter of the ball cactus. Wren took a big bite of the apple and strode out into the sun.

31

LITTLE PHOENIX

Wren paced east along the main street. The wooden buildings stretched for a hundred yards, after which it was all construction; what looked to be a library going up, a sports center with an outdoor swimming pool pre-dug, camp-style cabins, a church. Last time he'd been here all this had been concrete foundation platforms, left behind after he'd burned the wooden buildings down.

He kept walking. His head throbbed and raced, but the sweet nectar of the fruit helped. He licked sticky orange juice off his fingers, feeling the sun burn down on his face and arms. After the new construction ran out, there were the graves. Large granite slabs inscribed with the names of the Pyramid lost.

Maggie had been searching for them for almost two years by now. Digging up bones from the remnants of the Apex's pits. All his experiments. Executions. Femurs and ribs scattered to the winds and feasted on by coyotes and dingoes. She'd gathered them, DNA-tested them, consecrated then reburied them.

At the far edge he stopped and looked back, noticing for the first time a new town sign at the limits.

LITTLE PHOENIX

He smiled. Why not?

He peeled the second orange and bit into it directly. Cold sweet juice ran down his chin. How many times had he stood here as a boy, hands full of black stones, looking at the fake town as if it was the whole of the world?

He couldn't imagine how it would feel for the children here, now.

"Mister."

He turned, and for a long moment thought he was staring into some kind of time-slip mirror. A boy was right there, around twelve years old, nut brown from the sun with a fuzzy crop of black hair standing up in a mud-flecked shock atop his head.

"Hey," Wren said.

"You're not supposed to stand there," the boy said, pointing.

Wren looked down. He was standing on one of the Pyramid graves. He hadn't even realized, had just taken up his old position, looking out to where the sun would set on the other side of the town.

"Sorry," he said, and shuffled sideways.

"Say a prayer," the boy said.

"Amen."

The boy frowned. "That's not a prayer. But that's OK. I remember you."

Wren swallowed that down. There was only one place any of these children would remember him from, the Pleasure Island slave-ship he'd rescued them from.

"You get to do pretty much what you like around here, far as I care," the boy said. "After all that."

Wren just nodded; he didn't trust himself to speak. All that. This boy had witnessed him killing hundreds of Pinocchios, one after another. He must've been one of the throng of kids following after him, killing the men he'd left wounded behind.

Now here he was; healthy, fit, free, and giving Wren permission.

"Shouldn't you be in school?"

The boy just looked at him. Looked through him, really. Thousand-yard stare in a child. "You want some more fruit? Seems like you're awful fond of those."

Wren looked at his hands. In one hand he still held the bare nub of the apple core, in the other he held the orange peel. Back in the Pyramid days, the Apex had hated nothing more than untidiness. Litter was strictly barred as a sign of an untidy mind; the greatest crime possible.

"Sure," he managed.

"And water, maybe?" the boy asked.

"Yeah." It came out as more of a gasp.

"Meat too? Bread?"

Wren nodded.

"I'll be back."

The boy scampered away a few yards, then turned back and looked at him a long moment. "Thank you. You know. For what you did."

Wren couldn't think of anything to say to that. The boy turned and ran before he could remedy it. For a minute or two he stood there, battling old emotions. Hellion had sent him here on purpose, he figured. There were countless other places he could've holed up within range of LA, but she'd decided this was what he needed. It showed an impressive degree of empathy, at least for Hellion. Maybe she'd learned something from Dr. Ferat, after all.

The boy came running back soon enough, holding a wicker picnic basket. He grinned.

"Swiped these off Coral. I heard you met her? She's awful."

Wren smiled. "We exchanged a few words."

"She said you took her knife."

Wren winked and patted his pocket. "It's my knife now."

The boy laughed and set the basket down. He opened the top and pulled out a red check picnic blanket which he smoothed across the sand, then set atop it a plastic tub of what looked like roast pork, a slab of cheese, half a loaf of bread, a generous pad of butter, a tub of steamed broccoli, a glass bottle of milk and another of water, two more apples and a steaming corn on the cob.

Wren laughed as the items kept coming. A plate, a glass, a knife and fork. The kid had done speedy work.

"Here you go," the boy said when it was all out. "I figured you were hungry. I saw them bringing you in last night. I had most of this ready in the pantry; been watching for you to come out all morning. I thought you'd never get out of that kitchen."

"They tried to make me chop onions," Wren said.

The boy laughed. "Coral's a tough one, I'll say that. She topped up your milk though, added the best cream. You did good to slip away, though."

"Sounds like you did too."

The boy shrugged. "I'm fast. And they're not all that bad."

That was good to hear. Wren surveyed the picnic. It was a real feast, but only one plate. One glass. "Aren't you going to join me?"

Again the kid flashed a smile. "I'm supposed to be in school. You said it yourself. Maggie won't be pleased if I get caught out here lollygagging."

Wren smiled. "How is it here? Do you like it?"

The grin became a halogen beam. "Best place I've ever

been. Now, you eat up, and I have to go to class. See you, Mr. Wren."

The boy turned and ran. It took Wren a second to call out for him to stop. "Wait. What's your name?"

The boy turned. "They let us pick, if we wanted. Our old names were busted, you know? Used up." Wren's throat went dry. He could guess what was coming now.

"So?"

"I chose Christopher Wren," the boy said, "after you. Just like you chose it after another great man. I like it. It suits us both."

He ran. He didn't stop again, didn't even look back, just disappeared into the hotel, to join his classes and get on with his life and move forward.

Everything was moving forward, and that buoyed Wren up. Out here in the fake town, in Little Phoenix, hope felt like a real thing. The Apex's madness had been purged and the things that were growing in its place were truly beautiful.

The meal was beautiful too. Wren was famished. He sat cross-legged on the town's outskirts, beside the graves, and tucked in.

32

MAGGIE

Within an hour Wren heard the drumbeat of an approaching helicopter. A few minutes later it coalesced on the northern horizon, an ultralight two-seater, looked like a Robinson R22. He packed up the picnic basket and dropped it off outside the kitchen, then strode west to where the helicopter was touching down.

Sand blew in his face as Maggie got out and the rotors spun down.

"Christopher," she called over the dying chop of the blades.

"Maggie," he said. He vaguely remembered seeing her the night before, but that was little better than a dream. Now in the full light of day, wearing her outfit of layered browns and tans, she looked like some kind of mythical djinn grown out of the desert itself. She was beautiful in her way, with dark almond eyes and thick black hair, but it was the strong sense of calm command that made her larger than life, like she was utterly at home in herself, in this place. He imagined the children here adored her.

"How are you?" she asked, and put her hand on his arm.

"I'm fine," he said, and his voice came out more of a

growl than he'd intended. She didn't seem to notice, her dark eyes took it all in stride. "Thank you for coming to get me last night. I was..." he trailed off. "I hit a low."

"I know," she said, with a slight smile. "I've seen footage from the Wilshire. What you did there was phenomenal, Christopher. It makes me incredibly proud, and I want to thank you."

He got the sense that she wanted to go on, but she stopped there anyway, and that was fine by Wren. He didn't want to talk about any of it, really, especially with the way she was looking at him, like he was one of her children in Little Phoenix, damaged to the core. Like maybe she could 'save' him.

"Have there been any more videos?" he rasped.

"Not yet," she said, and kept on gazing at him. "I did speak with your hackers, though. Isabella gave me a shopping list of items you would need, and I prepared them."

Wren was on the verge of asking who Isabella was, when he remembered. "You mean Hellion? How did you get her to tell you her real name?"

"I asked," said Maggie, with a twinkle in her eye, then held out a canvas bag. "Your shopping."

Wren put aside his disbelief and took the bag, fished around inside and came up with several packs of tiny batteries; for the earpiece, the bodycam and the phone. He set to work slotting them in place.

"She told me your people are in danger. I'm so sorry about that, Christopher. If there's anything we can do, please let me know."

The phone battery snapped satisfyingly into place. "You too, Maggie."

She smiled, and it cracked her warm brown cheeks like the clouds parting after rain. "Don't I know it." She paused for a moment, watching him work a clasp on the earpiece. "I'd attempted suicide three times before I came out here, Christopher."

It took him a second to register that, then his eyes snapped up to focus on her. She continued in the same warm, even tone.

"I don't tell people that. Despair about my family, I suppose, getting ready to follow in my uncle's tracks. He killed himself when the Pyramid stole my mother and father away. There are cut marks all over my forearms, dating back to my teens." She smiled. "It's why I wear long sleeves. Then I came out here. I used to think about you a lot, when I was growing up. I didn't know you then, of course, just your legend. If my parents had brought me here with them, maybe I would have known you. I wondered if I would have survived the fires at the end, like you." She paused a moment, looking into some private past. "Thinking like that, it made everything feel so thin. Like, not real. Do you know what I mean?"

Wren nodded mutely. He didn't trust himself to speak.

"I don't know, though. On one level, I figure I'd come out here to die. But somehow, being here, it made me feel better. As if this was a good place. So I didn't kill myself." Another knowing smile. "This town, I know it's full of horrors for you, but that's not all there is. It's also capable of so much healing."

Wren didn't know what to say to any of that. There was something more in her eyes now, a sense of yearning, perhaps, that made his cheeks hot. He wanted to say something meaningful in return, but the words didn't come.

"It's OK," she said, and spread her arms. "I found my purpose, now. It's this place, these people. I look after them, they look after me, and you look out for us all, still fighting the Apex after all this time."

His mouth went dry. His eyes prickled again; the desert heat. He cleared his throat. "I-"

"You have to go," she finished for him, and touched his arm again, sending a shudder up his spine. "Just remember, this is your home, now. It'll never belong to him again, and it will be here waiting any time you want to come stay."

He nodded, managed a swift, "Thank you, Maggie," then strode off toward the helicopter before he had time to think about it too much. The rotors fired up as he approached. He slotted the earpiece in, strapped the bodycam around his chest and booted the phone.

Maggie was watching, out on the sand. Her eyes said so much.

"Where to, boss?" the pilot shouted. A rangy, toothless old guy with a scraggly white beard.

"Up," Wren said.

33

GRACE

The Pyramid dug down.

It was another scorching summer day, after another long procession into the wilds of the desert. Little Pequeño 3 walked solemnly this time, thoughtful and afraid, weighing his two memories of the last pit, those two versions of the Apex. For months he'd taught himself to hibernate like a cicada, and he'd learned a lot.

It was one thing to survive without air for three minutes. But three days? He didn't know what that meant, and it scared him.

So the Pyramid dug. This time the bright spirit of the first expedition was gone, replaced by the hush and shush of shovels biting into hardpack. The Apex said nothing, only watched, and the walls of the pit sank. Flat stones were found and mortared in for walls. Pequeño 3 found himself looking around, in between ferrying sand in buckets away from the pit, past the spiky Buckhorn plants and the riotous explosion of yellow Palo Verde, searching for the hole that shouldn't exist.

He couldn't see it. Perhaps that meant it never had existed.

The Apex had told the truth. 'You know what's real, don't you?'

He yearned to be so sure.

Across the pit he exchanged glances with Grace-In-Our-Times. She wore a polite little girl's smock and polite little girl's expression. In the fake town, she was always different. Only when they were mixing mud into pies in the desert together was she really his Grace.

By dusk the pit was complete. The Pyramid circled around it, fires lit, watching the shadows flicker, waiting for the Apex to give his decree. He kept them waiting long enough for the stars to shift position in the sky, and when he spoke it was a list of names.

"Aden-Of-The-Saints.   Galicia-In-Her-Mother's-Heart. Zachariah-Of-The-Marsh.   Chrysogonus-With-Bared-Arm. Gabriel-In-Extremis."

Pequeño 3 stared, along with the rest of the Pyramid. Five youths. The five elder Pequeños, gifted sacred names on their ascendance. His brothers and sisters, who spent their days taking the Apex's essential barometers.

A moment of silence passed, but the Apex was not finished. His mouth opened, and again he spoke, and this time he was looking directly at little Pequeño 3.

"Grace-In-Our-Times," he said.

Pequeño 3, Christopher Wren as he would become, only stared. He didn't open his mouth. He didn't dare. The Apex watched him closely. He nodded once, as if satisfied. Then he waited.

The Pequeños descended one by one. Chrysogonus was first, eldest, strongest in faith, with a bold jump straight down. Sixteen, he was entrusted with measuring the declinations of the horizon. Galicia followed, and the rest. Some leaped. Some dangled from the edge and dropped. It was too high to climb back out.

Soon the five of them stood arms spread at the bottom, faces alone lit by the firelight, eyes dancing with pride at being chosen, wide with fear of the ordeals to come, bright with faith in the Apex.

"No!" called little Grace, on the other side of the pit. "I don't want to!"

No longer a polite little girl. She was lifted and dropped. Chrysogonus caught her, lowered her to the cool, damp sand, where she began to cry. Her eyes caught Pequeño 3's and terrified him. He thought of cicadas beneath the earth, the whole desert breathing in and out like a single lung, the Apex's blazing blue eyes in the dark of the desert, and looked away.

She wept alone.

The Pyramid dragged in sleds to cover the pit. The Pequeños stood in the bottom, arms spread, as they'd seen their father do before. Little Pequeño 3 watched, and felt the Apex's gaze on him, and waited. Waited until the third sled was coming in, and the pit was almost sealed, then he sealed his fate. Two steps, and he jumped. Slotted in the gap, fell into the dark, and took the impact so hard it felt his shins might crack.

There was no sound. The sled blocked out the last of the torchlight from above. The Pequeños didn't speak. There was no sound at all, and Wren waited, waited, waited for the sleds to be pulled back, for the arms to reach down and snatch him out, but they did not. Instead there came the steady, shushing backfill of sand covering over the sleds.

The dark grew darker.

He moved amongst the Pequeños, standing like statues of stone, until he found Grace. She was sobbing silently on the hard, cold ground. He wrapped his thin arms around her as the sand kept filling in the spaces between the sleds overhead, drifting down through fine gaps like a dry rain. The sound continued until all the work was done, and the darkness was total, and the only sound was Grace's fading sobs and the steady, one-lung breathing of the Pequeños.

In those long moments he felt the world tumbling around him. What was real, what wasn't.

"It's gonna be OK," he whispered in Grace's ear, not really knowing what he meant. "I promise."

She couldn't say words back, could only snuffle her face against his chest, and that more than anything wrenched the world the rest of the way around. He was young, but he knew that three days without air would kill you. Three minutes was enough, and no measure of faith could change that.

The world finally righted itself. He did know what was real.

"There's a way out," he whispered in Grace's ear. "We'll find it."

That stopped her sobbing. Wren felt her head raising up, though he couldn't see a thing.

"A way out?" she whispered.

"We just have to find it. We have to dig."

"Dig?" He felt her eyes brimming with tears again.

"Not down," he soothed. "I swear it. Out. There's a tunnel, like a sand pipe. We can crawl right out. In an hour we'll be home, eating all the strooberry mud pies we can manage."

"I don't want strooberry mud," Grace managed in a small voice.

"Don't you worry, we'll have only the fat bugs then."

She chuckled a little.

"You'll see. We'll be out of here in no time."

"I hope so," she whispered.

Little Pequeño 3 stood then. Surrounded by his elder Pequeños. With their help, they'd find the tunnel in no time. They'd all go out together.

"There's a tunnel," he proclaimed, loudly. "The Apex used it before. Dug into the wall, stretching out into the desert. We just have to-"

The slap came out of nowhere. He didn't see it coming, not even a whistle in the wind, and it swiped his face completely to the side, almost rocked him off his feet. He gasped. The pain filled up his whole head.

Then another slap came, from the other side. A backhand, chipping his teeth and bursting the taste of blood in his mouth. Somebody was holding him by the scruff of his tunic, now, lifting him up. His head spun woozy with the pain.

"This is our testament," came Chrysogonus' angry voice. His hot breath burned across little Pequeño 3's stinging cheeks. "You were not called. You defied the Apex. We will not be tempted by you or your make-believe."

"But-" he tried, and another slap came, then another.

He was dropped. Bands of silver veered across his vision. Stars burst in the black. His mouth moved in agony, but no sounds came out. He didn't understand. The Apex had done it.

"Shh," came Grace's little voice. Her arms encircled him. "You hush now."

"Hush now, Pequeño 3," came another voice. Galicia. The nicest of the elder Pequeños. "Don't move. Don't speak. You will not ruin this for us, like you ruin everything else."

He opened his mouth. Grace's hand was already over it, muffling him from speaking. He tried, but she held on tight until he gave up, and they lay curled together in the dark of the pit, listening to the unified breathing of the Pequeños above.

He'd already perfected his experiments with breathing. He knew aortal flutter, and going as still and cold as the dead, and he knew that no matter how well he drove his heart into overdrive, he couldn't survive without breathing fresh air for three whole days.

They were all going to die.

34

GHOSTS

Wren's earpiece chimed as it paired with the Pixel, and it only took a second before the familiar sound of Hellion's voice came through loud and clear over the chop of the R22's rotors.

"Christopher. I hope you have enjoyed your spa treatment. There is work to be done now."

Spa treatment? He let it slide. "Point me in the right direction."

"North-west, and may I say, that is a very fine woman you have inherited."

"North-west," Wren said to the pilot, and completely ignored the bizarre notion that he had somehow 'inherited' Maggie. "What's my destination?"

"She may be a little too strong for you, though, as I know you like the frailer type."

Wren frowned. She was trying to rile him, he figured, see just where his mental state was at. He decided to let her have it with both barrels. "You don't know a damn thing about my type, *Isabella*. Fact is, neither of you emotionally stunted wunderkind would recognize an actual human relationship even if it DDOS-attacked your server. Now stop trolling me and get on point. Where the hell am I going?"

He heard her chuckling, repeating 'emotionally stunted wunderkind' to herself. "This woman has made you so passionate, Christopher."

"Did he call you Isabella?" B4cksl4cker asked in the background.

"Do I have to come to Europe and set you to work?" he barked. Sometimes you had to lay the smack down. "Two tasty little oysters tucked away in their convoy shells, you think I can't shuck you nicely? I've got a brand new knife and you'll go down a treat with a twist of lemon."

Now Hellion was laughing openly. It took all sorts.

"Is he comparing us to oysters?" B4cksl4cker asked. "These are shellfish, yes?"

"You are shellfish," he shouted over the helicopter rotors. "Filter feeders in the muck of the ocean floor, trying to drag me down into your BS. Now you've had your fun, let's get on with the debrief!"

"We are weathernet," B4cksl4cker said, sounding aggrieved. "If anything, Christopher, we are butterflies on jet stream, not shellfish."

"I don't care if you're pretty little unicorns riding rainbows! I've been blind for over twelve hours; tell me what's going on."

B4cksl4cker laughed low.

"Ah, Christopher, we have missed your charm," Hellion said, after she stopped laughing. "And you are welcome. Now, yes, that is enough fun, you are right. To business."

"To business," B4cksl4cker agreed. "Very great deal has happened while you were unconscious. The Foundation has mobilized like never before. Theodore, Teddy as you call him, has ordered up activation of member base. There are now four Foundation strike teams standing by around the world, waiting for your command. Threat has become existential, this is the word, yes?"

It took Wren a second to catch up with all that. "What are you talking about? Strike teams?"

"Strike teams," Hellion repeated. "Four. In China, Russia, Malaysia and standing by for Gruber. We have mobilized, Christopher." She paused a moment, letting that sink in. "Logistical effort to prepare this on such short notice has been impressive. Through night we sent eleven jets out of private airfields to get them in position. We faked storm of documentation to throw your government off. The Foundation is fighting back, and it is great joy to see. Teddy has certainly earned himself coin upgrade."

Wren stared for a second out of the R22's curved glass, down to the sands of the Hopi Reservation below, trying to absorb this information. "You're kidding. This is a joke."

"It is not joke. It is very real."

"But..." he hunted for something to say. "I didn't approve anything like this."

Hellion laughed. "Oh, Christopher. You were one coin minus and potentially locked away for life. The Foundation had to think about what was best for itself."

What was best for itself? One coin minus? "How am I one coin minus? When did that happen?"

"Christopher, please. Take a look at your outcomes."

"I stopped the Reparations! The Blue Fairy too. How is that worth one coin minus?"

"And lost your family," she answered, sounding bored. "Got yourself arrested. Turned the heat up on whole Foundation and left us alone against this latest threat."

He opened his mouth to protest, but couldn't really argue with that. It was all true. Still, he felt totally blindsided.

"The Foundation wanted me to fix things with my family, so I did," he said, but even to him his tone sounded churlish.

"But not get arrested," Hellion explained patiently. "Some might call that selfish."

Selfish? He wound himself up to argue further, then let it go with a sigh. Maybe she was right. He hadn't really thought of it that way.

He hadn't thought about anything. Things had changed a lot in three months.

"This was Teddy's idea."

"Putting you one coin minus?"

"Forget the minus coin! I'm talking about the strikes."

"In which case, of course. And technically, you did approve this. Dr. Ferat's training camps?"

He remembered that. Teddy had said something about operationalizing the Foundation, maybe setting up training, before he'd hit the Reparations. He'd agreed at the time just to get it out of the way, thinking he'd deal with it later, but later hadn't come. Now they were taking on terrorists around the world, after only three months of training. He tried to imagine Teddy running an obstacle course. Firing a rifle. Even Cheryl?

"Who's on the teams? Give me names."

"They are all adults," Hellion said, "they made their own choices and-"

"Names, Hellion. They're my members."

The sound of keys clacking shifted, becoming deeper and more forceful. Wren recognized it as B4cksl4cker. "Henry Bragg," came his deep Armenian accent, "former Marine from Nevada. Doona Joy, Namibian child soldier. Alejandro Gutierrez, he was Qotl cartel. In China and Malaysia we have drawn heavily on members from Sunlit Dawn, the Taiwanese cult you cracked four years ago. In Russia Theodore is leading a team with a sniper and supplemental mercenaries."

Wren blinked. Teddy was leading a mercenary sniper unit. It was outlandish.

"Who are they going after?"

"Assorted mercenaries," Hellion said. "Darknet hackers, propagandists and coders. It turns out, we know many of these people, Christopher. It seems this whole 'Ghost' attack has been outsourced, dreamed up in head of one single, masterful troll. All false flag killings, conspiracy, setting two parties against each other, these are preferred tactics of Internet troll."

It took Wren a second to figure out what she was saying. "A troll. You're saying it's just one guy?"

"Evidence suggest it is; one man in 'God mode' using data teams to amplify his influence. Real-world exposure has been strictly limited. Only three people were taken, using asymmetric phishing techniques to draw them out. Gruber basically kidnapped himself, and it looks same for the others, though there may be good news here also."

Wren felt about five steps behind now. His heart hammered crazily. "What good news?"

"We are beginning to see patterns of their ghosting overwrites," B4cksl4cker said. "This is how we tracked them back."

"Ghosting overwrites?" It felt like he was catching only one word in every three.

"It is complicated," B4cksl4cker said. "Essentially, every time they deepfake themselves out of CCTV or Federal records, we are able to build picture through what is missing. Really, it came from your idea to map 'ghost' cab by comparing it to known record of taxi movements in LA."

Wren was just about hanging on. He had no idea where this was going, but he knew where they were up to now. "You mean the way we found the Jeddah Mill?"

"Exactly. Signal out of noise. Now we are finally using weathernet as it should be used; mass infiltration and desecration of privacy."

Wren winced. "Don't enjoy it so much."

"This is groundbreaking, Christopher," Hellion crowed. "It is incredible accomplishment. We have constructed baseline environment that models data traffic across select portions of Internet. Through comparisons with 'ghosted' record, we can start tracking where these Ghosts have interfered. Their shadows show them, and they cannot hide from us anymore. Data technique is intensive, but works."

Wren ran that through internal translation. "You're saying you've invented a ghost hunting tool?"

"Yes," said B4cksl4cker cheerfully. "Now we are inventing ghost-blasting weaponry."

Wren rubbed his head.

"Particle beams," Hellion added. "Proton packs."

"Do not cross streams," B4cksl4cker contributed helpfully.

Wren ignored the reference. "But how? Before you said they were untraceable."

"That is bat box data!" Hellion cheered. "Our custodian friend delivered footage from his cameras, which Ghosts were clearly not aware of, because these cameras were not on any networked system. Therefore they could not interfere with them. This data has helped make key for our current ghost-detection algorithm, version 3.2. With it, we found mercenaries, and we're currently modeling route for truck that took Steven Gruber from Jeddah Mill. It went north, Christopher. We expect to narrow down final location within next few hours."

"And I'm heading there?"

"You are heading there right now."

Wren sat and breathed.

Things had definitely accelerated in the night. It seemed the dynamo was only going to go faster now. Mercenaries spread around the world, with Foundation strike teams closing in. Gruber somewhere up the West Coast, with Wren en route. It was a lot to take on board.

"What else?"

"A lot," B4cksl4cker said. "Importantly, there may be good news about Sally Rogers. Brace yourself, Christopher."

"Out with it."

"We think that footage of her death may have been deepfaked." He paused. "'Ghosted' is better term, as this technology is far beyond deepfaking. It is functionally indistinguishable from genuine footage. But you mentioned something about her seemed unusual?"

He cast his mind back. It was only yesterday, but so much had happened since. "Right. I didn't think she would break like that. Not so soon."

"Exactly. Well, Hellion has seen your Sally Rogers in action, and she did not believe it either. She decided to dig into footage herself."

"So?"

Hellion picked up the thread. "So we applied ghosting algorithm to test it. Just like with finding Gruber's taxi, we first had to build baseline model that we were certain was objectively 'true'. We gathered many hours of Sally Rogers captured on film; CIA training, in background of recorded operations, recorded on your own bodycam at times. We built behavioral model from her mannerisms, speech patterns and personality, then compared that model to death video."

Wren's mouth went dry. When he'd suggested the taxi modelling idea to rule out false positives, he'd never anticipated it being used in this kind of way. "And?"

"And it is clear that somebody died in this specific fire, though we do not believe it was Rogers. She did not behave as model anticipated."

Wren's heart skipped a beat. Rogers, not dead? Thanks to a data key derived from the bat box cameras? There could easily be a lot wrong with their hypothesis, but he'd take good news where he could get it. Adrenaline gushed through his system in a cascade.

"Are you sure?"

"We are refining ghost model, but yes. Reliability in double-blind test cases has proven extremely high. Behavioral patterns are very consistent, Christopher, as you know. Moments of extreme stress only make deviating from patterns near impossible."

"So, she's alive? Then what on Earth happened? Where is she?"

"Our current theory is that she must have escaped. If real-world action of these 'Ghosts' is what we suspect, tiny real-world force, with footprint augmented vastly by outsourced hackers using ghosting technology, then it should not have been too difficult for her to escape. As highly trained operative, it's possible that she could have overcome single troll."

Wren's head spun. If she was alive, what did that mean? "Tell me we're looking for her. We have to find her first."

"We are in complete agreement. We have sent discreet Be-On-the-Look-Out BOLO requests through various sheriffs stations all along projected route of Ghosts up West Coast. If she is found at any one of them, we will be first to know."

Wren sat back. It was hard to breathe. He couldn't have asked for better news than this.

"That's amazing."

"Yes," said Hellion. "We thought you would like that. Now, there is one more matter we must address before moving on."

"Go on."

"Agent James Tandrews has been reaching out to us. There is no doubt that he is being monitored by the CIA, but since we are using ghosting technology to disguise ourselves now, we are doubly untraceable. Do you wish to speak with him?"

Tandrews? For a moment Wren suspected foul play, but there was no way Humphreys could have flipped him. If he wanted to speak directly with Wren, it had to be something of vital importance; something he wasn't worried about saying in front of government oversight.

"OK. Maybe." He ran back through everything he'd just learned. "First, what's the timeline of our strikes?"

"Ideally, within next two hours," Hellion said. "The Ghosts have placed countdown timer on their feed, we assume before the next burning video."

"Will we have Gruber's location by then?"

"We believe so. Foundation Board decided we should hit three mercenary cells in few minutes before we descend on his location, wherever that is. If we go too early, Ghosts will have warning. Too late and God mode will remain operational against us. Prime goal is to generate maximum shock and awe, giving Steven Gruber best chance of survival. We expect we will know his location by time you are closer."

Wren nodded. There were details missing, but he had to trust them to the Foundation. "The timeline sounds good. Hit the hackers, hit the Ghosts. Is there anything else I need to know?"

"This is full summary."

"Good. Then let's get Tandrews on the line."

"Placing call. We will be listening, if you need us. Good luck, Christopher."

He took a breath. Far below the outriding lands of the Pyramid raced by. In his ear the comms line trilled until it picked up.

35

TANDREWS

"It's me," Wren said.

"Christopher," came James Tandrews' familiar voice, rough and raspy. "I am sure your team have made you aware that this call is being monitored."

"I get that. Did Humphreys give you much trouble?"

"I'm with the Director right now, Christopher. It's only through his generosity that this call has been allowed."

Wren laughed out loud. That was funny.

"Yes," said Tandrews, appreciating the irony.

"Humphreys, you touch one hair on this man's head, you know what happens, don't you?"

"Christopher," warned Tandrews.

"He's seen what I did to the Pinocchios. Now he figures I'm behind those mutilations too, so let's make that a threat. How's that sound, Gerald, I cut you up and string you out, will that be enough to earn another catch/kill order?"

"Christopher," said Tandrews. No longer chiding. Resigned.

"Humphreys knows me, James. I know him. Is he giving you his new look right now, the flat cliff face, nothing doing, white as alabaster? I call it Director-chic."

Tandrews sighed but answered anyway. "He is."

Wren could just picture it. A small room, recording equipment, cameras, his adoptive father James Tandrews cuffed to one side of the desk, Director Gerald Humphreys on the other, face as blank as a cue ball. Nothing better to be doing than chasing his own tail. It made Wren furious.

He'd thought that after the Reparations, Humphreys had finally accepted he wasn't a threat. Sure, he had to go to the black site for killing all those Pinocchios, but that wasn't personal. They'd had an understanding. Then Humphreys had changed all that with his flat blank face, his blanket condemnation of the Foundation, and it stung. "This fool should have been watching over my people. He should have protected Rogers. Anyone could see they were prime targets for my father."

"He still thinks this is you," Tandrews said.

"And that's the problem, isn't it? Your Deep State's blind, Humphreys! You're opening yourselves up to these kinds of attacks by over-reacting. My hackers are calling this latest batch Ghosts; they make a minimal interaction with the real world. They snatched, what, just three people? With only the visuals from that they've pumped the country up like a zeppelin, and there you are, holding your lighter out like you think the Hindenburg was some great light show. He's not using his head, James, he deserves to have it cut off when the people storm the bastille!"

He panted. He hadn't expected all of that to come out.

"Are you done, Christopher?" Tandrews' voice was tight.

"I could go on all day. But we don't have time."

"Quite right."

Wren rubbed his temples. Enough acting out. "OK. Tandrews. There's a lot to catch up on, but they said you were calling me. What is it?"

"They want the location of Rogers' body."

He laughed. "Her ashes, you mean?"

Tandrews' voice grew tighter still. "Yes. I told them you don't know, because this isn't you."

Wren weighed this new intelligence in the balance. He was done trying to earn the trust of the Deep State, whether it was Humphreys and the CIA or the FBI, the NSA, DHS, DOJ or any one of the alphabet soup agencies. At the same time, persuasion now could be a powerful tool. His father was never going to stop, but Humphreys might. At least he might hold back or retarget more closely, giving Wren and the Foundation breathing room. He had to wield Humphreys like a blunt club.

"OK, so let's deal. I tell you what I know, there have to be changes."

"They're not going to bargain with you, Christopher."

"Doesn't matter what they say, it only matters what they do. Train a dog to come at the sound of a bell, it'll come. Humphreys is my dog. So listen up. My best intelligence says Rogers is not dead. Her death was a new level of deepfake video, we're calling it 'ghosting'. There's a trick to detect it, but we're not telling you what it is. We think she escaped, so that's one in our corner. It means all they've got now is Steven Gruber, and I'm en route to free him now. Once I have him safe, I'll give you the location of Jay Durant's ashes."

There was silence for a long moment.

"He's not happy with that," Tandrews said.

"He's a sourpuss at the best of times. Tell him I could have killed him in that Chinook. Toss him out the door, he's dead. Why didn't I?"

Another silence. "He's steering me, Christopher. He wants more."

Wren laughed. It was never enough with some people. "Shall we talk about how I slipped him in the desert? I heard his voice on the bullhorns. He never sounded more stupid.

'Christopher Wren, surrender yourself immediately'. Tandrews, if this is all you wanted to call me for, I'll have to step off."

"Wait," Tandrews said. "No, it isn't. Let me frame this properly. They think it's you, Christopher. I think it's the Apex. So let's speak to that. We're all putting the puzzle pieces together here; the Saints, the Blue Fairy, the Reparations, they're all skirmishes in a larger war. Are we agreed?"

Wren blinked. Finally, something they could agree on. "Agreed."

"To what end? That's what they're all asking themselves here. They want you to tell them."

"Because they think I know."

"Because they think you must have some kind of demand. It's how most negotiations work. They're spitballing wildly, they think maybe you want an island of your own, to run your cult in privacy. A mini nation, Wrenlandia, whatever. If I'm honest, they're getting desperate, Christopher. Humphreys is not happy I'm telling you this, but they haven't cut me off, so let that tell you how desperate they are."

Wren listened, waiting for the tell-tale click of the transmission being cut, but none came. Tandrews was right, that was a potent sign.

"They're terrified."

"That's the sense I'm picking up, though they'll never admit it. Terrified. Enraged. Calmly professional on the surface, but it's a fake out, Christopher. You think Humphreys has a new face? It's just we've never seen him pushed this far before. Beyond breaking point, and no one's equipped to deal with it. Then you put on your show at the Wilshire? It cuts them to the bone. Their people are turning loyal to you. It's Christmas in July for nightmares here. The whole damn building is falling apart."

Wren considered that. Good, really.

"So they want to deal."

"They're open to it. If you stop."

"Except you and I know that whoever's behind this attack's never going to stop."

"That person is particularly single-minded, I'd say," Tandrews agreed.

Wren sighed. For three months in his cell he'd avoided thinking about any of this, along with all the other miseries of his life. Loralei and the kids. Betraying Rogers. The Apex resurgent. Now though it had to be faced.

"The endgame."

"The endgame," Tandrews went on. "We have the basics already. All throughout these attacks, they've been splitting the country apart along old fault lines. Breaking down our beliefs: that we're one people; that your neighbor will stand and fight for you, not against you; that we're good, and exceptional, and unified."

Wren grunted. He hadn't sat down to game it out, but the pieces of this grander puzzle were all right there. "Simple," he said. "It's mass cult indoctrination."

"On an unprecedented scale," Tandrews agreed. "The most ambitious act of brainwashing imaginable. But where's it going?"

Wren grunted; that was the question. He ran through the stages in his head. They were intimately familiar, he'd lived them, he'd used them on others, he'd seen their lasting effects in post-cult recovery, as the faithful gradually allowed the scales to fall from their eyes. It could take years, cost tens of thousands of dollars per person, to fully deprogram a broken way of thinking.

"Stage one, assault on identity," he said.

"Right out of Lifton's theory," Tandrews confirmed. "Followed by guilt, self-betrayal, then breaking point."

"We're far along that track already, if people are ready to turn on their own government."

"Precisely," Tandrews said. "People's hopes and beliefs are shattering. The Saints started the ball rolling, fracturing us on the basis of race, and each further attack just drove the spike in deeper."

Wren squeezed the phone hard against his head. It still galled that Humphreys thought he was responsible for any of this, the methodical delivery of tortures to irreparably damage peoples' minds, conducted on an industrial scale.

"The new crisis reduces the value of old beliefs," he said, nearly quoting the theory verbatim, "because the old beliefs can't solve the current crisis. People become sick with worry, they're afraid, and they're looking for answers."

"Then a savior emerges with all the answers," Tandrews added.

"And that savior gives them enemies to blame," Wren said.

"Enemies and answers," Tandrews went on. "The enemies die with the old beliefs, and the answers offer a hopeful future."

"Then confession," Wren said. The word sounded like a tolling bell.

"Confession," Tandrews repeated. "Admit and accept that all you thought before was wrong. The Judas moment."

Wren winced. He hated the Judas moment more than anything, when people abandoned logic and the evidence of their whole lives, and started in on groupthink because it made them safe. Four lights became five. Big Brother became not your tormentor, but your savior.

"Next comes internal harmony, a new balance and rebirth."

"Rebirth," Tandrews repeated. "That's where everyone here is stuck. What's the Apex's end point?"

Wren ran everything he knew back and forth through his head like an old spool of tape. The Apex thrived on chaos, but not because he loved chaos in itself. He'd always been the most obsessive compulsive, organized man Wren had ever known. He just hated reality.

Wanted to bend it for himself.

All his experiments in the Pyramid had been aimed at exactly that. The constant recording of the minutiae of life, all for the sole purpose of trying to somehow 'catch out' the world in a mistake, and thereby bend it to his own will. But reality was stubborn and did not bend. All he could change was the human conception of the world.

He'd achieved it at the fake town. Those people had eaten out of his hand for years on end. They'd died for him year after year until the final fiery end, when the Apex had fled.

"Death," Wren said.

"Death," Tandrews agreed. "But whose death?"

Wren could feel Humphreys leaning in across the distance, straining for this answer too. It made Wren feel oddly distanced from himself, like he wasn't in the helicopter but out in the air floating among the clouds.

"Everyone. All America, at least to start with. Maybe the whole world, down the line. It's the only way he'll feel better. Bend everyone, all at once, in the most total way possible."

There was silence for a time.

"That's not something they're prepared to negotiate over," Tandrews said.

Wren snorted. Of course not. But the Apex had always dreamed big. Twenty-five years ago he'd reaped a thousand souls, and it had fed him until now. It had kept him going. Now he had to be jonesing bad. Like any junkie, the next high had to be higher still. Aiming for the whole thing. Creation. Insert himself where God should be and bring things to an end.

It reshaped everything for Wren. With stakes like that, matters couldn't continue as they had been. The Apex had already brought them to this heightened point where it only took a single death to spark riots. If anyone could brainwash the world, it was the Apex.

Divided they would all fall.

"We need to get on the same page here, Tandrews. Convince them."

"I'm trying."

"Divided we lose. We all lose."

"They're not buying it. They think you're the devil here, Christopher. They can't get in bed with the devil."

He needed proof. Something solid linking the Apex to the deaths. And perhaps now, unlike any other time before, he had the ability to do just that.

Evidence. His heart boomed. It was really the only way forward. You had to live your values, after all.

"When this is done, when Gruber's free, I'm coming back in."

There was a long silence.

"He wants to know more," Tandrews said.

Wren sucked in a breath. If these were the stakes, then this is what he had to do. There was no playing around anymore, going rogue. He had to go all-in with all the chips available.

"Me. My Foundation. Everything. We come in, we share what we know, and we take this on together. Regardless of what you think, you need me, Humphreys. I'm the best weapon you've got against what's coming. You dunk me back in the black site, that's on you. You lock up my Foundation, that's on you. If we're fighting each other, he'll sweep us away like a tsunami. We need to unite."

Another long silence. Wren imagined Humphreys talking to other heads of agencies, to people in government, maybe the President. This went all the way to the top. This was all that mattered right now.

"They want proof, Christopher. Proof that this isn't you. Proof that your father is behind it."

Wren grimaced. Fresh anger dumped corticosteroids into his system, making colors brighter and his mind tick faster. Really, he hadn't expected anything else.

"I'll get it. Tandrews. Punch him in the face for me, will you?"

He rang off.

The phone lay in his palm before him. His whole body felt like it was trembling. Twenty-five years ago he'd fled the Pyramid, he'd traveled the world, he'd brought down countless cults, but everything had always been leading back to this. The moment of truth.

The old pilot was looking at him. Wren looked back.

"Heavy," the guy said.

Wren looked away to the horizon. Heavy. Yeah.

36

PROOF

"Let me understand this," B4cksl4cker said, summarizing while Wren's chopper churned west. "You want us to build ghost model from twenty-five years ago, but actually perhaps dating fifty years back, focused on one man, but not only one man. You want us to track everything he might have done, everyone he met, everywhere he went across that time period, but since there are no records of him anywhere, we'll need to use ghost-hunting technique to build up world around him. Is this correct?"

"It's a little more than that," Wren corrected uneasily.

"Oh, little more?" B4cksl4cker asked. "I have clearly not understood then, Christopher."

"You have. You know exactly what I want."

"Proof."

"Proof, that's right. That the Apex survived the Pyramid. That he was behind these other attacks. That he's behind this one.

B4cksl4cker sighed, took a deep breath, then sighed again. "Christopher. It is too much. This, in addition to tracing back Ghosts, and coordinating our strikes on hacker outposts, all before you land and retrieve Steven Gruber? You have been watching countdown, I think?"

Wren grimaced. The Ghosts' countdown was under ninety minutes now, leading up to 6 p.m.; everyone out of work and out onto the streets just in time to watch Steven Gruber go up in flames.

"I know. But this is important."

A brief silence. Below a small town whizzed by. "Hellion, can you talk some sense into this man?"

"Delighted," said Hellion. "Christopher, what you are asking is beyond impossible. On purely practical level, the vast majority of records we need to build ghost model for your father will not be available in digital. They will be stored as paper records in hundred different warehouses, filing rooms, basements spread across whole state of Arizona. We cannot access those, and even if we could, it would take forensic team of hundreds to make sense of them, then army of hundreds more to put these pieces together. This data is simply not available."

Wren was ready for this. "So don't get all the data. I just need enough."

"Enough to find ghost inconsistencies, yes, Christopher, but to find ghosts there must be enough reliable data to see those gaps! The record must be near perfect to spot them, and there is not nearly enough data, or we would already know where Apex is."

"Not good enough. You haven't even tried."

Another moment passed. "B4cksl4cker, he is all yours."

"Christopher," came the older hacker's Armenian bass again. "This is not Hellion and I trying to persuade you because it is difficult and we are lazy. It is impossible, and no amount of bullying will change that. There is no place to start. Finding ghosted taxi cab in LA, this is possible thing, in current data-rich world. But the movements of one man in desert thirty years ago? There was no data then. The world was thin, Christopher. One tenth as many satellites. No street view. No social media. Far fewer cameras, no date stamps or GPS built in, no blogs. There is not enough raw information to build model."

Wren's mind raced. "So you're telling me you need more information."

"Christopher, no. Do not try to spin this. There is not enough data in whole world to do what you're asking."

"The data silos. Hellion just mentioned them. Records everywhere on paper, in warehouses, filing rooms..."

"These are air gapped. Inaccessible. No amount of phishing techniques can extract metric ton of paper folders. We would need semi-truck trailer just to store one tenth of these. They are more secure than best cryptography."

"So I'll get you ten semi-truck trailers. I'll get access."

"You cannot get access. Perhaps to some. Not all."

"So I get some, then. Narrow it to the records for the counties around the fake town. Traffic violations, DMV records, cop beat reports, land deeds."

B4cksl4cker sighed.

"And hundreds of people to process this?" Hellion asked, taking up the baton again.

"With a few dozen you could scan a semi-truck in a few days," Wren argued. "Smart AI processes it and builds the model. Where people were. What they were doing. Money flows. Vehicle flows. And we scratch the fifty year window, focus on the years right around the end of the fake town. Or scratch all that, and focus on the now. If he's behind the last three attacks, there has to be a record. We're data rich now, right?"

Hellion sounded exasperated. "Yes, Christopher, but-"

He tuned out of the explanations, momentarily flashing back to the attack that had begun all of this; Richard Acker, head of the Order of the Saints. As he'd stepped back into the flames of the Whipple Building in Minneapolis, he'd talked about meeting with the Apex. He'd known Wren's Pyramid name, Pequeño 3, that he'd never told anyone.

"Richard Acker," he blurted. "He said he met my father. I thought it was BS at the time, just to get in my head, but what if it wasn't? We could track him back. The Blue Fairy too, Lance Gebhart, he must have known my father. The Reparations, what was her name?"

"Yumiko Harkness," said Hellion wearily.

"Track those three. Their paths crossed with the Apex somewhere, I guarantee it."

Hellion sighed. "As you have already said, scanning alone will be work of days. It is not possible within ninety minutes. It may not be possible in ninety years, Christopher. He is needle in this haystack."

"So narrow the haystack. Harness the second skin and the weathernet. I'll get you the resources you need, just tell me what they are. There really is nothing else more important right now. If my father's endgame is to kill everyone, it's going to affect you too. I don't care how well you like the hacker lifestyle, you'll like it a whole lot less if you're dead."

Hellion chuckled. "Dead? How will he kill us, Christopher? Brainwashing will not work. I will never burn myself alive."

"I think you would, if he had you locked alone in a room for long enough," Wren pressed. "But he doesn't need everyone to be brainwashed, just enough to carry the rest with him. Imagine he gets hold of just one nuclear missile facility. He fires at Russia, do you think Russia will hold back from mutually assured destruction? I'd like to see your hacker lifestyle then, rocking a convoy through a global fog of radioactive fallout."

There was a pause.

"This is good point," B4cksl4cker said.

"So come to me with solutions. What do you need?"

"All this data," Hellion said at once. "On your Pyramid, on last three organizations, gathered together in one database."

"Good. What else?"

"What else?"

"Human resources. Computing power. Money. Who and what?"

"Best forensic data scientists in the world," B4cksl4cker joined in. "Dozens of them. Best AI programmers and pattern analysts. Entire research staff of MIT."

"So get me a list of names."

"Even preparing this list will take longer than three hours, Christopher," B4cksl4cker countered. "It will take many hundreds of hours just to gather and process data. It will cost millions of dollars, and even with all this, breakthrough may never come. It may take months or years to find his trail, if it exists anywhere."

Wren seized on the positive. "But you might find it?"

B4cksl4cker made an uncomfortable noise.

"It is highly unlikely," Hellion said. "But it is possible."

"Good enough. I'll get you what I can. Start moving pieces into place."

"Using Foundation assets?"

"Spend it all. Gather your team. Start with the Pyramid and set up a system; we'll expand it outward to the Saints and the rest when we can. Remember, nothing else matters here."

There was a silence.

"Humphreys will never give you what you're asking for," B4cksl4cker said. "Not without proof first. Argument is circular."

"So we don't ask," Wren said, as the plan formed up in his head. "We just take."

37

HELICOPTER

The helicopter flew on and Wren watched updates
pouring in on his phone. The backlash to his speech
at the Wilshire was already setting in like a bad
hangover: anger at the police, at the protesters, at Wren. A
new theory was being constructed as he watched, from
memes and fringe theories, backed up with circumstantial
'evidence' fabricated from whole cloth: that he'd been co-
opted by the Deep State.

'Look at that fight in Gruber's apartment!' one argument
went. 'It's clearly fake. He pulled all his punches. And
bodyslams? What DELTA agent does that in the real world?'

That was true. It didn't help that viral gifs supported the
theory, showing Wren tossing the FBI guy around
accompanied by big comic-like 'BANG!' and
'KRRAAANNG!' speech bubbles.

'Are we really supposed to believe he was in a black site
for THREE MONTHS and didn't flip?' another went. 'No one
can stand up to torture for that long, and come out looking as
good as he did.' For this there were time-lapse graphics of his
face before and after, getting thin. He was flattered they
thought he looked good.

'Everyone's saying he did this miracle at the Wilshire," went another, over video footage of Wren pulling capoeira moves, "the crowd was going wild, but he was there beating up FBI agents just an hour before he 'spread peace' through the masses. The man's a charlatan just like his father!'

He scrolled on. The news channels were documenting the outcry with gusto, anchors repeating the charges for all they were worth. Talking heads popped up in split screen like firecrackers, variously applauding or decrying what Wren had done. Presidential candidate David Keller stood at a podium, Hollywood handsome in an unbuttoned shirt, cuffs rolled up, salt of the Earth.

"Something's sick in our society," he said, vigorous but restrained. "I was his first advocate, but even I have to question what we're seeing now."

Wren switched channels.

In LA people were coming back onto the Wilshire parking lot. Across the country the same thing was happening. This time they would be better prepared, Wren knew. Better armed. Reporters were jostled in their midst. National Guard forces gathered at the edges, racking rubber bullets. In turn the signboards grew darker. RELEASE CHRISTOPHER WREN became CHRIS-TRAITOR WREN. DUMP THE DEEP STATE became DESTROY THE DEEP STATE. FREE THE FOUNDATION became F**K THE FOUNDATION.

The Russian propaganda factory, hard at work. He brought up his mission brief on the first of the Foundation strikes.

The propaganda factory was a purpose-built black hat unit out of Vladivostok, suspected of frequent use by the Kremlin to undermine foreign elections and spray out fog of war memes. Stolen intelligence suggested there were over a hundred workers hard at work formulating memes, conspiracies and fake evidence within its squat, windowless box warehouse.

The Foundation team there included several ex-CIA assets, an old SEAL associate who went by 'Abercrombie', and Teddy riding herd.

Wren placed the call, and within seconds Teddy came up on video. He looked even thinner than the last time Wren had seen him, almost skeletal. It lent him an uncanny intensity, like the bullet to his brain had burned off all the nonsense.

"Christopher," he said. Even his voice was different, deeper and more assured.

"I'm asking you to hang back when the strike goes down," Wren said. "The Foundation needs you."

Teddy stared at him for a moment. "You don't know what the Foundation needs anymore." There was no anger in it, just a flat statement of fact. "I'll remedy that, as soon as this is over."

Wren re-appraised him. Teddy had always been a man of overwhelming charm. It had spoiled him with an excess of every kind of pleasure imaginable, making him rich and soft. Now he was hard, like hammered iron.

"So survive, then. I expect a thorough debrief."

"You'll have one. Get this done, Christopher."

He ended the call and sat for a moment staring at the phone. He hadn't expected that. Teddy had always wanted a cult of his own. Now he had one, and the weight of responsibility had only made him stronger.

He scrolled to the next brief, a down-at-heel fifth-floor Internet café in a textiles district of Beijing. Video overwatch was provided by a hacked civilian drone. Intelligence suggested it contained a twenty-strong team of black hat propagandists operating under the iron rule of Pang Jiao Shou, Pa-Shou for short, which meant Fat Unicorn. She was a long-time thorn in the Communist Party's side, having propagated a number of infamous pro-democracy videos that briefly pushed through the Great Firewall. Now she ran a mercenary crew focused on manufacturing virality for the Ghosts' death videos.

The Foundation team there included three paramilitary ex-members from Sunlit Dawn, a god-emperor cult he'd cracked in unprecedented collaboration between the CIA and the Taiwan National Security Bureau, along with Alejandro, his ex-Qotl cartel coyote and undercover hook-up.

Wren scrolled to the last mission brief, live footage from a surveillance cam watching the Malaysian hacker nest, concealed inside the donut hole of a large Kuala Lumpur block in the shadow of the Twin Petronas Towers. A cabal of several dozen elite graphics hackers were at work within, apparently operating using a Titan2-level parallel supercomputing array, capable of 100 petaflops. They were responsible for simultaneously 'ghosting' all trace of the abductions.

The Foundation team included another two from Sunlit Dawn, three Foundation Army Rangers Wren had extricated from an Afghanistan fraud scheme, along with Doona, the ex-child soldier who'd helped him raid the Reparations' Anti-Ca compound.

Everyone was in position. Ghosted themselves by Hellion and B4cksl4cker. Waiting for the signal.

The R22 put down, as scheduled, just north of LA in Oxnard airfield, and Wren transferred to a waiting luxury Airbus ACH175, the largest commercial helicopter available on short notice. American-built, it could lift seven tons with room for fourteen passengers. Wren cranked the rear door open.

The interior had been completely stripped, luxury

recliners torn out and replaced with wall-rack seating, making room for twin Yamaha YZ360 dirt bikes down the bay's middle, with a large pallet in back loaded with squat red cylinders.

Wren stared.

"Corporal," came a familiar voice, shouting over the beating of the rotors.

Henry was standing right there, saluting. Wren hadn't seen him since their joint operation against the Viking biker gang in Utah.

"Hot dang," Wren said, and matched the salute sharply. "Henry, it's good to see you. How are you?"

"Better for seeing you alive, Sir," Henry reeled off, as uniform as a military roll call.

"Likewise, soldier," Wren said, barreling through the catch in his throat. It had been too long since they'd had a coin meeting. "Your family?"

"Well, Sir! And yours?"

"Well," Wren answered, though he didn't know it. Better off for not being near him. "At ease."

Henry broke off the salute and stood smartly, arms clasped behind his back as if for inspection. Wren looked down the line at the rest of the team; all Foundation members he'd recruited over the years, from drug deals gone sour, black ops that went wrong, cartels that broke apart, gangs that fractured under DELTA-level tactics.

Mason was there. It took Wren a second to pick out his dark eyes within the mass of scar tissue branding his cheeks, chin, forehead. SAINT, those brands read. Mason, who'd turned on the Order of the Saints just in time to save Wren and the country.

"Oh God," Wren murmured.

"Not quite," Mason said, with a shy smile.

The man had been in the hospital for months, getting treatment for the bullets Sinclair had put in his chest, followed by months more in private therapy with Dr. Ferat for the mental scars the Alpha had put in his brain. They'd had a coin meeting since Ferat's death, spoken some about small things, and Wren had arranged for fresh mental health support. He'd never expected to see this.

"Are you sure you can-"

"I'm sure," said Mason. His voice sounded thick. "I owe this."

There was the weight. They all carried it. Mason had killed Wendy, the love of his life. Cult indoctrination broke people in all the worst ways, made them traitors to themselves.

"I was a Marine," Mason went on, justifying his presence. "I can fight."

Again Wren pushed through the tightness in his throat. "I'm glad you're here. We're lucky to have you."

Mason just nodded.

Wren surveyed the others; people he hadn't expected, who weren't military or even police-trained, who shouldn't be there at all. Chuck the office worker, who'd fallen into the Foundation after being caught out in a basic marijuana buy. He looked thicker in the chest than before, filled out with muscle. Abigail, a brilliant triathlete who'd been sucked into a pseudoscience cult at 21, then pressured to give up her ambition and 'serve' as a lay preacher to squeeze the masses. Luke the ex-State Congressman, who'd fallen from grace on deep charges of white collar fraud, only kept out of jail by his decision to testify against the CEO of a major oil corporation. It had briefly made the national news. Larissa Bray, a surgeon he'd caught out in the run-up to graduating to an Angel of Death, padding out care packages as a sadistic Munchausen-

Syndrome-by-Proxy addict, staring back at him with those dark eyes that always gave him goosebumps.

They were a band of misfits. Only three months of training for some of them. Chuck who'd never seen combat in his life. Mason barely recovered from deep trauma. Henry still scarred by the sacrifice of Abdul, saving his life against the Order of the Saints.

That was over a year ago now. To Wren it felt like a lifetime.

He stood in the dark and thunder before them, struck by the power and unity of the Foundation, such that it could bring these people together. For some reason they believed in him, and what the Foundation stood for. They weren't out on the streets sharing bullshit memes, lost in some hunt for meaning when meaning was right there in front of their eyes.

Loyalty mattered. Actions rather than words. These people were the Foundation upon which he now stood. The shoulders of giants.

In that moment, Wren realized his plan was wrong. Would have to be completely re-thought. He was needed elsewhere, and they had the matter in hand. He nodded at Henry, then surveyed them all. Explained the new plan. Took receipt of a few pieces of gear in a deployment bag, then shook their hands one by one.

"Thank you," he said, looking around at his Foundation, then stepped off the helicopter.

The rotor sped up. The Airbus rocketed into the air.

Sometime in the last few minutes his mission brief had shifted. Maybe it was the slow punch impact of seeing Teddy, out there on the front line. Of seeing Henry and Mason. Injuries healed. Loss could make you stronger. Loyalty counted for something.

There were so many frontlines, now, and this was not his.

"You need another helicopter?" B4cksl4cker said in his ear.

"I thought you'd never ask."

"We have one on standby. Strictly civilian. Also, we're working on a location."

It was music to Wren's ears. "Lead on, maestro."

38

BOLO

The first BOLO had come in twenty minutes earlier, from a farmer's market in the tiny desert podunk of San Felipe, fifty miles south-east of San Jose. A wild-looking half-naked woman stalking the market's produce aisles, snatching up a guava in one hand and an avocado in the other, before making off through the back with a shop apron plucked off a coat rack.

No attempt to play the Federal agent card. No effort to request a phone. No identifying details at all, other than female, stocky, blond.

It told Wren everything he needed to know: the Ghosts had abducted Sally Rogers the same way they'd taken Steven Gruber, by exploiting a known connection. They'd phished her and drawn her out. A text message from a trusted source, maybe, citing some emergency. It was the only explanation why she hadn't immediately called in to local authorities.

She thought the CIA was compromised. She thought the Ghosts had a mole high in the CIA.

Wren thought so too.

His helicopter sped just west of due north, parallel with the Pacific coast, an R44 four-person. Wren sat beside the pilot, eyes glued to the Ghosts' countdown on his phone. Just over an hour left.

"You got them all?" he asked Hellion.

"All the BOLOs were intercepted," she replied. "No one else knows where she is."

The second BOLO had come in swiftly on the first's tail; a sighting of a woman wearing a navy shop apron boosting an ATV sports vehicle from the ostrich farm two hundred yards down the road from the farmer's market.

It was going to be tight. The crowds across the country were already heating up in the run up to dusk. The strike teams in Russia, China and Malaysia weren't going to stay undetected for much longer. The countdown timer on the ghost's feed was ticking down. Gruber's life hung in the balance, and with it peace across America.

"Any sighting on the ATV since?"

"I have a drone array up, shifting satellite overwatch."

"Can we project her potential route?"

"Already done. Modeling predicted routes now. Twenty percent ruled out so far; she's not on any known roads. The remaining eighty percent are routes through the wild."

"So she's off-road?" Wren brought up the map on his phone and scrolled the screen, looking for her angle. Rogers thought like him. If there was a mole in her organization, she'd look to root it out herself. Her first thoughts now had to be money, clothes, weaponry and a way back in.

So where would she be headed? On an ATV with thirty minutes to play with, she could have covered maybe thirty miles over rough terrain. Immediately to the north, east and south of San Felipe lay the thick barrier of the Henry W. Coe State Park, a chaparral coated ten-mile tranche of the Diablo Range mountains. Only to the west and southeast lay roads leading out down narrow valleys.

Wren zoomed in. If it was him, he'd head for a cache-point; a place he'd secreted money, weaponry, clothing. He had them in every state, tucked away like buried treasure in parks, highway sidings and open scrub. It was highly unlikely Rogers had anything like that, though.

So where?

The answer came fast. She'd overseen the placement of his family in Witness Protection, which meant she'd had access to a range of Federal safe houses. Any capable agent would have memorized as many as they could, against a rainy day, and Rogers was far more than just a capable agent.

"Can you get me a map of CIA safe houses?"

"What?" Hellion came back. "Safe houses?"

"Witness Protection, stations for the FBI, anything like that."

A second passed. "That's deep within the Deep State, Christopher."

"Is it a paper record?" Wren pushed back. "Will I need a semi-truck to carry it away?"

"Of course not," Hellion snapped swiftly. "With the second skin, I can steal this information in moments; but we will no longer be invisible. This action cannot be ghosted from Humphreys, Christopher. They will know whatever I look at."

He weighed that for about a second. Every bit of his new plan depended on the element of surprise, but you couldn't control for everything.

"Acceptable risk. Do it. Apply what you find as targets in the ghosting protocol for Rogers. I need to get to her first."

Keys flew and clattered immediately. "B4cksl4cker, can you activate a botnet to crunch the crypto?"

"Yes," said B4cksl4cker, "activating."

Wren sat in the thundering helo hunched over his phone screen. Somewhere a hundred miles north the Airbus was closing in on Gruber. A hundred miles south the crowds at the

Wilshire were gathering mass and anger. All across the country, people stamped toward the precipice.

"No video whatsoever," he said. "This is a dark strike."

"Understood," Hellion answered. "We're through their first firewalls. Hang tight, Christopher, let us do our job."

Seconds ticked by, long enough for Wren to second-guess himself multiple times over. Intelligence was a gamble. You looked at your opponent's MO and you made predictions, like the ghosting protocol.

"Got something," Hellion said abruptly. "Not a full listing, we're inferring a lot, but there looks to be a witness protection building forty miles northeast of your current position, the town of Dos Palos, across from the Circle K. Our bet is that's where she's heading."

"Is it built up?"

Keys flew. "Population five thousand, but there'll definitely be witnesses to a helicopter coming in over the mall."

Wren cursed. Always too slow. "No witnesses then. I intercept her in the desert. Get me her position."

"Fine-tuning. You're en route. Given the timings, we anticipate," a brief pause, "seven minutes until live intercept. She's not going to stop for you, Christopher."

"I know."

From the Airbus deployment bag he extracted a safety harness and a two-hundred-foot rappel spool; a large coil of slim black Nylon 4 rope with a large carabiner-style donut ring for anchoring. He shrugged on two black double-leather palmed gloves then held the spool up in front of the pilot, whose eyes bugged.

"Here's what we're going to do," he said.

39

DOS PALOS

Three miles out of Dos Palos Wren saw her; a half-dressed blond woman racing an ATV through green and ochre fields of budding pistachios. Wren sat half out of the passenger side door, feet on the skids with the wind rushing hard around him.

"Lower," he shouted to the pilot, and the helicopter dropped.

The pilot hadn't wanted to do it. Wren had bargained, cajoled, and finally settled on a form of compulsion.

"I am going out of that door. If you don't land me right, I'll die. You don't want that."

The guy had turned to water.

Two hundred feet of line. An impossible maneuver. Rogers' head whipped around at the sound, sighted the bird in the sky, and at once the ATV began jerky evasive maneuvers, zigzagging side to side through lush crops.

"Stay with her," Wren barked, then jumped.

Helicopter rappels were hard. They were only ever supposed to be conducted with a rappel master in back, from a stationary helicopter, but Wren had already broken both those rules when he'd bailed out of the Chinook, so this was nothing.

The nylon rope sped through his hands, and the wind battered him, swaying him hard into the helicopter's backdraft and setting him off at a dizzy spin. He squeezed the rope and briefly slowed his momentum, but it did nothing for the mad pirouette as the air resistance tumbled him crazily.

He saw Dos Palos, he saw the Diablo Range, he saw Dos Palos then the Diablos and a tiny glimpse of Rogers' face staring back at him in disbelief, then he squeezed the rope again and slowed his descent further; still seventy feet above the ground and choppering ahead at forty miles an hour, keeping pace with the ATV.

Rogers banked hard right.

"Right," Wren shouted, his earpiece keyed now to the pilot, but the helicopter overshot wildly. The pilot corrected swiftly. Rogers was fifty yards to the right, thirty down, and the tail end of Wren's rope was trailing through the bushy low pistachio trees.

He released his grip and rappelled the final length until he was down at the level of the top branches, tearing down an open aisle in the long parallel ranks of trees, then slid further still until his feet were barely inches above the ground. That was crazy enough in itself, but the pirouette was only picking up speed, so he slid the final stretch until his feet touched and corkscrewed into the dirt.

The friction halted his spin. He clamped hold of the rope and picked up his feet and began to run. At forty the pace was far too fast, but he landed big strides that kept him poised and facing forward, ahead to where Rogers' face had spun back to see him, a mask of disbelief.

"It's me!" he shouted at her. Barely thirty yards between them now. "Christopher Wren!"

He couldn't imagine what she was thinking. Last time

she'd seen him, it was in Great Kills before dropping the black bag on his head.

She revved the ATV and swung hard left.

"Left," Wren shouted, and the helicopter banked hard, yanking Wren into a swing. Only too late did he realize he was heading straight for a pistachio tree. They weren't thick around, no wider than a street lamp, but a street lamp could wreck a vehicle at the speeds he was going. He'd wrap his body around it like a pretzel.

"Stop!" he shouted, but the pilot couldn't possibly react fast enough, leaving him with one shot. As his feet touched down just ahead of the tree he kicked off the ground with everything he had, while also yanking on the rope. He cleared maybe five feet and veered slightly to the left; enough to send him crashing through the branches rather than splattering into the bark.

Raspberry red pistachios burst around him like confetti at a wedding, branches whiplashed across his face and chest, then he dropped down hard on his nylon line. The pilot must have felt the drag, because the helicopter's speed died and Wren was left swaying and spinning out of control, so fast he couldn't make anything out, feet bare inches above the ground.

He dropped the distance and turned just in time to see Rogers coming right at him in a cloud of dust. He barely picked his legs up in time, the ATV flew by underneath and Rogers' shoulder hit his chest and stripped him off the rappel line like a shelled pea.

For a second they flew together, then he hit the hard clay first and tumbled, air forced from his lungs, with Rogers controlling the roll. He tried to get his legs underneath him but she had the initiative, wrenching his arm up behind his back and forcing his face into the dirt so hard he could hardly breathe.

Damn, she was strong. For a moment he thought she was going to break his elbow, probably dislocate the shoulder joint with it, and if not that then maybe just throttle him in the dust.

"Christopher Wren," she barked instead. "What the ever-loving hell?"

"It's a …. long story," he managed to wheeze out.

"You've got two minutes."

He started in. One minute later she was on her feet and backing away, his own Glock trained on his face. At two minutes her already-pale face lapsed as white as Humphreys'.

"What are you talking about, Ghosts?"

Wren grunted and rose to his feet gingerly, brushing twigs and ripe pistachios off his scratched up shirt and jeans, rolling his shoulder. She'd definitely tweaked it. "Ghosts. Spooks. Specters. On account they're invisible."

"I get the synonyms," Rogers snapped dismissively. "I'm talking about the number. You're saying Ghosts, but it's just one guy, singular, Ghost."

Wren blinked. The helicopter's downdraft massaged them both. "What? One guy?"

"One guy. He's a beast, bigger even than you, and CIA. It's how he brought me in."

Wren's head spun. "What?"

"He posed as a Company man standing guard on your family, said he had intel you were preparing a breakout followed by a 'rescue'. My eyes only, the Company was infected. He called me and I came." She spat. "More fool me."

Wren struggled to catch up. CIA? And rescue? It sounded just like with Gruber, drawing the target out to self-abduct. "He phished you."

"So maybe I'm a phish," she spat, the anger burning off her, the dark barrel hole of the Glock trained on his face like a third eye. "But now I'm thinking. He said there was some 'Deep State' conspiracy to set you free." Her eyes narrowed. "He said you'd come for me, extract the location for your family, and now here you are. So what do you want, Wren? And how the hell did you get out of a secure black site?"

He stared. She was dead serious. More BS, black psy ops just to sell the phishing tale, but how could she know that? "I fought my way out, Rogers," he began. "It wasn't some conspiracy. I almost died just to get out of my cuffs, almost took Humphreys with me, jumped out of a Chinook pretty much like I did just now, then started some crazy nonsense all over LA to get to here." She didn't look convinced. "Listen, Sally, you're right about a lot. The Company are compromised, this guy definitely phished you into a kidnap, and maybe other parts of the Deep State are rotten too, but that's a problem for a later day. Right now riots are about to hit the fan across the country, Gruber's about to burn, and I need your help."

Her eyes narrowed. She squeezed the trigger bar on the Glock, releasing the safety. "Help with what?"

"With stopping this thing before all hell breaks loose! Like the good old days. Are you in?"

40

HEAVENS ABOVE

For long moments little Pequeño 3 lay in Grace's arms in the dark of the pit, waiting for the pain to pull back, for his lungs to stop catching in his tight chest. All the while, she stroked his head and whispered about mud pies in his ear, her touch hot against the clammy cold.

Above them the Pequeños breathed, in then out, like the whole Earth was alive. In the deep dark it felt like the walls of the pit were expanding with every breath, were shrinking with every breath in.

Except he knew that wasn't true.

"We're gonna be OK," Grace whispered.

He pushed himself up, off her legs and into a sitting position. He had some dull sense that Chrysogonus stood above them, Aden to the left, Galicia to the right, the others around the back. Stuck in the middle.

He moved his head closer to Grace, pressed his lips against her ear, waited until the Pequeños were breathing in and whispered.

"We have to dig."

He felt her stiffen at the words. Let her head move beside

his, cheek to cheek as her lips came to his ear, waiting for the moment.

"They ain't gonna let us."

Another slow, rolling exchange.

"You pull the stones," he said, and waited. "It's easy. They come right away." Another pause, breathing. "Reach one hand in, feel for the tunnel." Breathing. "We don't need to dig much."

Her head rolled gently around his. "They'll hear." She was cold with fear. He felt just the same. "They'll hear us and stop us."

"They won't hear you."

It was a simple plan. She said she didn't like it. He didn't give her the time to argue.

It began with him pulling both his legs in tight, snug like a bug, then shooting them out as fast as he could. His heels hit Chrysogonus' calf so hard it knocked his foot back. Chrysogonus yelped, then shouted, then bent down to snatch up little Pequeño 3, but he was already gone, scampering on all fours.

One knee fell on what could be Aden's foot and pulled out another cry, his head bumped into a knee and he rolled away before swooping hands could grab him, using all the skills he'd developed outrunning his minders amongst the desert cacti. Within seconds he was at the wall, thin body pressed into the corner, while all the elder Pequeños were pushing and falling and letting out frenzied whispers.

While they fought he dug at the wall. Flat stones pried away easily, as his elders grappled with each other. Beyond each stone he felt only damp sand. He pushed against it, remembering how the thin barrier of sand had crumbled away beneath the Apex's hand, but that sinking sensation didn't come.

Then the Pequeños were silent. He realized it too late. His

head felt a little foggy, maybe from the slaps. He kept digging too long, prying out the fifth stone with his fingernails, maybe a black stone, perhaps a white stone, when he felt the vibration of heavy footfalls coming near. He tried to roll, but it was too late.

A booted foot came sweeping in and struck him hard in the belly. It forced all the air from his chest, sent him thumping off the wall and back to the sand, curled double with an incredible hot pain surging from the pit of his gut to the top of his neck, sucking emptily for air.

Nothing came in. Panic poured through him. Somewhere above Chrysogonus was panting, shouting between pants, and the other Pequeños were arguing. About killing him, maybe. He rolled to his back, desperate for breath, sucking as hard as he could but getting nothing.

It couldn't be so soon. Running out of air. He'd watched the experiments drown in the vats behind the hotel, seen the terrible panic in their eyes, filmed them for the Apex.

"I saw the light," those men and women would say after their experimentation, bowed low before the Apex. "Thank you."

Those that survived.

Footsteps stamped in and he curled, but no kick landed. Instead there was a thud, followed by other thuds, and the voice of Galicia rallying above the others.

Protecting him? He couldn't be sure. Finally a trickle of air worked into his throat, and the excitement almost blacked him out.

"Come on," came Grace's whisper, and her touch on his shoulder. Leading him away. She pulled and he followed, making it back to his knees while the elder Pequeños fought and panted overhead

"Did you ... find it?" he asked in whispery gasps.

"We'll look together," she answered. "Just like the pies."

"Just like ... the pies."

The fighting dwindled, but all the elder Pequeños were groaning now. At one point they bumped into Galicia, lying on the floor. She didn't move at all, and they crawled over her body. Chrysogonus bellowed at times, about his testament or calling to Pequeño 3, but he sounded strange, sucking in air too hard and staggering around.

"He's drunk," Grace whispered in Pequeño 3's ear.

"What's drunk?" he whispered back, between, rock pulls and sand punches.

"It's when you get older, and scary."

They avoided Chrysogonus, and worked their way around the circle. It wasn't large. Whenever one of the elders came near, they froze, or scampered away. Their previously unified breath had become a staggered rasping.

"There's no air," said Grace.

"So how come we can breathe?" he answered.

"'Cos we're small," she answered, like it was obvious. "Like a mouse. We don't need much."

That made sense to him.

Then they came upon tumbled stones. It took him a moment to realize what it meant. Damp sand in the wall. Flat stones by the corner. They'd been around the pit walls one whole time.

"Dig more," he said. It was all he could say. It was getting harder to breathe. Up in the air of the pit, Chrysogonus was wheezing loudly, sucking hard.

They sped up. Sound didn't matter now. They worked a second circuit, and Pequeño 3 pulled more stones out, and dug deeper into the sand. His fingertips got cold and raw but he couldn't stop. They were just little shovels, he told himself, like the mud pies were strawberries and cream.

At some point Chrysogonus stopped staggering and dropped to his knees with the others. There they all wheezed, until they fell back into synchrony. Like one giant lung, breathing in the earth, breathing out the earth.

Pequeño 3 didn't realize he'd stopped moving until Grace's cold touch came on his cheek.

"Come on," she whispered. They kept on. They dug a second row up, then a third. They went over Galicia's body, and she didn't move. The wheezing of the others faded. Pequeño 3's breaths came in tiny, panicky pants. Sometimes Grace pulled him along, sometimes he pulled her, until finally his hand broke through.

He was up to his shoulder in the wall. Fingers worming in the sand. Suddenly there was no resistance. He pulled back, and felt a cold blast of fresh desert air blow into his face. At once it woke him up. His eyes brightened. He grabbed Grace and pulled her over.

It didn't take long to open a gap wide enough to crawl through. The other Pequeños were stirring. They crawled out. Still it was pitch black, but there was a hint of light ahead. Pequeño 3 took the lead, feeling rough wooden staves at his sides, over his head. He crawled and crawled, until at last there was faint moonlight, and he saw his hands, and he emerged through the crust of the Earth into the open desert.

The sky had never seemed so immense. Stars were everywhere, sparkling like a million dreams. He rolled and helped Grace come through. To the right they saw the Pyramid, clustered around the low mound of sleds and sand, lit by flickering fires. He thought he saw the Apex, standing in their midst, staring right back at him, but he couldn't be sure.

"What about the others?" Grace whispered in his ear. "The elders?"

"They'll be fine," he answered. Afraid now. Afraid to have survived. "Come on."

They crawled, then they walked, then they ran. Not to the

fake town, but to the red rock. There they stayed by the muddy water pool, and drank the juice from prickly pears and ate hand-roasted bark scorpions and Mexican red-kneed tarantula and once even a big pink Gila monster.

In the days they climbed the rock and made mud pies, and in the nights they cuddled close in a shelter of torn ocotillo necks. They talked about the Apex and the other Pequeños. Where they might be. They imagined Chrysogonus roaring his way around the fake town, looking for them, and laughed.

On the third night, as dusk fell and the stars shone up in the sky, they returned. The Pyramid remained circled around the mound, listening to the Earth suck in and out. They entered the tunnel and crawled along it, expecting a beating on the other side.

Chrysogonus would be furious they had ruined his 'Testament'. The laughter stopped as they reached the end of the tunnel, in the total darkness, and found it blocked up. Pequeño 3's heart raced. It was easy to dig through, pulling some sand, pushing the rest. He was first through, into a sour, musty smell.

He recognized that smell.

"Cover your nose," he whispered to Grace.

Soon after that, the sound came of sand shushing above. They were being dug out. Together they filled the tunnel in, and patted the big flat stones back into place to cover it. They went around and around the walls, faster and faster as the foul air grew thinner, pushing stones back into place, covering up every sign of their escape, until finally, standing together in the middle of the pit, the first of the sleds came off and light poured in.

Chrysogonus lay in front of them, pale as the grave. Galicia lay by the wall. Aden lay beside her, with Zachariah and Gabriel nearby. All pale, and still. On some level, little

Pequeño 3 understood what must have happened. They'd sealed themselves back in.

The Pyramid wailed and cheered. So many dead. Two still alive. It was a triumph of faith. It was a tragedy. It was proof that the Apex was a great man, the greatest of them all.

They were raised out to such clamor, and promises of a celebration mixed with a wake. Throughout it all, the Apex's eyes remained pinned to those of little Pequeño 3, sparkling blue like furious stars in the heavens above.

41

ROGERS

With thirty minutes left on the clock, Hellion nailed the Ghost's position down.

"He's in a big rig, semi-trailer truck," she said sharply in Wren's ear as the helo tore through the sky. "Or he was two hours back, heading north on the 99. It's ghosted, but I ghosted our satellite overwatch and picked it out."

Wren took a sharp breath. Ghosts fighting ghosts.

"Destination?"

"No way to know. We're tracking forward via satellite, but algorithm predicts he pulled east. Our best target is shuttered school at edge of Angels Camp, little town west of Stanislaus National Forest. Nothing near but creeping desert. We will know for sure soon."

Wren squeezed the phone tight. Good news at last. "Anything on his ID, his link-up to the CIA?"

"Working. Rogers' description helps. It is deep bench."

"What about backward tracking? Any idea where he crossed with the Apex?"

"Nothing yet, Christopher. Taking him backward will take time. For now we are working on location."

"Good." He took a shaky breath. "How far out's the Airbus?"

"Twenty minutes ahead of his last known location. They are low on fuel, but they will make it to the school in twenty minutes."

Twenty minutes until the school. Thirty minutes until Gruber burned. It was going to be tight.

"How much lead time does Teddy want?"

"The plan was five minutes, in advance of Ghost hit."

"Shorter," Rogers said abruptly. She looked at Wren urgently, listening in on her own earpiece, sitting by his side in the back of the R44. "This guy, he's on the ball. You start cutting his links to the network, it won't take him five minutes to read the tea leaves. Gruber will be dead in seconds."

"Call it two minutes," Wren said. "Hard strikes, priority on cutting lines and shutting them down."

"I'll relay to Theodore," said Hellion.

Wren felt his heart kick up a notch, eighty beats a minute rising to ninety. It was all going to happen soon, and everything had to be ready. He tapped the earpiece silent and turned to Rogers.

She looked sick. Maybe pneumonia, early-onset, compounded by deep post-traumatic shock. After what she'd been through, the physical damage would be the least of it. He hadn't even tried to address that yet, too busy pumping her for all the information she could muster; what the guy looked like, what his habits were, what he'd wanted. It wasn't going to be enough, though, if this thing went the way he thought it was going to.

"What?" she asked. Glaring at him now, angry almost.

He wanted to reach out, touch her elbow, knee, but knew that wouldn't be welcome. All the anger she was feeling, no small part of it fell at his door. She'd be twisted up inside, knowing she'd been tricked with lies about him, that she'd had to watch Jay burn because of him. In some sick way, his father had made all this about Wren.

"Nothing," he said, then quickly corrected that. "No, not nothing. I was thinking about the guy. The Ghost, what he wants. But mostly I was thinking about you."

Rogers' eyes blazed. It was easiest to rely on anger, after what she'd been through. "Don't think about me."

"Because we're nothing to each other?"

"Because we were teammates, and you abandoned me. You shot me, dumped me, gambled with my life."

"I'm here now."

She looked away. "Not for me."

He couldn't argue with that, but it wasn't quite fair. "For what it's worth, I'm sorry I shot you."

"It's not worth anything," she snapped, staring out of the window. "You set my career back five years. I could have died. On top of that, you killed hundreds of Pinocchios. You appointed yourself judge of them all, and you made me complicit in the crime."

He took that on the chin. Maybe it was a mistake to bring any of this up, but then he needed her. He looked at his phone screen. The minutes raced by.

"The people I killed were monsters, Rogers. We're talking about serial child abusers, the worst of the worst."

She glared through the window so hard he thought she might burn a hole. "I'm not going to discuss it."

"And shooting you was an operational risk. It was a mistake. I should have found another way."

She spun her eyes back to him, hot and hurt. "You'd do it again in a heartbeat."

"Betray you?"

She said nothing, boring a hole into his eyes. There were things he could say further, probably better off unsaid. He held his tongue. She turned away. Orange desert rushed by below.

His phone chimed and he brought it up. Confirmation was coming in, the Ghost had gone to the school in Angel's Camp, though his trailer truck was gone. They were tracking it. The Airbus was closing in, getting ready to deploy its dirt bikes. Five minutes until the overseas strikes began.

Five minutes. A lot could change. No point holding back now.

"You weren't the only one who was betrayed at the Anti-Ca compound," he said.

Rogers spun on him like a left hook. "What the hell you say to me?"

He hadn't said anything like it until then. Had avoided saying it, because it was so much easier just to let her hate him, but hate wasn't going to cut it now.

"You turned on me first, Rogers. You pulled your gun, aimed it at me, told me to stop."

Her cheeks blushed scarlet with rage. Thrown back into the memory. "Because you were threatening a pregnant girl! You were trying to make her drink cyanide."

"It wasn't cyanide," he said quietly.

"What?"

"It was apple cider vinegar and orange juice. I faked it. You were my partner. You could have trusted me."

Not should. Could. Should might be too much. Still she stared at him for a long second, eyes burning, maybe figuring out just how furious she was, whether she wanted to kick him out of the helicopter right there and then. "Trusted you? The way you were talking back then, about the Apex, about your father? It was like you'd gone mad, Wren! You were obsessed, out of it completely."

He looked at her, feeling the sadness of it now, a sadness

he hadn't allowed in since she'd renditioned him, about what they'd both lost in that moment.

"But I wasn't crazy, was I?"

She opened her mouth. Didn't say anything. Closed it.

Three minutes on the clock.

He turned back to his phone, bringing up the visuals from the three strike teams. He tapped his earpiece and immediately heard the chatter of mission prep, then scrolled through bodycams of the Vladivostok squad until he got a bead on Teddy's thinned out-face, backdropped by the canvas wall of their forward operating truck.

"Teddy?" he interrupted.

"All go here, Christopher," Teddy said, holding one hand to his ear in a practiced gesture, like he'd run a hundred ops before this. "We're synced."

"Good luck. Don't risk yourself. We need you."

"It's all risk," said Teddy and cut the line.

Wren brought up the Airbus video feed, shot from the belly of the chopper. The rectangular complex of the school was coming up ahead, surrounded by baking red sands.

"Henry, are you go for assault?"

The line crackled and Henry's sharp voice came back, matched by the bodycam visual from a team member across the way. Henry looked cool and commanding in the dark of the cabin. "Yes, Sir!" he shouted over the roar of the Airbus' blades. "We put down three miles out, Mason and Abigail are en route via dirt bike. I'll lead the rappel charge. We'll hit simultaneously, should be two minutes after Theodore."

Theodore. That killed Wren. First thing when you join a cult, they give you a new name.

"Take them alive if you can. Priority is Gruber. We're almost in position. Shut down any and all live video feeds. Our worst case is not just that he dies, worse is that they screen it."

"Understood, Sir."

Wren leaned back, and the red light in the corner of the bodycam feed blinked out.

He went through the same process for the two remaining strikes: Alejandro hunkered with his team on the rooftop of the Internet café in Beijing, sheltered by a silver water tower; Doona at the roof edge of the donut block in Kuala Lumpur, looking down on a traditional Malay building in the midst of jungle-like overgrowth, thatched roof and raised on stilts.

The feeds locked down. The teams were ready. Everything looked to be five by five. Wren checked the clock, a minute left. He felt Rogers glaring at him and turned. The fury in her eyes was overwhelming. Like she wanted nothing more than to stab him fifteen times and dump the corpse out the door.

"That isn't fair," she said. More a hiss, like the last air deflating from a withered balloon. "You didn't give me any choice."

There was nothing to say to that. He said it anyway. "There's always a choice."

Ten seconds until breach.

42

BREACH

Teddy's team hit first by a few seconds, a fast charge out of the truck and across a parking lot up to the door of the meme factory in Vladivostok, like any other large office block, and Wren watched it all on bodycam. Abercrombie hit the secure glass door with a handheld ram and the glass burst inward, unleashing a caterwauling alarm as the squad of Foundation members raced into a brightly colored double-height lobby with their rifles raised.

Fast on their heels came the Beijing hit; the Sunlit Dawn members led by Alejandro racing down two flights of stairs from the roof and charging pell-mell into the Internet café. Faces flipped up from their screens, shouts rang out, and Alejandro reached the door to the rear room where virality chief Pang Jiao Shou was holed up, just as-

Doona rappelled off the roof in the shadow of the Petronas Towers, leading four more Sunlit Dawn members to the ground where they cut their lines, hoisted AR-15 rifles and ran at the ornate carved exterior of the wooden box, raised up on timber legs in the tight green jungle, hidey-hole of the ghost-tech hackers.

"Clear," came Teddy's bass, and Wren shifted to the

Vladivostok hit. He was standing at the edge of the curving, molded lobby, decked out with bright geometric shapes like a Silicon Valley campus. A receptionist stood behind his desk, arms up, wearing a cute blue cap. Teddy's team rolled over the security gates and took up position either side of a double card lock door leading deeper in, hit it with the ram and crashed through into-

Alejandro tried the metal door to the café's back room but the lock held in the reinforced frame; he signaled and two Sunlit Dawn members moved up in perfect synchrony, wielding ten pound sledgehammers. Alejandro gave a fast three count and they pulled back, swung the hammers and struck the door either side of dead center. There was a huge double bang and the lock's face tore away from the strike plate, the bolt dredged out of the frame and the buckled door swung wide open into-

Doona bypassed the door to the incongruous house ensconced in jungle palms, instead climbing a stilt and attacking the wall head-on; four pads of C4 explosive tacked into place with adhesive strips. She dropped back down, took shelter amongst the trees then hit her phone to detonate. The wall blew out like a backfiring engine, with a burst of flame chased by fat gouts of gray smoke. Doona was climbing and plunging through the ragged hole into-

An office expanse lay ahead of Teddy, sectioned off into dozens of octagonal cubicles like a human-scale bee hive, each with low walls in bright primary colors splashed with exhortations to BE CREATIVE! and USE AMERICAN SLANG! In each octagonal cell faces turned to the interlopers, like drones at the advent of the beekeeper. Hands went up like a Mexican wave, creatives bowing out easily.

"Eleven o'clock," Wren snapped in Teddy's ear, picking out a scrap of stray movement on his bodycam, "maybe the Queen."

Teddy swung; Sunlit Dawn members were already moving through the passageways cored into the hive, deploying plastic zip ties on the worker drones.

"Got him," Teddy answered, and set off at a sprint toward a door in the rear wall. Either side hung huge posters laying out near-mathematical equations for pumping out propaganda in English: a mish-mash listing of famous names, apocalyptic predictions, outlandish conspiracies, dark religious quotations and past political scandals. His name, the Foundation and the names of his key members were everywhere; a shopping list for sowing nonsense in the minds of the American people.

He'd seen equations exactly like them many times before, had written the guidance himself on occasion, in black psy-ops against rival states; all the ways you could launder lies and control a populace.

He dragged his focus dead ahead, where Teddy was almost at the door in back. Hanging above it was the largest banner yet, this one written in Russian Cyrillic, though the translation came easily; a familiar reduction of Lifton's theory on indoctrination.

CONFUSE. DISCREDIT. REPLACE.

The propagandist's credo.

"Careful, Teddy," he cautioned, as Teddy laid hands on the rear door and wrenched it open.

Alejandro shot through the reinforced door into a private conference room in the back of the Internet café, where a short round woman wearing thick black spectacles stood at the head of a long desk, screeching something in Mandarin and punching a whiteboard covered in calculations. Her eyes widened on Alejandro as the busted door clanged off the inner wall.

At the conference table sat a dozen kids, none older than twenty, each set up with a twin-monitor array atop buzzing fat desktop towers.

"Phones down!" Alejandro barked as he stalked in, rifle levelled on the Fat Unicorn at the fore. Her eyes were phasing now to anger. Sunlit Dawn members in back barked out the command in Mandarin and Cantonese, then the woman gave a sharp nod.

"Six o'clock!" Wren shouted.

Alejandro spun and took sudden incoming fire. There was an explosion of distorting sound, the bodycam abruptly reeled back and Wren saw only the ceiling, then chair legs, then terrified faces low to the fuzzy gray carpet as the kids hit the deck. Shooting and shouting came through in a cacophony of jumbled sounds, and Wren flicked between bodycams on the various members of his strike team.

All were down.

"By the door," he shouted. "Two guys with handguns. Alejandro!"

Alejandro's feed spun to the ceiling, back to the fuzzy carpet as he got to his hands and knees, then scrabbling forward until he came upon a pair of stockinged feet. The camera jostled, rose, pressed against brown fabric, then Wren caught a glimpse of the Fat Unicorn's toad-like face in close-up, her gimlet expression a blend of hilarity and terror.

"Tell them to stop!" Alejandro shouted at her, rifle to her head while the shooting and screams crescendoed, but the Fat Unicorn just let out a high, panicky laugh.

"Your team's down, give me eyes, use the bodycam," Wren ordered, as clear and precise as he could.

It took Alejandro a second, then his palm closed over the bodycam lens, plucked it, reversed it, and raised it up above the line of the conference table. It gave Wren just a second of visual before one of the guards picked off the lens and flung the screen into darkness.

"They're flanking you left and right, one high, one low,"

Wren said rapidly. "Roll left and take the one guy, pop up and get the other in transition."

No answer came, only loud rasping sounds, breathing, then the abrasive sound of two gunshots, three, four. Wren raced through the cams of the Sunlit Dawn team, seeing only mold-damped squares of ceiling tiles.

Doona plunged through the smoke into some kind of ringing outer corridor; so narrow she had to advance side-on.

"Go, go, go!" she ordered, sending her team left while she went right.

"Insulation skin," came Hellion's voice. "To disguise the heat mapping within. I recognize this set-up."

"We use it," said B4cksl4cker.

The cam jogged up and down as Doona ran to the corner, where she angled and looked out; nobody was there, just another featureless wooden corridor bar one security camera in the far corner.

"No sign of any doors."

"Security procedure, single access," Hellion said, the sound of keys flurrying. "They have you on camera now."

"Let's see what they're hiding," Doona said, extracted another two strips of C4, peeled the sticky tabs and stuck them to the wall.

"Back," she ordered, retreated beyond the corner, hit the phone for another tremendous explosive bark, then sprinted back around and through a fresh wound in the wall, into a space that held-

- nothing.

No people. No desks, computer towers, chairs, or anything at all, except an unobtrusive red workman's tin in the center of the floor.

"Bomb!" Wren shouted.

Doona ran, out of the fresh hole, along the corridor, until

her bodycam jerked abruptly sideways soundlessly, driven through the wall and sent flying through the jungle while bright purple lines of static skirled across the screen. Just before her cam hit the ground there was an almighty crumping sound, air impacting under explosive force, then the video died.

Wren flicked rapidly through the feeds of her squad, all down.

"Get them help, Hellion," he said urgently.

"I've called local ambulance services. Our on-site doctor can't handle this scale. We can extricate them later."

"Good," said Wren, his mind whirring. "Pay off anyone you need to pay."

"Who?" Hellion asked.

"Anyone you can reach. All of them. The guy with the stretcher. The surgeon. The local politician. Flood the zone with money."

"Flooding," Hellion answered. "Christopher, we're also scrambling for Alejandro."

Wren flicked back through the feeds.

"Alejandro, report!"

Alejandro's bodycam was looking down on the bodies of two guards. Thickset, one was dead, the other had a hand clamped to his shoulder.

"I'm shot in the thigh, Christopher," came Alejandro's pained voice. "Binding it now. We cut transmissions from the building ahead of the strike, nothing in or out."

"And your team?"

"Three injured, one dead."

Wren cursed. "Exfiltrate," he ordered. "Take the Unicorn, the gear, the kids. Get to the safe house."

"We're on the move."

Alejandro nudged the guard. Somebody shouted a command in Mandarin, and he grudgingly got to his feet. In the background came the sound of the Fat Unicorn bleating something in rapid half-English.

Wren flicked over. Rogers put a hand on his arm, staring at him. "They knew you were coming."

He ignored her for the moment, bringing up Teddy's feed.

"Where are your Ghosts, Wren?" Rogers insisted.

He didn't have an answer for that.

"Teddy, report."

Teddy stood in a small office, in front of a thin man who'd been gagged and bound, sitting behind his office desk. "We're clear. No pushback at all, Christopher. We're documenting everything, like you said."

"There was a bomb in Malaysia. Doona's whole team is down. Be careful."

Teddy nodded. "I saw. She's tough. There's no sign they had any warning here, looks like we got their whole complement, top spec equipment, millions in value. These people, though, there's too many for us to hold them."

Wren knew it. "We dump it on Interpol."

"We'll finish extracting data, call them in."

"Run it fast," he said. "Before Russian police get there. I'm switching to Henry."

"Good luck," said Teddy.

Wren blinked, rubbed his eyes. The chopper was soaring over buildings now, suburbs rushing by. Almost there. It didn't make sense, though; if the Ghosts had had warning, why not share it with the meme factory and the Fat Unicorn?

"Henry is breaching," Hellion called in his ear. "They need you."

They needed him. He blinked hard, trying to get the image of the empty Ghost compound out of his head. If there'd been no warning, then had there ever been Ghosts in Malaysia, and if there hadn't been, who the hell was running their invisibility protocol?

"Wren!"

He looked up. Rogers was glaring at him; fierce now, chiding, worried. Almost like back when they were partners, keeping him on track. It made him heartsick. "We'll deal with that," she snapped. "Now get on point!"

43

HENRY

Wren watched from the Airbus's belly camera, hovering fifty feet over the outskirts of Angel's Camp. Sparse clumps of closed-cone pines encircled the abandoned middle school like circling sharks in an ocean of wild tan pampas grass. The roof was shot through in places, knotweed throttled the drain pipes and dead brown kudzu vines had swallowed the parking lot.

There was a two-tone roar, then the dirt bikes pincered into sight, coming at the school from opposite directions.

"Exterior looks clear," came Henry's voice. "Bikes report no outliers. I'm going in."

Wren picked him out, an ant-like figure in tactical black with a thick red cylinder on his back, leading a three-strong team up to the west exit.

"There was a bomb in Malaysia," Wren said urgently, "don't cluster up, retreat at the first sign of threat."

"I'm not retreating," said Henry, and hefted a pair of long-handle bolt cutters. One of Hellion's drones hovered close and Wren scrolled through his feeds to pick up the transmission. Instantly it zoomed him into the thick of things, holding position just over Henry's shoulder.

The west exit looked to be custodial; metal plate, shuttered with a thick chain and padlock. Henry brought up a pair of bolt cutters and clasped them around the chain.

"Infrared?" Wren asked.

"Nothing clear," Hellion answered. "The roof insulation's blocking any signal."

"But there is heat?"

"It could be the boiler. Somewhere in the middle. Overlaying school plans, it looks like the gymnasium. Middle of the basketball court."

Wren cursed. Center of an empty space; another bomb blast would have clear sightlines to rip through the whole school. Support columns would be left standing, tissue and bone would be shredded like corn before a thresher.

"Tell me the drones are in position," he said.

"They are," said Hellion.

"All of them?"

"All of them."

The bolt cutter's jaws closed with a clunk and the chain split. Henry pulled it through the door handle.

"Hellion, take the lead," he ordered. "Henry, in back."

"Following," Henry replied, and pulled the door open.

The drone flew headlong in. The interior was sun-dappled, with afternoon light shafting through the ruptured roof. A corridor stretched away, lined with busted lockers, doors hanging slack like lackluster flags. Motes hung thick in the air, a gray layer of dust carpeted the floor, and the drone flew on at a sprint.

"Something's off," Wren said. "Keep your team staggered, Henry."

"Copy," said Henry.

"Running analyses," said Hellion, taking the drone's speed up a notch. "No movement anywhere at this end."

"So take us to the center."

"Aye aye. We'll take the scenic route."

The drone swerved abruptly off the corridor and hung hard left into a classroom. Wren briefly saw sand-dusted desks piled up, surrounded by beer cans, needles and broken glass shards catching the afternoon light through shattered windows, then the drone pulled another sharp turn and went straight into a hole torn in the wall. It passed through the wall cavity in a split second and shot back outside, for a second zipped over dry red clay scrawled with the crazy paving of heat cracks, then entered again through another broken window.

Short cut to the gymnasium.

Tiered bleachers lay along the north side, scoreboard over the basketball hoop to the west, backboard glass and net long gone, stage to the east, light streaming in like tiny sky beams from what had to be bullet holes in the roof, and in the middle, Steven Gruber.

Wren cursed.

Gruber stood in the center of the open space, naked skin shiny, with a wooden barrel beside him, a paintbrush in one hand and a lighter in the other.

"Napalm!" Wren barked into the system. "Henry, he's rigged to blow."

"Understood," Henry replied. "Relaying."

Wren just stared. He'd been right in this place before, looking at skin glistening like morning dew at dawn, with Yumiko Harkness at the Reparations' arena, with the Pyramid spread throughout the fake town, people doused like stolen cars ready to burn out. He smelled the bitter kerosene stink even though he wasn't there, rich and overpowering. Gruber's eyes were red with it.

Barrel at his side. Paintbrush in his hand. Just like it had been before.

Gruber shuddered. He had the same old Steven Gruber

face; uncertain, afraid, worried he was overstepping some unknown boundary.

"Where's the Ghost?" Wren barked at Hellion.

"Not here," she answered. "We're tracking his truck north. This is it for heat, there's nobody else here."

"Eliminate any signal coming out of this place. Nothing gets out. The people will not see this."

"Wireless is a cone of silence. Mason and Abigail already cut the standard hard lines, but I can't speak to any other wires, if they laid their own."

"Take me in, nice and slow."

Gruber's napalm-smeared, shuddering face drew closer as the drone scrolled in. Short brown hair, puppy fat on his cheeks, the light stubble of a beard. 'Man says drive, I drive'.

Not now.

This wasn't that same Gruber. Close enough now, he saw that the eyes were transformed, like the deepfake of Rogers but worse. Madness shone through the misery; wild ferocity of a new certainty. He'd come out the other side of a Judas moment. All the willing Pyramid faithful had shared that same look, the day they'd burned alive.

Wren's pulse racked up to one-twenty, one-thirty. Here was the Apex again, rewriting every life around him as just a reflection of his own. Just like Yumiko Harkness, except one death was only the beginning, now.

It pissed Wren off.

Gruber flinched as the drone drew in, pulling the hand holding the lighter closer to his head.

"Stop," Wren ordered, and the drone stopped dead.

"Put me on speaker."

"You're on," Hellion answered.

"Steven," Wren said, holding the phone up close to his mouth. He heard his own voice ring back through the drone's mic, tinny and time-delayed. "It's me, Wren."

There was a panicky flash in Gruber's eyes at that: recognition, terror, maybe a glimpse of hope, then the new programming crashed down and the old Gruber was crushed beneath it, releasing a maddened kind of glee.

"You mean the ungrateful son?"

Gruber's thumb jerked.

The lighter sparked.

44

GRUBER

"Wait!" Wren shouted.

Gruber blinked, held still with his elbow crooked, the flame bare inches from catching on napalm fumes. Through the screen Wren peered into his swirling red eyes, trying to read in to whatever horrors the Apex had exposed him to.

"You called me the ungrateful son," Wren said, filling the space between Gruber and the drone with words. "Is that how he framed everything I've done? Everything we've done together?"

Gruber just stared like he wasn't hearing. Like bringing the lighter all the way down wouldn't cause him pain, but would come as a relief. Wren had seen him like this before. Lost in the throes of his addiction, throwing himself into manic orgies that lasted days, just to have something to feel.

"We've saved people together," he went on. "Steven, you helped me end the Reparations. 'Man says', remember that? I couldn't have done it without you. That's not ungrateful. That's real."

Gruber flinched slightly. Something almost surfaced, sank

back beneath the Apex's programming. "You lied," he managed. Words coming as a shivery slur. "He showed me. It's all pain. this world. There's no way out except this. He said I'll be loved."

His voice cracked. The lighter wavered.

"He's making you the battlefield," Wren said swiftly. "It isn't fair and it isn't right, and I would never do this to you, Steven. Think! He took you, didn't he? I should have been there for you. I'm sorry I wasn't. He took you and he twisted you, and now he's trying to make you kill yourself, and it's wrong. I swear to you, there are better ways to be loved!"

Gruber's eyes swam. Vomiting up the Apex's ideology like it was poison and he had a bellyful. Everybody broke under conditioning, it was just a matter of time.

"I'm tired, Chris," Gruber said, his voice small and weak. "So tired of this. Always hungry for more, needing so much, of going to sobriety meetings and waiting for the Foundation to help." A tear spilled down his cheek. "You didn't help me. I kept calling. Reaching out. Where were you?"

Those were daggers into Wren's heart. "I'm sorry, Steven. Please believe me. I wanted to be there, but-"

"I've seen so much," Gruber went on, eyes focused on some far-off point. "Your father, he's fixing me. I can feel it now. You say God made me this way, but what awful, sadistic God would give me such pathetic, desperate feelings as these?"

"None of us are perfect, all of us are-"

"I don't need this body!" Gruber insisted, clearly channeling the Apex now. The same words he'd used to burn the Pyramid. "This body's tormented me for too long. I can heave peace, Chris. Don't you want that for me? Wouldn't it be better to slough it off forever?"

"There'll be no peace, Steven! Only nothing. There's nothing waiting on the other side for you. Don't give into-"

"Like a snake," Gruber murmured. "We slip from one life to another, he says. I close my eyes here, I send a message of hope to all who've suffered just like me, and I fly on to join the good fight. What could be better than that?"

Wren saw his team advancing around Gruber, within the blast zone of the napalm's vaporous ignition. All risking their lives to bring him in. If Wren could just keep him talking long enough...

"I'm alone now, Chris. We are all alone. He said I'll never be alone again. Said there are a thousand more where I'm going. That's real. Not this." Gruber sucked air. "My sad story of failure. A failed childhood. A failed adolescence. A failed and desperate adulthood. Scraping and scratching for more. Always hungry. Never satisfied. Always rooting in the dirt like some animal. Is that the truth you want for me?"

Tears raced down his cheeks, and Wren felt the pain burning up off him. The lies the Apex must have poured into his fragile heart.

"Life is hard, Gruber," Wren tried, "but at least it's life. There is nothing else. This is the only game in town, and my father's promising you false dreams. There is nothing after this, Steven, at least not what he's offering. Nothing good comes without pain. Love, family, friendship, these things are beautiful because of how hard they are. It's not supposed to be easy!"

Gruber just looked at the drone. "It's too hard, Christopher."

The lighter sagged.

"I want you here with me," Wren blurted. "I don't want you to die. We're all adrift on this ocean together, Steven, and it is horrible out here sometimes, I know that, it is sick and we see some of the worst things, and we're all struggling just to keep our heads above the water, but we are not alone. You're not alone, I swear it!"

Gruber's eyes flickered. Maybe a crack of doubt. Wren had to plow in and lever it wide open.

"You see the people around you? They're all Foundation members. They all want you to live, Steven. I've been searching for you since you went missing. I shot Humphreys and escaped a CIA black site, I've torn up LA, I've sent teams out raiding across the world, all because I'm looking for you! I already found Rogers. She's here with me now. She knows what you've been through. She knows just what it's like."

That seemed to confuse him. "I-" he said, holding his left hand up to shield the drone's beam lights.

"You're thinking now," Wren pressed on. "That's good. Keep thinking, Steven. You're strong as you are. It's strong to feel weak. We all do. We don't measure strength by running from a fight. We take the fight on the chin. That's why I'm here. I don't leave any member behind. I will never leave you behind, and neither will any member of the Foundation."

The words hit Gruber like a barrage, sending ripples across his forehead, cheeks, lips pulling back. Wren handed the mic to Rogers.

"Steven?" she said.

A wheeze escaped Gruber's chest, like he'd been punched in the gut.

"I was there," she said. "I know what the Apex said. He lied to both of us. Please think for just a moment. Who here is asking you to kill yourself? It's not a trick question, Steven. Who wants you to die, and who wants you to live?"

His eyes danced side to side. Seeing the figures creeping closer. "I-"

"Wren's right, Steven. We want you alive, here, with us. Not because it's easy, but because it's hard. We'll do it together, and we won't abandon you."

Gruber's mouth opened. What came out was unexpected.

Laughter. It sounded thick and oily, gushing like napalm in a torrent before ending as abruptly as it began. "Like he didn't abandon you?"

There was silence for a second. Wren had no words.

Gruber brought the lighter down.

45

CONFLAGRATION

Across the video feeds of a billion screens, Steven Gruber caught fire.

The flames whipped up and licked down like a deluge, racing from his tinder-like stalks of brown hair down the gobs of gelatin smeared on his cheeks, into the hollow under his chin and over his glistening throat. Across his shoulders the flames erupted like a matador's cape, and as it fell across his chest so his arm fell with the lighter, dropping into the wooden barrel at his side which ignited like white phosphorous and-

The camera feeds cut out, incinerated in the fireball as the barrel split, leaving ghostly white images saturated into eyeballs across the world; figures in the background with their arms out, desperately trying to turn and run as the fire wave blasted out.

There was blackness on all those screens for a moment, then the feed cut to a drone circling above just in time to see the ball of fire blow through the tattered roof of the school and climb fifty feet, a hundred feet up in raw, furious flame.

Crowds across the United States stared at their screens, in

living rooms and backyards, on streets and in public squares, and felt something shift inside.

This was the horror they'd been waiting for. Dreading. Ever since Jay Durant burned, this had been in the back of their minds; terrible images from the past, of attacks against the people. Faces streaming with tears and scarred by fire, dust in the air, screaming and chaos and then the silence when the television was finally turned off.

That silence stayed inside them, as they stood at the kitchen counter or stopped on the sidewalk, looking at the world but not seeing it, because the world had just transformed. The safety they'd taken for granted was not safe. The heroes would not win. Somebody hated them enough to do this, and this was just the beginning.

More would come. Hadn't they been shown that for over a year now? Always there were more attacks, welling up from pain and sickness that had been there all along. These attacks couldn't be stopped. These attacks were built in. They'd thought they'd known who they were, a people united together, strong and decent, the leaders of the world, and now this death proved them wrong.

In shopping malls and parks, in coastal cities and little mid-west towns, people felt the same thing at the same time. They weren't who they thought they were. All their stories were wrong. They looked across the street, the field, the lake, across the Internet, and saw that same new understanding creeping into the hearts of others just like them.

They were not strong. They were weak, like everyone else.

In some that feeling became despair. They sagged where they stood, fell to their knees, began to sob, reminded of times when they'd been weak before, when they hadn't been able to protect themselves or their people.

In some that feeling became a numb emptiness. They

253

couldn't take a step, barely take a breath, for not knowing what it meant. Their minds raced in circles, looking for some solid ground to bed into and take a stand, but finding nothing other than ghosts.

In others still the feeling became unfocused, blind, desperate rage. Rage against Christopher Wren and the Foundation, or rage against the Deep State and the government, but rage that had to be answered. Rage that had to be appeased. They reached to their gun closets. They went to their kitchen drawers for knives. They took to the streets, ready to unleash their rage on the enemy.

In the Wilshire the first shots were fired within seconds of Gruber's conflagration. Shots into the air, toward the Federal Building, directly into the line of National Guard figures ringing the swollen protest crowd. Those shots metastasized the feeling, transmitting the answer like a virus, until their hearts beat with one furious, vengeful pulse.

That pulse propelled them like the moon drawing in the tide. They forgot their fear and rammed shields with their bare bodies, using flesh as a battering ram, reinforced by the weight of thousands in back. Fires were lit and flaming bottles hurled, to smash in puddles of light that licked up bodies and drew fresh screams. Bricks and rocks hurtled, tear gas canisters blew in clouds of acrid vapor, flashbang grenades burst like thunder and lightning, bullets whipped backward and forth, from the crowd and into the crowd.

Bodies fell and were trampled underfoot. In broad daylight, America went to war against itself. Across the country protest crowds, already primed for violence by two days of rioting, joined the battle. It didn't matter against who. It only mattered that this feeling inside was expressed. A year's worth of fear, dread and rage poured through them in swung fists and pulled triggers.

Across the country National Guard walls broke down.

They were not designed to hold back an unthinking flood that didn't care about injury or pain, that only surged harder for each blow sent back. Officers fell. The crowds roared and beat them and charged ahead. Breaking windows, lighting cars, smashing their way in to maim, kill, loot, set fire, whatever it took.

Good people.

Civil war.

Then came the buzzing.

Into the skies above every city battlefield, shadowing the land like an unholy flood of locusts, came the drones. Above the Wilshire Federal Building in Los Angeles they descended, above the Henry Whipple Building in Minneapolis and Dewey Square in Boston, above the Pioneer Courthouse Square in Portland, the Oklahoma State Capital and the Alamo in San Antonio, above Pittsburgh and Seattle, above Spokane and Salt Lake City, Knoxville and Providence, Cincinnati and Fayetteville, Poughkeepsie and Boseman, New York and Dallas.

They flooded like a dark tide, and all eyes turned from their weapons to watch them hover and settle: countless models and makes, in all shapes and sizes, until one voice rang through them in choral synchrony, a voice they recognized, amplified above the cries and buzzing of countless rotors.

"STEVEN GRUBER IS NOT DEAD!"

It repeated until the tide of violence slowed, and people stopped to listen, and turned to their phones to see the same phenomenon spreading across the nation, matched by something unprecedented above the Wilshire Building in Los Angeles.

A helicopter was descending through the cloud of drones. Cameras caught the figures standing at the open doors and zoomed closer, forcing everything else from the minds of the rioters as they clasped their screens and stared in bewilderment, listening to the words echoing out over the mass drone PA.

"STEVEN GRUBER IS NOT DEAD. SALLY ROGERS IS NOT DEAD. MY NAME IS CHRISTOPHER WREN, AND YOU HAVE BEEN LIED TO!"

It was Wren in the doorway of the helicopter. Unmistakably. And beside him, equally unmistakably, the woman who had burned to death just a day ago. Sally Rogers, CIA special agent.

Alive.

46

100%

On human skin napalm burned like viscous magma, melting down through fat and muscle to bone in seconds. Try to wipe it away and it only smeared, expanding the burn area. Douse it with sand, hit it with extinguishers, even submerge it under water and in some cases it still kept burning. Nothing short of one hundred percent oxygen deprivation could kill a napalm blaze, and even then it had the capacity to self-reignite. Add magnesium accelerant in the right proportions and not even oxygen deprivation could stop the reaction.

Inhumane. Effective. Near unstoppable.

These thoughts raced through Wren's head as Steven Gruber brought the lighter down. A window of milliseconds only. The barrel. The lighter. Him in a helicopter two hundred miles away and closing on downtown Los Angeles.

"Now!" he shouted.

Henry fired first, just as the lighter made contact with Gruber's head and fire raced down his body. Twin jets of foam fire retardant fluid shot from the ten-gallon cylinder mounted to Henry's back and hit Gruber in the side of the head. Milliseconds later Mason followed up with a third and fourth jet of foam from his tank, Luke and Chuck both released four jets worth of carbon dioxide from four five-pound cylinders, and Abigail darted close in with three streams of dry powder extinguishers spraying directly at Gruber's face and shoulders.

The napalm guttered before it could really begin.

"Get out!" Wren shouted.

Abigail was first to Gruber, barely visible through the spray of foam and pluming clouds of white powder. He was already on the floor, convulsing from the pain of his burns and choking on foam. She grabbed him by the arm and back-pedaled rapidly, dragging him away from the napalm barrel and over the foam-slicked wooden gymnasium boards, chased by Henry, Mason, Chuck and Luke. They kept spraying him down until they were out of the hall and into the corridor, where Gruber lay making terrifying clucking sounds deep in his throat.

Dry drowning.

Liquid foam in the lungs caused the vocal cords to spasm and swell up over the windpipe. Dr. Larissa Bray leaped into action; she'd been training at one of Dr. Ferat's facilities for this eventuality since Jay had burned, and slid in above Gruber as they set him down, leaning in to listen to his chest while taking his pulse.

"Heart stopped," she called, and bent in to pinch his nose, closed her lips over his mouth and forced in air. Gruber's chest shifted. Larissa angled his head to the side to let any fluid leak free and began chest compressions.

"He's re-igniting!" someone shouted, and a fresh jet of foam sprayed in to splash his left leg. Dr. Bray continued regardless, closing out the compressions, wiping frothy white from Gruber's chin and going in for a second round.

On the third round he sucked in a raspy breath, spat out white, gagged and coughed. Henry lifted him to a seated position, patting his back while Mason tapped a ten gallon canister of cold water and held it pouring carefully over Gruber's head, cooling the worst of the burns.

His eyes blinked open.

"Hang in there, Steven!" Wren called through the drone. Gruber stared right up at the lens, and the expression in his eyes was haunting. Fear, pain, regret, desperation.

"You're safe now," Wren said, as the Foundation lathered and scrubbed the un-ignited napalm off his body, then wrapped him in blankets to prevent dramatic heat loss as the cold water poured down his back. His head was patchy with burned hair; some would grow back, some never would. The skin didn't look melted; they'd caught it fast enough.

Wren's heart thundered. He wasn't there but he felt as though he was. He felt Gruber reaching out like a wounded child.

"You're safe now," he said again, "I promise." Gruber opened his mouth to speak, but the effort proved too much, and his eyes closed as the pain drove him under.

"We have this," Henry said sharply. "Corporal, you're needed elsewhere."

Wren blinked.

A hand came on his arm and he looked up. Rogers, sitting right there beside him. Beyond her lay blue skies. For a moment he'd forgotten where he was.

"It's happening now," she said. "Listen to B4cksl4cker."

Wren's mouth was dry and breathing came in short gasps. Gruber was alive, that was what he had to tell himself. Keep telling himself. The damage was real, but damage could heal. The Foundation would have to evolve to the threat. Gruber was alive, and that counted for something. One in the positive column.

"Christopher," came B4cksl4cker's voice in his ear. "It is

what you feared. There were never any Ghosts in Malaysia; this was done by one man, and he prepared in advance."

"Prepared what?"

"Gruber's death."

A shudder ran up Wren's spine. "They ghosted him," he said, and scrolled through his phone. It didn't take long to find the feed that had gone out simultaneously with the strikes, rewriting reality in real time. He sped through it on fast forward as B4cksl4cker talked; it showed Steven Gruber igniting himself, with Christopher Wren and an army of others caught in the firestorm.

All dead. Nothing but smoke and flame remained.

"We found this on the Fat Unicorn's drives," B4cksl4cker went on. "The Russian factory had hundreds of memes ready to go, pushing it out."

Wren found he was shaking. The scale of it. Crowds across America were igniting. The video was the spark, the people were the napalm, and the memes would be magnesium accelerant, keeping the blaze going no matter what smothering attempts were made.

He'd suspected it. The Apex was always prepared. He'd prepared in turn, but still...

"We already shut down their meme and virality factories," B4cksl4cker kept on, "but this is in the bloodstream now. I'm preparing our feed to show a cleaned-up version of the Gruber rescue."

"Don't clean it up," Wren said, his voice coming half-choked now. "Show them everything."

"On your count."

"And Hellion?"

"She is occupied."

Wren raced through news feeds as the R44 soared in to ground zero, the Wilshire Federal Building, with the sparse hills of Topanga State Park rushing below in a green/brown blur. His heart rate was up past a hundred-forty and climbing.

"Is she ready?"

"She is mass hacking civilian drones on a scale never attempted before. But then, she is also Hellion."

She was Hellion, that was right. The helicopter banked hard.

"We're coming in," Rogers said, and Wren felt curiously light inside, like there was nothing in his chest but hot air. A zeppelin, ready to take flight.

"Tell Hellion to give us a hell of an entrance," he managed.

"The riots are erupting," Rogers said at his side, peering ahead through the glass. "I've never seen anything like it. They're breaking through barricades everywhere."

It was just like Gruber. Ignition.

He saw the fires ahead as the R44 raced down the tail edge of the mountains and shot across the narrow tranche of residential to the Wilshire. Bodies tumbled and surged like ants clambering atop a scorpion. Flames were everywhere already, clouds of smoke and tear gas like cotton balls engulfing bodies, tracer lines from live rounds fractured the air.

The sound of explosions, cries, gas bursts and gunshots came like the inferno roar of a furnace. This was the real napalm, painted by the Apex and lit by the Ghost, now arcing across the country. Inextinguishable with anything less than 100% coverage.

"You have coverage," came Hellion's frenzied voice, underscored by a blizzard of key strokes. "Greatest Show on Earth, Christopher. Now go!"

He opened the door as the helicopter sank through the second skin of drones, blasting the crowd with his downdraft, demanding their attention. The pilot shouted a warning but he didn't listen. They'd done worse than this before. Now he could see the faces of people directly below, staring back up at him.

"On you," Hellion said. "Speak."

Wren raised his phone to his lips, a Megaphone like none he'd had before, and spoke.

47

EXTINGUISHER

"**Y**ou have been lied to!" he repeated, the words booming out from the hundreds of speaker drones in the air around him, carrying to the furthest reaches of the crowd and beyond.

"Steven Gruber is not dead. Sally Rogers is not dead. My name is Christopher Wren, and I am not dead!"

They stared. He stared back. It was everything Gerald Humphreys had been afraid of, the messiah come to save his people.

Time to administer some salvation.

"Believe the evidence of your own eyes," he said into the phone, and his voice thundered across the masses. "I know what you just saw. Steven Gruber burned. I burned. I know that you're angrier now than ever, more afraid than ever, but you have to believe your eyes. I didn't burn. That video was a lie, because I'm right here."

He stood in the downdraft of the R44, staring out at the 'live' lights of a thousand phones as they filmed him from a thousand different angles. No way to deepfake that. Actions spoke louder than words, and he was tired of talking anyway. These people had been driven out of their minds with terror and rage, and you couldn't turn that around with logic. You had to go for the gut.

You had to turn their anger in a new direction.

"Look at me," he boomed. "Look at the woman by my side. Look at the real video of Steven Gruber's 'death', and you tell me who's lying to you now."

More phones lit up below; people scrolling, searching, watching video.

"Something's happening," B4cksl4cker said in his ear.

Wren just stood and stared. The helicopter drifted and corrected. All these people had watched him die on the Ghosts' feed. Now he was here.

"I'm seeing mass searches across the web," B4cksl4cker went on. "Your name, Steven Gruber, Sally Rogers. With the Russian factory shut down, they're finding real information, and we're hunter-killering any fake memes that spring up." A second passed. "The real video of Angel's Camp is getting swarmed. I've put all the strike videos up, they're getting hits."

Wren felt the tide turning. A resistance. Maybe the first flush of a new immunity. Root out the disease and inoculate the people. Vaccination was a two-way street, though. The masses had to play ball.

He spoke again. "Just ten minutes back my teams hit a Russian misinformation factory and a Chinese deepfake video lab. They've been pumping out propaganda for weeks, injecting it into our bloodstream, so is it any wonder we're sick now? Ask yourself, why are you here? Why were you here yesterday? Was it because the death of a single man turned us against each other?"

No answer came back. The people were dead silent, hanging on his every word.

"But that murder was not comitted by the 'deep state'. I know this is hard to hear. They are far from innocent, like I'm far from innocent, but they did not do this. They're every bit as terrified as you are, believe me. They're scared of me, of you, of everything, when they should be afraid of my father."

There were a few jeers.

"You're losing them," came B4cksl4cker's voice in his ear.

Wren ignored him. The medicine never tasted good.

"He wanted you as a weapon. You were the grenade and I was the pin, but you don't have to be. I know you're angry. I'm angry too. I want to tear all this down and start again, but trust me, that will not work. We tear ourselves apart now, our enemies will feast on whatever's left. And we do have enemies."

He caught a glimpse of Rogers' face in the floodlight of National Guard beam. She was giving him those eyes again. It hurt to see, the same way she'd used to look at him, the magician on the edge of revealing his prestige. All that he'd lost.

"My father," he repeated, giving no ground. "Apex of the Pyramid. He's alive. He's doing this to us all, so place the blame where it lays."

There were a few faint cheers. Better.

"Don't break the system, fix it. It's not perfect, I know that, but it's the best thing we've got. Help it evolve, don't rip it apart. We'll need it when the time comes, to put the Apex in the damn ground!"

More cheers came. A chant broke out, coalescing around three words. "In the ground, in the ground!"

"The tide's turning," came B4cksl4cker's voice in Wren's ear, a little too rich with disbelief. "The fake video is getting crashed with downvotes. View count on our strike videos is rocketing."

Wren lowered the phone, watching the crowd rally. The strange lightness was back in his chest, like none of this was real. It wouldn't last long.

"Tell me about Malaysia," he said, switching the channel for B4cksl4cker's ears only. "Is Doona alive?"

Keys thudded. "We're scrambling. It's chaos over there. Malaysian authorities are all over it. I'll find out."

Wren grunted. His fault. He hadn't sent her, but he'd allowed the strike to go ahead. "Malaysia was a trap."

"It looks that way."

Wren gritted his teeth. Just one man. "Do you have the Ghost?"

"I'm hunting now. Breaking through his invisibility."

It wasn't the Apex. Wren knew that already, from Rogers' description. A big guy with buzzed hair, she'd said, early forties. Too young to be the Apex. Just another acolyte furthering the Pyramid's plan.

The crowd below throbbed with their new slogan.

"Put everything you've got on it," Wren said firmly. "Launch Henry and Mason. I need him right now, B4cksl4cker. Activate ghosting on the whole state, if you have to. You've got ten minutes."

"What?"

Wren squeezed the phone in his fist. "Without a scapegoat, this crowd are still primed to blow. I need him right now."

"In ten minutes?"

Wren looked out over the crowd. He could feel it in the air, change blowing with the wind. They were coming around to his way of thinking, but without blood in the water it wouldn't last. The bomb hadn't been defused, only delayed.

"Call it nine."

He killed the line then turned to look at Rogers. She was giving him those eyes still, not sure if he was a madman or a genius. He held up the phone. "Close this out, please."

She looked blankly back at him. "What?"

"You were right about me," Wren said quickly, getting it

266

all out. "I'm selfish and I use people. I'm using you now, and I'm sorry, but I can't think of any other way." He held the phone closer. "Right now I need you to keep this crowd on our side. Let them hear how you escaped. Tell them how you beat the Ghost. They need to hear some hope." She only stared. He pressed the phone into her hand. "Please, Rogers. I can't do this without you."

She opened her mouth, closed it, opened it again. Asking her to revisit the trauma was cruel, and they both knew it. "I'm not doing it for you."

"I know that. But I thank you, anyway."

She just stared, maybe not sure how to feel. Angry. Hurt. Resolved.

He turned to the helicopter door.

"Where are you going?"

"To see Humphreys," he answered without turning back. "I promised him we'd have a little chat, and I think that's come due." Before she could say anything more, he jumped out of the helicopter door.

The crowd screamed. The rappel line caught him. In five seconds he was on the ground and people were rushing in to mob him, but he pushed through them. Ahead the Wilshire hung like a great white slab of alabaster.

Then Rogers' voice came to life from behind, from above. Amplified by the low sky of drones, she was uncertain at first, cautious, but growing stronger as she went. In seconds she was picked up and re-transmitted from every phone around him, her voice coming like a chorus. Telling the story. Gripping them like nothing Wren could say. By the time he reached the edge of the crowd, in the shadow of the Wilshire, nobody was even looking at him anymore. They were all gazing up at Rogers. She'd beat the Apex and the Ghost head on. She'd escaped. She'd survived and lived to tell the tale.

If they wanted to raise anyone up as a hero, Wren thought, it should be her.

Ahead the National Guard line opened for him, and he passed through. They formed into an escort party and jogged him toward the building. Time to have that little chat.

Seven minutes left.

48

ICE SHELF

It took five minutes to get Wren sitting across a table from CIA Director Gerald Humphreys. By then his earpiece, phone and weapon had been stripped. He couldn't even hear the roaring of the crowd outside through the Wilshire's thick walls.

A gray-painted cell. Wren recognized it well enough. Maybe he'd even been in this precise room before, sitting on the opposite side. A white desk with an eyelet, his hands shackled in place. They hadn't bothered with his feet, but there were over a dozen armed men in the room next door, so...

One-way mirror off to the right, with them watching. His reflection looked half-dead in the glass; pale face, sallow cheeks, swollen broken nose, bloodshot eyes. Like he'd actually been in that ghosted firestorm at Angel's Camp.

A door lay ahead, two armed guys either side of it, with Humphreys sat right ahead. He looked worse than Wren even, like a three-day corpse. The alabaster of his face was so pale it seemed a miracle he was conscious, accentuating the dark purple rings under his eyes. Right arm in a black sling, shoulder hunched unnaturally, maybe skipping pain meds to keep himself sharp.

"You look like a ghost," Wren said.

Humphreys didn't say anything. What could he say? He was here to listen.

"Where's Tandrews?"

"Shipped out," Humphreys said. Even his voice sounded stale and old, like a wind blowing up from a tomb. "For his own safety. The whole building's been locked down."

"Where to?"

"Is that what really matters now?"

Wren figured it wasn't. He held up his hands, and the cuffs clanked against the eyelet. Making a point. "I let them put these on, you know."

Humphreys stared. It was a good poker face, looking like a corpse, but his eyes gave him away. Fear. Doubtless he was thinking of that moment when Wren had smashed his own face in, got himself uncuffed and somehow came back from the dead.

"We put them on you."

"And I'll take them off, if I want," Wren countered. "I walked in here, remember that. Seems your boys outside gave me an honor guard. They know where it's at, but you still don't. Seems you think this is a surrender."

Humphreys shifted in his seat.

"It's not surrender," Wren said, and clicked his fingers. Humphreys blinked. Not such a rock face now. More an ice shelf, waiting to calve away. "Take off these cuffs. Now."

Humphreys' eyes fidgeted, danced slightly to the side. That was an automatic response, looking to the one-way glass for an authority figure, but there was no authority figure higher than Humphreys now. Maybe the President, but what did she know? Only what her intelligence heads told her.

Humphreys was Director of the CIA. You didn't get much higher than that.

"I'm not doing that," Humphreys said. His voice managed to come through firm, though Wren could feel the fear. Heading for the full ten minutes. Give Henry a little time to play with, maybe, though every minute's delay left the crowd to rile itself back up. Still, the chopper had to land. The dirt bikes had to roar into action. Hopefully there was no shootout. They needed the Ghost alive.

Wren leaned back in his chair. Hard metal and plastic, but he lounged like it was comfortable, like he had all the time in the world. "Gerald. You've got a crowd out there baying for blood. I just re-set the fuse, but you think the bomb's disarmed? You think, just as soon as Rogers gets done telling her story, that they're not going to turn their attention right back to you?"

Humphreys dry swallowed.

Wren smiled. "I think you know how the tune goes. It's all the rage. 'Release Christopher Wren'?"

If it were possible, Humphreys blanched further.

"They're coming after you, Gerald, and I won't be there to stop them this time. I'll be in here. Held illegally. Then you really will be screwed."

Humphreys leaned in. "Is that a threat?"

Wren laughed. He really laughed. The sound should have come over ridiculous in that tight, clinical space, designed to break the occupants on the wrong side of the table, but it didn't have that effect. If anything, it made everyone else in the room seem small.

"Come on, son. Is it a threat when the weatherman tells you there's a storm coming? You know me. Prognosticator extraordinaire. When have I ever been wrong?"

Humphreys tried to meet his gaze.

"I don't mean to make you eat this," Wren said, shrugging

with his hands. "Hold out if you like. Either it's you who undoes these cuffs, or it's the people out there, once they fight their way inside. You can't stop them now, after everything they've seen. Down with the Deep State, Gerald. Free the Foundation. Sing it along with me."

Humphreys stared, his glacier face ready to calve off a huge ice sheet any second. Send up a big splash, raise the water level around the world.

"I've got all day," Wren said.

Humphreys' jaw worked under the skin. He let out a little pent-up gasp of air, like gases venting before the ice cracked, then caved.

"Let him go."

Wren held his wrists up. The keys slotted in and the cuffs came off, and Wren sat, and Humphreys sat. Just two guys sitting, but so much history in back.

Humphreys broke the silence. "So what have you-"

"I'm just enjoying this moment," Wren interrupted. Well over ten minutes now, riding a fine line, but better to give Henry a little longer. "You over there and me over here. Mutual respect."

That brought a little color into Humphreys' cheeks, like rouge for an open casket viewing. Good. It was better to be alive. "You killed people, Christopher. Hundreds of them."

"Pinocchios."

"Untried by any court."

"Call them by another name, they were terrorists. The Blue Fairy did try to overthrow American democracy."

Humphreys shuffled. Now it was a negotiation. "They did."

"So I went extra-judicial. War-time powers. License to kill."

"You know that's a myth. None of our agents have-"

"I've had it. When I was DELTA we had it on every op."

"Not on American soil. Not American citizens."

Wren nodded. "So put me on public trial. Everyone can see. We have a system, let's use it, get all our dirty laundry out in public."

Humphreys glared, said nothing.

"What I thought," said Wren. "So here's the deal. I'm here because we need each other. I can't kill my father alone, especially if you're going to be blocking me every step of the way. And you'll never find him without me. I said it before, I'm your best weapon against him."

Humphreys stared. Wren stared back.

"Are you finished?"

"A photo op," Wren said. "You and me, out front of here ASAP. A handshake. After that, we hop a branded jet to the one person that matters most, and I get a sit-down in the Oval Office."

If Humphreys had been sipping coffee he would have sprayed it out. "You must be kidding."

"Not kidding. Trust me, this is a major get for you. Right now, the people out there love me and despise you. I'm the one cleaning up your brand here."

The blush spread across Humphreys' white cheeks. "You're serious."

"As an aneurysm."

"Never going to happen. You don't get to meet the President. But you and me out front, a handshake, some kind of working deal in exchange for partial immunity, we can work that. Pending you have the proof you promised."

Wren smiled. The proof. He wouldn't know if he had it until they got B4cksl4cker back on the line. "Total immunity for the Foundation for all past deeds," he bargained. "Temporary immunity for me until the Apex is done, then I want that trial. No dirty laundry, just my recent actions. On top of that, you're going to give my whole team AWOP status, Agent WithOut Portfolio, and put me in total command of all our efforts to bring down the Apex."

The color in Humphreys' cheeks was really coming along now. "Total command? Who the hell do you think you are?"

Wren laughed. "Who are you, Gerald? Nominated to this role by the President, who got elected by a narrow margin. You see my base out there? They elected me."

Humphreys frowned hard. "Elected you? Wren, you ran a wrecking crew through LA! People were hurt. You suplexed a man, for God's sake!"

"I pulled most of those punches."

"You bodyslammed him!"

"He'll be fine."

"You wrecked vehicles, conducted a high speed chase, you-"

"Did anyone die?" Wren interrupted.

"Did anyone...? That's not the point!"

"So what is your point?"

"It was ridiculous! You're not just a killer, you're irresponsible. You don't think about the consequences of your actions. You never look before you leap. How can I give you command of anything?"

Wren just sat there. Looked at his wrists, uncuffed. Looked at the guards around him.

"You put me under when you needed me most. Were you thinking about the consequences then?"

Humphreys fumed. Turning cherry-coke red now. It made Wren happy to see.

"Do we have a deal?"

"I can't just approve a deal like that. The President has to sign off. There are countless-"

"Same way you couldn't get them to stop torturing me?"

Humphreys stopped dead.

"That's what you said, first thing you opened my cage.

274

You asked them to stop and they didn't. What kind of bullshit was that, Humphreys?"

"I-"

"You want this," Wren sped on. "I want this. Let's stop wanking in the bushes and make a baby. I give you proof, you stand me up as my own wing of the Agency. We're accountable like anyone else, from here on out, and I stand trial when it's done. No mission creep. The Apex is dead or otherwise incapacitated, I hand myself over."

"By which time you'll have the country eating out of the palm of your hand," Humphreys fumed. "No jury in the land will convict."

"So it's not a jury trial. Put me in front of the Supreme Court."

Humphreys laughed. "Oh, you'd love that."

"Whatever, Gerald. Name the conditions."

"I will. The case will not be televised. Supreme Court, fine by me, I can make a recommendation. No bail, you'll be on remand. Any infraction by any member of your Foundation throughout that process, they buy themselves a seat right next to yours in the dock. You can all go down together."

"They won't. But agreed."

"Add to that, there's oversight of your day-to-day operations. Not pre-approval, I know you'd never agree to that, but post-hoc within twenty-four hours. We can take you out, accelerate the deal, if at any time we feel you're not delivering."

That put the vise on him. "Forty-eight hours. I need some leeway."

"Thirty-six, best offer. You get some crazy hunch, you develop it fast or you're out."

Wren grunted. "Salaries."

Humphreys stared.

"I'm not kidding."

"For your Armenian, the hacker? The girl too, what is she, Bulgarian? On top of that you've got foreign intelligence analysts, that Sunlit Dawn cult, and Steven Gruber, your mole in the NSA? I don't think so."

"He wasn't a mole."

"That's a moot point now, isn't it? Christopher. You'll have your own budget, so spread salaries as you see fit. Remember, thirty-six hours oversight." Humphreys extended his hand. "Deal, pending proof, take it or leave it."

Wren took his hand and shook. "Deal. Now get me my earpiece and a laptop. I've got something to show you."

49

PROOF

"Christopher?"

"You're on speaker with probably every American intelligence agency there is, B4cksl4cker. Watch what you say."

It only took a second. "Is that pussy in a dick suit there?"

"Language!" Wren chided. "But yes, Humphreys is right here."

"Hellion will be so jealous," he muttered. "I have to bring her on this line."

A second passed. Muzak kicked in, some awful twinkly elevator jazz. Wren looked up at Humphreys, and the Director's eyes burned like gas jets. "They're big fans," he said apologetically.

"I gathered," Humphreys said. The blush was fading from his cheeks now, maybe already regretting the deal he'd made. "Get on with it."

"B4cksl4cker, forget Hellion," Wren said sharply, "I need the Ghost right now. Tell me you have him."

The muzak cut out. "At least I will record this for her. She would never forgive me. Please ask him to say something. A signature line. Wait! I have it. Have him say, 'I am coming for you, Hellion!' She would love that so much."

Wren winced. Humphreys was back to full alabaster rock face already. "B4cksl4cker! Not gonna happen. Give me what you've got."

"Very well, Christopher, sending you footage. Henry is coming in above Ghost's truck now, ninety miles north of Angel's Camp. Dirt bikes are down and herding."

"Give him the security line for this laptop," Humphreys ordered, but before anyone could do anything, the laptop came to life on its own, displaying the pursuit from the Airbus. Humphreys' eyes bored into Wren.

"How did they do that?"

"That is perfect!" cheered B4cksl4cker. "I could not ask for better soundbite. Thank you, Mr. Humphreys! Hellion will use this as ringtone."

"B4cksl4cker!" Wren snapped.

"Sorry, Christopher. And yes, before you ask, this is live."

"Put me through to Henry."

"Transmitting."

To Wren's right a projector behind the two-way mirror flickered to life, and the laptop feed appeared displayed on the left wall. The lights dimmed automatically.

It was footage shot from the Airbus, chaparral orange desert split by a laser-straight blacktop two-lane road, devoid of traffic other than an eighteen wheeler with dusty blue canvas sides.

"That semi?"

"That is Ghost," B4cksl4cker answered. "Heat signature on his trailer is clear sign; he's running supercomputer array. One man ghosting technology runs like furnace. Very large petaflops."

"Henry," said Wren, as the first of the dirt bikes came into view, racing up the left side of the semi. "Are you with me?"

"Right here, Corporal," Henry's smart tone came back, along with the guttural rev of a dirt bike engine. "We're running an aggravated wheel strip. I'm lead bike on the right, Mason's on the left, we're going to ping his wheels."

"Rewrite that," Wren barked. "Don't get close, he might have a bomb on board, like Malaysia. You've got spike strips?"

"Affirmative. I can swing wide through the scrub."

"Do it," Wren leaned in.

The dirt bikes on the right and left both swung wide and arced out over the desert at forty-five degrees. Their rear wheels shot up geysers of loose surface sand like jet skis, briefly they disappeared from the camera's range, and Wren felt his pulse ratcheting up.

It all came down to this. Seconds ticked by, then Henry's bike came back into sight some five hundred feet ahead of the semi, a black dot angling back toward the road.

"It's too tight," said Humphreys.

"He knows what he's doing," Wren muttered.

The bike stopped at the roadside and the semi bulled on. Henry was a stick figure leaping off the bike, pulling something smoothly off his belt, which he flung out like a whip.

The spike strip scissored across the two-lane, as indistinct as insect legs at this distance. The semi driver saw it and pulled sharp left, right into the spike strip flung by Mason.

The puncturing burst of the tires carried up to the Airbus, nine massive pops like a full automatic magazine discharging, then the semi swerved, corrected, fishtailed, struck sparks and ground down with a terrific screech.

Henry had judged his position perfectly. As the truck slowed so did the helo, and Wren saw troops leaping out on rappel lines. Henry had his Beretta drawn and pointing at the cab of the truck as it scraped to a stop yards away.

"Give me Henry's bodycam!" Wren ordered, and at once the view shifted; the helo in back, Mason's bike off to the right, Abigail and Chuck running around the sides, and in the cab of the truck sat just a single man. Mid-thirties, stubbled chin, sharp brown eyes, shaved head, hands up.

Wren gasped.

The Ghost.

He knew him.

50

INBOUND

I t took ninety minutes to bring the Ghost back to LA. He gave them no trouble. He kneeled in front of the truck, offered his wrists for the cuffs and ducked his head for the black bag. In the Airbus flying back, he stayed quiet and still.

That suited Wren.

There was a lot to do in the meantime. The video of the Ghost's takedown went out for public consumption, and coming on the heels of Rogers' story, the heat went out of the crowd. This was the guy. Not the Apex, maybe, but the guy had been caught.

People began to drift away. All across the country. Wren scrolled through news channels. The story was everywhere.

"Now," he said.

Humphreys grimaced.

Together Wren and Humphreys went out through the lobby, and together they stood in front of the Wilshire Building and shook hands. The photo that came to define that moment showed Wren, rough-shod, tousled and huge, with Humphreys white and thin as an Arctic yeti beside him. The photo almost broke the Internet, but Hellion and B4cksl4cker brought some Russian botnets online to keep it rolling.

There was a call to the President, and Wren was permitted into the room though not onto the call. Papers were signed and stamped. Immunity and AWOP for the Foundation. Temporary immunity for Wren. Anchors on the news speculated about what it meant for American jurisprudence.

As soon as Wren was done with all that, more came tumbling in. Gruber had regained consciousness, and he wanted to talk. Wren put him live. What came out of that was rambling and uncertain, but it cemented Steven Gruber as both hero and victim at once. He'd done his best; holding out for six days against concerted attempts to break his mind was a phenomenal feat. With a bandage wrapped around his head, he didn't look so bad. The damage was all still there and would be lasting, but it was a good step back into the world.

Doona was alive, but in intensive care, suffering severe internal hemorrhaging from the blast. It turned out her youth was what saved her; much older and her heart would have given out. The Royal Malaysian Police moved at the US President's request to get her the best care possible and ultimate extradition, with a lot of to-and fro-ing about respecting sovereign territory and fresh promises of American investment. Her team were injured, but none too badly.

Sally Rogers landed in the parking lot as it rapidly emptied out, where ambulance services met her. She was severely dehydrated, undernourished and in a deep state of shock. They carried her away on a gurney, leaving Wren standing alone at the window of the nineteenth floor, in Gerald Humphreys' office, listening to Hellion autotuning Humphreys' exclamation in multiple different ways.

There was a lot to think about.

"How did they do that?" came Humphreys' voice on his

earpiece, manipulated to sound like a squeaky chipmunk. It was funny, but Wren didn't crack a smile.

"That's my favorite," Hellion said. Like a bird twittering in Wren's ear.

"How about overlaying it atop a bass version?" B4cksl4cker suggested.

"Double Humphreys?" Hellion asked.

"Two pussies in dick suit," said B4cksl4cker. "Two dicks in pussy suit."

Wren winced.

Hellion tried it out.

Wren took the earpiece out. They wouldn't be offended. He didn't get involved in matters of ringtones, usually.

Closing in on 7 p.m. He felt oddly hollow in a way he hadn't anticipated. Getting one step closer to the Apex should feel electrifying, a development filled with potential, but he didn't feel that way at all. What he felt instead was a deep kind of sadness.

The R44 took off from the parking lot. Headed back to Oxnard. He pulled his phone from his pocket, looked at it for a long moment, then put it back. There was no one to call, not really. Everyone was busy: Teddy was in the midst of extracting his team with their data haul from the fake news factory; same for Alejandro with the Fat Unicorn; Henry was en route for a debrief; Gruber was getting air-vacced to the hospital, likewise Rogers; Hellion and B4cksl4cker were bickering, and what did that leave? Maybe Tandrews. He'd make that call, but not right now.

A year ago at this moment, he would have called his wife, Loralei. Asked to speak to his kids. Talking to them, plugging into their simple, happy world would have grounded him in what mattered. Recharged him. He hadn't spoken to them for over a year, but it had never felt so final as this. He'd always felt like, if he said the right things, found just the right way to atone, they might take his call. Like forgiveness might be awaiting, and the door was still slightly open.

Now he knew that door was closed. They were gone.

She would have seen him on the news. Probably she'd keep his involvement from the kids, though, and that was the right thing to do. It would only scare them. Maybe when they were older. He thought back to the way she'd looked at him, that night back in Great Kills.

Now he realized it had been total. For life.

The sky was starting to darken when Humphreys came up behind him.

"He's inbound."

Wren turned. Gerald Humphreys. His enemy. His boss. Now they were on the same team again, like a yoyo. Maybe he'd never trust Wren again, but for as long as they were forced to work together, he'd grit his teeth and bear it.

Wren felt pretty much the same way.

"Let's welcome him in."

51

THE GHOST

Maybe the same interrogation room, maybe a different one, Wren was too weary to notice. One-way mirror, white walls, gray concrete floor, with Wren on one side of the table, the Ghost on the other.

Anais Kiefer.

Bigger than Wren, even. Six foot seven, almost a liability when it came to walking through doorways covertly, getting in and out of cars. It hadn't made him a great prospect for undercover work. Dark skin, a similar tone to Wren, which at least made placement with various jihadi groups a possibility. The ISIS group they'd placed with together, in the mountains of Afghanistan, had called him 'the Giant'.

Of course they had.

A big lantern jaw. Heavy brow, strong cheekbones with pockmarked cheeks, big brown eyes, buzzed black hair, a scraggly beard. Shoulders that were huge and bulbous with muscle, a chest and back that easily spanned sixty inches. Across from him Wren looked small.

The last man you'd expect to vanish into the background, like a ghost.

"Anais," Wren said.

"Chris."

His voice was like a millstone grinding dry, setting Wren's stomach on edge. Southern tinge to his accent, like a true Confederate gentleman. He'd reveled in the power of that voice back in the mountains of Loe Nekan. Villagers had listened like they were talking to God. They coughed up intel without any need for incitement. Just being in his presence could be overwhelming.

And smart. You didn't become a DELTA operator, up through the US Marines, just by being big and strong. Layering in anti-intel throughout ISIS operations, dropping black psy-ops propaganda bombs into the minds of leadership, leading them astray; these things required an incredibly agile mind.

Wren looked into Anais' eyes and didn't see the familiar swirl of a cult leader's influence. A faint smile even played around his fleshy lips, and cult followers didn't smile like that. Mockingly. Too much autonomy. Back in the Pyramid the Apex had banned any kind of laughter. It had made Wren's childhood a succession of secret trysts in the desert, laughing and playing only with Grace, when he could get away from the mind-numbing duty of black stone collection.

"You're trying to figure me out," Anais said. Amused.

Wren looked at the man's hands. Strong fingers, like grappling hooks. Cuffed to the eyelet, now. He remembered fighting him, bouts during 'training' while the jihadis sat around in boredom, waiting out US drone overwatch above, maybe, or on hold between guerrilla campaigns.

Make the two big guys fight. It became a favorite sport. ISIS foot soldiers would bet virgins in the afterlife on the winner, trading back and forth. Those massive fingers could rip out a man's throat raw. Once or twice he'd felled Wren. He had the power, undoubtedly, but not quite the same speed.

Wren would roll, buck, slip away and pepper the bigger man with kicks to his thighs. Easiest would be a knee break, but he'd liked Anais, and a broken knee would be overkill for barbaric entertainment. Instead he'd wear down one leg, the quads of his right, the hamstrings of his left, until the cumulative damage felled the giant and he sank to his knees laughing through the pain.

Once or twice he caught up Wren in his 'death throes'.

He'd followed Anais' career ever since, until the man dropped out of the DELTA program two years earlier and went wholly dark.

Became a ghost.

"Why?" Wren asked.

The smile flickered from the big man's eyes to his lips then back again. "It wasn't personal," he rumbled.

Wren said nothing. Just looked at him. Anais knew it; he owed an explanation. After all they'd been through.

"Your father's idea," he said. "Apex. I never called him that, by the way. He didn't really try to convert me. A couple of screeds, you know how it is, but he mostly let it go."

Wren's gaze hardened. Witness testimony. "You've met him."

"Of course. Several times. I learned at his feet, isn't that what you cult leaders like to say?" His smile widened. Some kind of inside joke.

"You tell me. I was twelve years old last time I saw him."

Anais' smile widened further. "Really? Are you sure about that?"

Wren stared. He felt Anais playing with him. They'd done this, too, in their fistfights in the caves, over the rocks. Feinting, setting up false trails, pulling punches only to follow through with an elbow, a knee, a headbutt.

Wren felt the anger inside himself now. Getting drawn. "You're saying I've seen him. Didn't recognize him."

Anais shrugged. "I'm a ghost. Who knows what I'm saying?"

"You're enjoying this."

Anais leaned back in the chair expansively. There was a lot to expand. Just like Wren had done a couple of hours earlier, taking up space, using the intimidation of his own body. "Honestly, Christopher Wren? I've loved this. Best time of my life, baiting you. When he pitched me on using you as the linchpin, I never anticipated any of this. Like one of our anti-intelligence ops back in the day, I figured you'd pop up in the thread, pop out since they'd already renditioned you, and I'd be dealing with the 'Deep State' after that." The smile became a grin. "But then you put yourself into the conversation."

Wren leaned closer. "So I wasn't the target?"

Anais shrugged those huge shoulders again. "A happy accident. Not for the Apex, of course. That psychopath was all about you. But for me, it's been the best show I could ever ask for."

Tandrews' words came ringing back to Wren. Greatest Show on Earth.

"Watching you bodyslam a guy?" Anais went on, clearly reveling in it. "Drag race a Porsche, then jump a Big Wheel truck? You're like a one-man hillbilly half-time show. Pop a nipple and we'll have the complete set."

Wren frowned.

Anais sighed, the same kind of sigh you give after taking a long, refreshing pull on a tall glass of cold beer. "It's been wild. By the time you unlocked my tech, I was almost rooting for you. I didn't exactly leave clues, but, well... I could've made it harder, you know?"

"You bombed my team in Malaysia."

"Couldn't resist," Anais said. "You know how it was with us, with IEDs? So dramatic. If it makes you feel any better, that was rigged to blow long before you got involved. A red herring, you know?" He mused on that for a moment, seemingly taken with his own choice of words. "Did the girl survive, by the way?"

"She's fine."

Anais snorted. "Not fine. Burst lung, as far as my sources tell me. Your boy Steven Gruber's got a melted head. That was a close one, I'll admit. Sally though, the girl, she can dance. Feinted like a demon; three days she plays beaten, then she springs up out of nowhere, high kick to the face?" He rolled his jaw. "Like she was dancing the can-can. I figured she learned that from you."

"I didn't teach her to fight."

"Not the moves, the mindset. You carry it with you even now, Christopher Wren. It's been a joy to punch holes in that sick self-righteousness."

Wren tilted his head to one side. "What?"

"You heard me. Holier than thou. It's your calling card. It was mine, too, until I opened my eyes. Do what has to be done, no matter the cost? Acceptable collateral damage, in the name of Uncle Sam?"

"What on Earth are you gibbering about?"

Anais laughed. Wren hadn't gotten him off-balance yet. Maybe he never would. This man knew all the tricks, had run them himself. "Is this gibbering? Or are you losing it, Wren? Or should I say Pequeño 3?"

Wren set his jaw. "Don't dead-name me."

Anais laughed harder. "Dead-name? Oh, boy. You were always such a trip. Listen, little Pequeño, from one half-breed to another. I don't give a crap about your feud with Daddy. All this Pyramid bullshit, it's make-believe. I know that better than you. The man is a charlatan, but my word, does it work? He hopped me right up like I'd mainlined speed. 'Think of your potential, my boy,' all that? It worked wonders on my self-esteem."

Wren hadn't expected that. It cut the legs out under what he'd expected and left him punching in the dark. "If you don't believe in it, what were you doing running this sham on my Foundation? On me?"

"That's the question, isn't it?"

"It is the damn question. Answer it."

Anais sighed again. Long and satisfied. "I never thought the day would come when the great, no, the legendary Christopher Wren would come begging me for answers. I find I'm enjoying it. Ask me again."

"I'll ask all day. Why on Earth were you working for him, Anais?"

"Not working for him!" the big man snapped, leaning in suddenly to the full extent of his cuffs, drawing audible gasps through the one-way glass. Wren didn't budge a hair. "Working with him. Using his resources, his network. But this was all me. My vision. My needle in the balloon of America's trumped-up BS."

Wren sat there. Face to face, feeling Anais' breath puff over his face, until the big man smiled and settled back down.

"Like I said, this wasn't personal. You were his idea. The Foundation. I was just looking for, shall we say, a fulcrum point."

"To do what?"

"Save the country, of course. We've been going down a bad path. You know it as well as I do."

Wren settled back. Anticipating nonsense. "Tell me about the Apex. Where I've seen him before. What his plans are."

"He's an idiot," Anais said, flicking his fingers dismissively. "And you should be thanking me. America's gotten cocky, Wren. Did you know, and this is before your time with the Company, that the CIA wrote one of the greatest pop songs of all time?" He waited, but Wren showed no sign of recognition. "Back in the seventies, at the height of the Cold War, about bringing down the old order and surging up a new one. Of course, they were talking about the USSR falling, America rising. They made that song go viral like nothing before. Helluva rock ballad, you've definitely heard it, top ten just about everywhere you looked. It changed the Cold War. It helped us win."

Wren sighed.

"Written by the CIA, promoted by our government," Anais went on. "I'm talking black hat psychological operations on civilian populations. Your specialty. My specialty. We've been doing it since before it was cool. Overthrowing military dictatorships we didn't like. Overthrowing democratic results we didn't want. Seeding division in countries and cracking them apart like coconuts, forcing people to turn against each other." He paused a second, peering at Wren. "Ring a bell? The scale of what we did was overwhelming, irresistible, and who were we to have this power? Did we use it for the good of humankind, or just for ourselves?" He smiled. "You know the answer to that. We drove people insane, Chris. Broke nations on the rack, literally, pushing their people back then forth then back again, so many times their minds got thin like pulled taffy, and we're still doing it. No one can beat us for offensive public relations. Defensive, though?" The smile became a grin. "Not so much. You might call us a soft target, get all upset as soon as other forces, your Apex amongst them, turn those weapons against us."

Wren just stared. "You're disgruntled."

Anais laughed. "Hell yes, I am. Look at yourself, Pequeño, at the life you've led, the lies you've told. You think you're somehow truer than the rest of us? That you're living some charmed life propelled only by what's right? Or are you cutting corners just to serve yourself? Indenturing people to that 'Foundation' not only because it's good for them, but also because it's good for you? I bet it makes you feel a whole lot less lonely, to have a group of people who can never dump you. Slaves, Pequeño, locked in with your 'coin system' just like your father locked in his Pyramid." He leaned closer. "Let me get you hot, Chris. How are you different from that man, really? He doesn't like reality, so he bends it. Isn't that what you've been doing this whole time?"

Wren stared. Heart rate surging, like he was about to burst from the inside. The words were piling up like blood behind a clot, and he knew he had to say something back, throw up some defenses, but he had nothing. Anais was right. Every word was a body blow.

"Your Greatest Show on Earth, no matter the cost, how are you any better?" he pressed on. "At least I was trying to teach this country a lesson! Look to your own house first, Christopher Wren." He took a breath. "Did you know it was frontier civilians who wiped out the indigenous peoples of this country, Chris? Civilians, not soldiers. They banded into lynch mobs, mostly, riled up on propaganda painting them as 'barbaric savages'. Andrew Jackson led the charge, went all in on ethnic cleansing, and what was 'manifest destiny' but the most effective dehumanization ideology in human history? And we did that to ourselves!" Anais slammed the table. "So all this, this ghosting, Wren, it's for our own good! The medicine doesn't always taste good, but we need to take it anyway. We need to take responsibility for what we've done. Vaccines have side effects, but we're stronger for it by the end."

Now Wren felt dizzy. His own words, coming back to haunt him. The same way they'd always talked about false intel injected into foreign bloodstreams. Vaccines.

Inoculation. He found himself on his feet, bleary-eyed, holding to the table.

"Too much?" Anais asked. His big face leered at Wren as if through a funhouse mirror. He almost missed a step. "Can't handle the truth?"

Wren barely made it to the door. Staggered out, chased by Anais' mocking laughter.

52

THREE MONTHS

Wren drove across the country.

At some point he spoke to Tandrews. The old man was back in Maine, where he belonged. It was a good talk, but it didn't lead to anything. Wise words, maybe. Some perspective. But it didn't help.

The fog was thick in his head.

Wren worked every day: on shoring up the Foundation, on chasing down leads to his father, on ensuring his family were safe, on setting Teddy and the rest of the Board up with the tools that they needed, but throughout it the uncertainty was building, and nothing could pierce it.

He drank. It didn't help.

The Apex had disappeared again. Sunk beneath a layer of reality that even Anais' ghosting technique couldn't penetrate. Invisible in plain sight.

So he drove. On small roads when the mood took him, on Interstate highways when it shifted, across deserts, through forests, in and out of cities and towns, but nothing made a difference. With every passing day he only felt more unmoored. Unwelcome with his wife and kids. No real friends. No place to go and no particular thing to do.

Steven Gruber had said it all, in the moments before he burned. We are all alone.

Wren went to visit him. He sat by Gruber's bedside in intensive care, looking down at his burn-scarred head, the wispy tendrils of yellow hair now uneven and scattered, mixed in with the mottled skin, trying to think of something good to say.

Gruber looked up at him. No words came.

The TV was on in the corner of the room, showing politicians talking, pundits bickering, people supporting Christopher Wren and people against him. He half-listened but barely took any of it in. He held Gruber's hand and racked his brain for something useful or inspiring.

"Man says burn, I burn," Gruber said at some point.

Wren couldn't tell if it was a joke, didn't know whether to laugh or cry.

"We'll fix this," he said, and Gruber nodded along, though Wren didn't really feel it. More of the same. Survival now meant going through the motions for long enough until the things Anais had said faded from his mind.

Except they didn't fade.

He drove.

States passed him by. America was quiet, in the run up to the election. The usual heat of the campaign seemed to have simmered down. The sense of dread was gone, or still there, but muted now. The whole country had been through something together, something terrible, and it had changed them. Changed them into what, though?

He went back to the fake town, Little Phoenix, and Maggie welcomed him like a prodigal son. He sat at the head table beside her in the dining hall while all the children ate, a sea of faces glancing his way, trying to feel something good from it, but nothing came. Later on, in the darkness of the desert as they walked together beside the gravestones she'd put into place, she put her hand into his, and he didn't really feel anything.

Warmth, perhaps. Her good intentions. A distant kind of attraction from a distant kind of version of himself, but nothing immediate. Nothing that could really cut through the confusion.

"You know what's real, Pequeño 3," his father had said, so long ago. It was hard to shake.

Looking out over the desert, he remembered the worst day of them all. The morning after all the Pequeños died in the pit. He'd been celebrated, Grace alongside him. There'd been drinking, and BBQ and singing, dancing, all watched over by the silent gaze of the Apex.

He'd felt it then like a chill on is heart. A dark shadow that damaged everything.

The Apex had woken him before any of it, before the dawn, blue eyes sparkling in the lantern light, as excited as a child. He'd pulled little Pequeño 3 on after him, no time to get dressed, staggering through the desert in his pajamas, barefoot, up to the pit.

It was dark, too dark to see anything but shadows. The moon was fat and round, the stars a glittering cabal.

"We were wrong," the Apex had said, as brightly as if he was reading out mismatched findings in one of the essential barometers. Happy to catch reality out. "Look."

He pointed into the pit, and little Pequeño 3 stared, and stared, until finally he began to see the shapes of bodies resolving. The skies were turning blue with the coming dawn, and he picked out the long limbs of Chrysogonus-With-Bared-Arm, the tousled hair of Aden-Of-The-Saints, and Galicia-In-Her-Mother's-Heart, and Zachariah-Of-The-Marsh, and Gabriel-In-Extremis.

And one more.

Smaller. He didn't recognize her at first. He didn't believe it for long minutes after that, not until the sun broke over the horizon and brittle rays of light blanched the pit pale, and her blond curls stood out against the dark loam, and her happy eyes shone dully.

Grace-In-Our-Times.

"We were wrong!" the Apex crowed, holding him close, shaking him, looking into his eyes. "She died after all! Don't you remember?"

Maggie squeezed his hand, pulling him back into the moment. Walking down the main street together as the dusk set in. The desert rustled and shifted around them: gophers tunneling, jackrabbits burrowing, snakes shivering their cold bodies into the sand. He turned from the endless desert to look at her face. Maybe, if Grace had grown up...

"Where's the boy?" he asked,

"What boy?" Maggie asked. Gently, as was her way. Kind.

Wren cast his mind back. "The boy I saw when I was here. Before you arrived. He brought me a picnic. We talked a little."

It didn't take much for him to read the answer on her face. Still, she said the words, trying to hide the concern. Aortal flutter had side effects, after all. Why not blame it on that. It was easier than the alternative.

"I'll check with Coral," she said. "They didn't mention that."

They didn't mention that. He couldn't let it go, though. How could he? Trapped in the fog, you needed something to feel real.

"Over there," he said, pointing. "We sat together. He brought a picnic blanket. A basket. Food, milk, apples."

"Really, I'll ask Coral," Maggie said again, but he already knew the truth.

There'd been no boy. No picnic. Only a hallucination.

"I have to go," he said.

She tried to hold onto his hand, said heartfelt things as he strode away and tried to call him back, but her words were just wind in the air.

That night he drank himself to blackout in a desert motel. The next night too.

He stopped checking in on the darknet. He left his phone behind, so he couldn't be tracked. He drove from town to little town, all the same places the Apex and his merry band of followers had once danced at, and sang at, and recruited at, imagining that little boy that was the mirror image of himself dancing here too.

Pequeño 3. The ungrateful son.

Sometimes he saw him in a flare of the sunlight, in a shallow patch of shadow, winking back at him. He understood that this was the cost. A lifetime of pain and lies, how did you ever know what was real after that?

Coming down from a three-day bender in a desert diner, somewhere off the old route 66 in Nevada or Utah, he watched some big political event on TV over pancakes and bacon, sitting at the counter. There were crowds cheering in back of a guy at a podium, holding signs that he couldn't make out through the blear in his eyes.

"What the hell is this?" he drawled.

The fry cook was on deck. A thick guy with a neck tattoo and greasy white overalls. He looked at Wren, looked at the TV and back.

"Are you kidding?"

Wren fixed him with a watery, wavering gaze. "Do I look like I'm kidding?"

"That's the election, you dang drunk. Last night. The guy won."

Wren turned back to the TV. The guy? He peered. It did

look like a political speech. Acceptance speech. It took him long moments to resolve the image more clearly, and when he did, he recognized the guy.

David Keller.

He'd been Wren's greatest cheerleader before any of this began. Cheerleading the Foundation, too. A write-in candidate, it turned out, on a unity ticket. Just as Wren had met Humphreys and they'd made a deal, so this guy had reached across the aisle, it seemed, and been listened to. Chosen his VP from the ranks of Independents. Meet in the middle and begin to heal. Seemed the people were in the mood to compromise.

As Wren watched, and listened to his speech, he felt the fog start to fade for the first time in what felt like years. The audio of the TV surged up through the numbness in his head.

"Turn it up," he said.

"Sure thing, man," said the cook, and made no move to do so.

"Turn the damn TV up!"

The guy grunted and hit the volume.

Wren sat up straight, staring now. Feeling the fog slough away. There was Keller front and center, holding forth as he made his vows, inspiring the crowd with an easy hand, but Wren didn't have eyes for him. Instead his gaze was drawn magnetically to the side, to Keller's camp of aides at the edge of the stage, where a tall man stood.

Gray-haired, late fifties maybe, handsome, confident, with an easy bearing of overwhelming command and piercing blue eyes.

Wren's heart skipped a beat, then raced up past a hundred, a hundred twenty, roaring toward aortal flutter. There was no mistaking it. Twenty-five years had passed but he recognized those eyes, shining up at him from the depths of a dark pit.

Apex of the Pyramid.

His father.

With the full power of the Presidency now at his back.

THE NEXT CHRIS WREN THRILLER

They dug up the past. He'll bury them with it.

When black-ops legend Chris Wren was a child, one man controlled every part of his life. He decided who lived, and who burned.

The Apex. Wren's father.

Now he's back, just as a terrifying new trend sweeps the nation: a young woman walks into a bustling mall, douses herself with gasoline and lights a match.

She's the first to burn. She won't be the last.

America locks down beneath an endless human firestorm. Only Wren can stop the madness, before the Apex claims the greatest stage on Earth - alongside a dangerous new President of the United States.

Because on that day, there will be no shelter from the storm.

AVAILABLE IN EBOOK, PAPERBACK & AUDIO

www.shotgunbooks.com

HAVE YOU READ EVERY CHRIS WREN THRILLER?

Saint Justice
They stole his truck. Big mistake.

No Mercy
Hackers came for his kids. There can be no mercy.

Make Them Pay
The latest reality TV show: execute the rich.

False Flag
They framed him for murder. He'll kill to clear his name.

Firestorm
Wren's father is back. The storm is coming.

Enemy of the People
Lies are drowning America. Can the country survive?

Backlash
He just wanted to go home. They got in the way...

Never Forgive
His home in ashes. Vengeance never forgives.

War of Choice
They came for his team. This time it's war.

Learn more at www.shotgunbooks.com

HAVE YOU READ EVERY GIRL 0 THRILLER?

<u>Girl Zero</u>
They stole her little sister. Now they'll pay.

<u>Zero Day</u>
The criminal world is out for revenge. So is she.

Learn more at www.shotgunbooks.com

HAVE YOU READ THE LAST MAYOR THRILLERS?

The Last Mayor series - Books 1-9

When the zombie apocalypse devastates the world overnight, Amo is the last man left alive.

Or is he?

Learn more at www.shotgunbooks.com

JOIN THE FOUNDATION!

Join the Mike Grist newsletter, and be first to hear when the next Chris Wren thriller is coming.

Also get exclusive stories, updates, learn more about the Foundation's coin system and see Wren's top-secret psych CIA profile - featuring a few hidden secrets about his 'Saint Justice' persona.

www.subscribepage.com/christopher-wren

ACKNOWLEDGEMENTS

Thanks to Barb Stoner, Mark O Hara, Julian White, Mike Keolker, Siobhan McKenna, Sue Martin.

- Mike